Femme Fairytales

Teapots and Stolen Souls Publishing

Teapots and Stolen Souls Publishing

Interior Illustrations by Nagimeras Copyright © Teapots and Stolen Souls Publishing

Cover Illustration by @zlivkun on Fiverr Copyright © Teapots and Stolen Souls Publishing

Canva images/edited/ Canva license held by Wednesday Andrews

First Edition First Edition: April 2023 This paperback edition was first published in 2023

ISBN 979-8-218-11552-4

Teapots and Stolen Souls Publishing contact information:

teapotsandstolensoulspublishing@outlook.com

Contents

FEMME
FAIRYTALES
Published by Teapots and Stolen Souls Publishing

Trigger Warnings

These stories all follow different protagonists and some may contain contents that some find uncomfortable.

- Death
- Thematic Violence
- Characters sustaining injuries
- Stories without HEA
- Blood
- Drinking
- Mentions of abuse

Femme Fairytales

A Poem by B.A. McRae

Bore the folklore that has caused an uproar on the enchanted forest floor.
Leaving curious travelers on a quest for encore, an exploration of more.
The inquisitive of them all, gusty and small, had finally tracked the trail.
A path that led to where the legendary fables were stored, a patch of the forest hardly explored, its own mossy veil.
The trees were thick with centuries of untold stories, their fallen leaves cushioning the traveler's feet.
Ominous yet inspiring, the forest was either singing or crying, but the pursuit must be complete.
Their pointed ears flickered towards an echo of a sound, crushing the leaves in the quick pivot on the ground; they ran to it without asking why.
The further they ran, the ground turned to sand as a gust of wind strolled in from a majestically winged creature decorating the now magenta phantom sky.
Out in the distance, a stone structure leaving them speechless was built within a mighty tree, an emerald glow surrounding its grips.
On they continued, as they took a deep breath through their petal tea-stained lips.
As their bare soles touched the platform, the whining of the forest collided into a single whisper caressed within the traveler's ear.
"Enter with a fair heart, take with you only the remembrance of words like art; the fabled Femme Fairytales lie here."

"ENTER WITH A FAIR HEART, TAKE WITH YOU ONLY THE REMEMBRANCE OF WORDS LIKE ART..."

The Tale of Night and Day

B.V. Beuge

Shards of shattered porcelain drenched in chamomile tea was a chaotic way to begin the day, but not the most uncommon for the Princess of Fayharbor. In fact, I could easily recall and have not enough fingers to count regarding the number of times an innocent teacup had been angrily thrown in just the past week.

It was, however, the first time it had occurred because of the princess' mother.

Queen Melantha loved her only daughter, the Princess Nesrin of Fayharbor, more than she had loved any other being (not including herself, of course) - therefore, it would be surprising for the Queen to be the cause of her daughter's frustration.

As I gently picked up scattered pieces of the broken cup and soaked up the lukewarm tea from the rug which Princess Nesrin stood on, the argument above me grew louder and louder with each hurled word.

"Never in a million decades would I allow this!" Nesrin's shrill, demanding voice grated on my poor ears. Only years of practice kept me from wincing.

The Queen's tone was much more controlled, but I could hear her patience slipping. "You do not have the luxury of turning down this marriage proposal, my dearest daughter. You are eighteen, and soon no one will want to marry someone so old."

I would never acclimate to the age that our kingdom considered acceptable for espousal. Most young ladies were betrothed or, at the very least, spoken for by the age of thirteen. To put so much pressure on someone so young was appalling. Not for the first time, I was glad to be rid of the societal demand.

I disposed of the mess into a nearby waste bin and brushed the remnants of the sticky, sugary tea onto my apron. Nesrin turned on her heel and smoothed out the ruffles of her dress, chin high. "Sol, with me."

I curtsied low to the Queen, whose face was turning redder by the second, then hastily followed her daughter out of the room.

"The *audacity*!" Nesrin hissed, striding angrily down the hallway at a hurried, angry pace. "You don't think eighteen is old, right, Sol?"

"Of course not, Your Highness," I said, struggling to keep up with her long stride.

Nesrin continued to mumble under her breath, cursing Queen Melantha all the way back to her rooms. As I reached out to open the set of double doors for her, she held her gloved hand up, shaking her head. "I need a moment to myself. Return later with dinner. I refuse to see my mother anymore today."

"But Your Highness-" The doors slammed closed, cutting off the rest of my words.

Queen Melantha was one queen of many in the Kingdom of Fayharbor, while Princess Nesrin was one of even many more princesses. The High King had taken many wives, resulting in a lot of children. So much so that there was hardly enough room to fit them all into one castle. Therefore, all wives were given the title of Queen and each took responsibility for different sections of land in Fayharbor. On such land was an estate where they raised and kept their children.

I was not at all knowledgeable in the royal family lineage or political histories (for I found it utterly boring), but it all seemed quite eccentric to me.

Though as ridiculous as it was, Queen Melantha's castle estate was the only home I had ever known. My late mother, having been a handmaiden herself, had assigned me the task of being Princess Nesrin's maid at the young age of eleven.

And Nesrin had tortured me ever since.

The girl was not *completely* intolerable. In fact, one could say that we were friends when we were children, having practically grown up together. But the passing of time, her royal title, and selfishness soon crushed that friendship into oblivion.

No, Nesrin might not be intolerable, but she definitely could be described as a headache that never went away.

Unfortunately, just because I had been banished from Nesrin's presence did not mean I had free time to myself. All tasks related to Nesrin were assigned to me no matter what they entailed. Currently, I was cutting and tending to the flowers that would have to be picked to be placed in her chambers.

The sun was hot without a cloud in sight. I was sure to get a burn on my arms but it felt nice to be outside. A slight breeze ruffled the wisps of pale hair that had escaped my bun and seagulls cried overhead, searching for the ocean that sat not too far away from the castle grounds. It was, all in all, a peaceful day despite the uncomfortable incident earlier.

"Oh, I bet she was livid. You poor thing," said a voice from above with a ripple of laughter. Someone had opened the windows of the Queen's parlor room.

The Queen let out a melodramatic sigh, sadness in her tone. "My poor Nesrin. It's not like I'm happy about the decision either. I would rather she just stay with me her entire life. But who will look after her when I'm gone?" There was a snap of a fan, the paper ruffling with movement to stave off the heat. "I'm just doing what's best for her."

"Yes, but to Prince Erevos of all people? One might think you're sentencing her to death," cackled the second voice. I recognized it as one of the courtiers the Queen favored.

Not prone to eavesdropping, I tried with all my might not to listen in.

But Prince Erevos? That's who Princess Nesrin would be engaged to? I could not summon an image of the Prince of Faygrave, but from everything I had heard he seemed to be the worst person to ever exist on the large island of Fay.

"Stop it. You're making me feel worse," the Queen whined. "Besides, I'm sure all the rumors about him aren't true. Who could possibly ever believe all of that?"

In the confines of the garden where no one could see me, I rolled my eyes to the skies above. As I gathered my bundle of fresh periwinkle roses that I had snipped from the bush, I stood up to leave and one last snippet of conversation from above caught my ears and leeched the sun's warmth from my skin.

"Well, you aren't sending her alone, are you?"

"Of course not," The Queen sounded further away as if she had moved throughout her room, "I'll be sending her maid with her."

How had that not even crossed my mind?

The dread swirled through me for the remainder of the day, all the way up until I was carrying Princess Nesrin's platter of dinner to her chambers.

Of course I would be going with her. I was her sole handmaiden. I had been naive to think of it any other way.

The doors swung open after one knock as if she had been waiting for me. Without me to assist her all day, Nesrin was still in her morning clothes. Her shoulder-length golden hair was a mess on one side and I assumed she had slept all day. A sliver of pity coursed through my heart for this girl one year my elder. "Your highness-"

The platter in my hands went flying.

The doors slammed shut in my face for the second time that day.

And as split pea soup drenched my hair and the remnants of the dinner lay at my feet, I decided:

Princess Nesrin of Fayharbor was *definitely* intolerable.

I wasn't quite sure what I had expected, but a lot more fighting was at the top of the list. However, Nesrin had accepted her mother's orders the very next day with a smile so fake I wasn't sure how anyone believed it.

Perhaps they were just ignoring it - just happy that the princess had agreed.

Before I knew it, all of Nesrin's belongings were crammed into a wagon and sent ahead to the Prince of Faygrave's home. The day after that, Nesrin and I were preparing to leave.

I stood by our two horses, checking the straps on the saddles and comfortingly patting their noses. Fay was not large, yet it would still take a day's journey for us to reach Faygrave. The horse I chose was a simple brown mare, fat from lazing around the estate and looked about as excited as I was to set off. The other, however, was a gift to the princess from the High King.

It had a beautiful lavender coat and a pearlescent horn protruding from its forehead; Felix, she had named it. More unicorn than horse, I would say. I resisted keeping my hand on its nose for longer. Fay unicorns were notorious for mind-speaking and it always unnerved me. I ignored its knowing eyes as I patiently waited for the princess.

Queen Melantha was sobbing loudly and holding her daughter in a vice. She blew her nose into a handkerchief and Nesrin took her chance to quickly back away. The queen turned to me and pointed threateningly. "You are responsible for the princess, you hear me? If anything happens to her-"

Nesrin swatted her mother's hand as dread pooled into my stomach. I bowed low, my gaze on my worn slippers. The woman was never terrifying until it came to her only child. "I will care for her with my life, Your Majesty, I swear it."

I helped Nesrin onto her horse and she waited for not one second longer than she needed. With a wave of her hand and a kiss blown to the queen, she forcefully flicked the reins and left me (quite literally) in the dust. I coughed and struggled to mount my own horse, my short legs failing me once again to catch up with the princess.

And so a new chapter of our lives began.

The further away from the ocean we traveled the more my shoulders tightened from the anxiety of leaving home. Having long since disappeared behind the hills, the castle was no longer in sight behind us. I could not hear the waves crashing on the beach nor could I see any seagulls flying above. My grip was so fierce on the pendant around my neck that it dug into my fingers. Distracted, I hardly felt a thing. As I always did, I tried to draw strength from the necklace my mother gave to me before passing away but this time it did nothing to help.

Nesrin kept a measurable distance ahead of me. She hadn't said a word since leaving and I imagined it would be like that for a while. We were not prone to conversations and I never minded the blissful silence.

The sun was at its highest point now. Unlike on the coast there was no soft, ocean breeze to cool the air. Sweat gathered in every crevice and soon I was uncomfortably shifting so much that my horse was starting to shoot me annoyed glances. I gave it an apologetic pat.

An hour passed of complete torture before Nesrin finally slowed her horse to a stop by a small river and grove of trees. "Let's stop here for a moment. Help me down."

"Of course, Your Highness," I said, hurriedly dismounting and assisting her to do the same.

Nesrin stretched and sighed, glancing around at the scenery with a bored look. "Get me some water from the stream."

I dug in my satchel for a cup and kneeled by the water, filling it up completely. As I turned and held it out to the princess, she grabbed it and poured the contents out on the grass all while meeting my gaze. Her blue eyes cut into mine as she handed it back. "Fill it again."

My fingers gripped the cup and a shiver of unease coursed through me despite the heat. "Yes, Your Highness." I knelt again and filled it up. Same as before, once I offered it to her, Nesrin dumped it out again.

My patience was starting to slip but I kept my anger in check. My tongue, however, I could not. I tried my best to keep any attitude out of my voice as I said "Is something wrong, Your Highness?"

Nesrin made a noise of disbelief and tossed the cup aside. She took a step toward me and I took one backward, causing one of my slippers to start sinking into the thick mud of the stream's bank. The princess before me was nothing like the one that had said goodbye to her mother this morning - proper with all smiles. This was the version of Nesrin that I received the most. Her face was contorted into annoyance and disgust. "You must be enjoying yourself," she scoffed.

"What–"

"I have to leave my home and be forcefully married to someone probably twice my age and you get to come along on an adventure. This doesn't affect you at all. You have the utmost privilege of watching my entire life be ruined."

I was smart enough to hold my tongue this time. When in a jealous fit, Nesrin would never snap out of it with just consoling words. And besides - what was I going to say to all of that? Of course I would never want to leave home. I never had a choice in anything, but I would also never wish ill towards Nesrin.

Her fingers gripped the front of my dress. Physically fighting with Nesrin never frightened me. Even though I was a head shorter than her, I knew I could overtake her. Nesrin's petite frame would never hold up against my own. As tempting as it was, I instead lowered my gaze and said nothing. To my dismay, her hard shove caught me off guard and I landed on my backside in the shallow stream. The shock of the cold water was enough to dampen my anger and twist it into hurt. Nesrin stood above me on the bank, arms crossed and haughty. With a twirl of her skirts, she left me there.

The sun dipped below the horizon and took the heat of the day with it. Fortunately, my dress had mostly dried by then. Only the streaks of mud lingered. I had glared at Nesrin's back for the first hour since setting back out on our path but now the scenery around us stole my attention.

I quickly realized what I thought had been the sunset was instead a thick fog that had crept up on us, shutting out any trace of sunlight. The sky transformed into a swirl of gray and dark blue, the icy breeze bringing goosebumps to my skin.

We slowed our horses and Nesrin gave me a panicked glance. "Is it a storm?"

As if on cue, a sign appeared out of the fog.

"It's no storm," I muttered, my eyes roaming over the elegant letters. *Faygrave.*

We had been informed the weather in Faygrave would change but I had no idea that it would be this drastic. I wondered if it was always like this.

I went to snap my reins to urge my horse back into a trot but Nesrin's hand shot out and gripped my forearm. "Wait," she said.

A spark of annoyance flashed through me as her long nails dug into my skin. "Yes, Your Highness?"

"We must stop for a moment."

I was not about to live through another fall into a stream. Not in this weather. "Your Highness, we're going to be late-"

"Then hurry up!" Nesrin snapped. I schooled my face into what I hoped looked a lot more passive than what I felt and slid off my horse. When Nesrin's feet had touched the ground, she dragged our horses and me under a grove of nearby trees off the road. Unease coursed through me. Images of buried bodies and missing girls flashed unbiddenly through my mind.

She stood in front of me, hands on her hips, looking every bit the demanding princess she was. "I need you to listen to me very carefully." When I kept silent, she continued in a rush. "I am not about to be married off to some horrible, gross man I don't love, much less one I don't even know."

I watched, utterly confused, as she rummaged in the pack tied to Felix. When she yanked out one of her dresses and shoved it in my direction, I merely blinked.

"Your High–"

"Take it, you idiot," she snapped. My fingers closed around the soft fabric and I watched as she tugged out another heap of clothing.

"Is that mine–"

"Quickly, change into that before someone comes," Nesrin said, nodding sharply at the bundle in my hands.

Still absolutely confused, but nervous about getting caught mid-change, I obeyed without question. The dress she had handed to me had definitely been hers. Not only was the bubblegum pink fabric softer and of higher quality, but I had remembered washing it several times before.

Nesrin and I were anything but the same size though and I was confused when the piece of clothing fit me perfectly. As I watched the princess slip on my own plain, brown dress and have it fit her as well, rather than being too big in the hips and bust, I realized she must have had them tailored.

We stood there and faced each other then, both in the other's clothes. Rather than looking displeased by wearing a dress she would have never even given a second thought to, Nesrin seemed ecstatic. "Oh good, they fit."

"Your Highness..." I trailed off at the mischievous gleam in her eyes, the question dying on my lips. She began to shove our old dresses into the pack, her back to me.

"Where is your beloved necklace, Sol?" Nesrin asked nonchalantly.

Confusion toppled onto even more confusion as my fingers went to grip the chain around my neck. When they closed over nothing, however, my confusion quickly turned to panic. My necklace! "Where–"

"I believe you dropped it in the water."

"The water..." Ah, right, where Nesrin had pushed me.

"What a shame."

"A shame..." I repeated the words slowly, as if in a trance. My mother's necklace was not just a trinket left behind to remember her by. She had given it to me for protection. The small gem that had been looped onto a simple chain was enchanted to keep anyone from casting magic on me. I raised my gaze to Nesrin, who had turned to look at me smugly. The girl before me was the only person to ever know what the gift from my mother truly was. "You knew I lost it when I fell." Even my own words sounded unsure.

"Getting rid of that necklace was the hardest part of this whole plan. Of course, you know by now, that no one but the wearer can remove it. I had to get you to lose it yourself." Nesrin's smirk was proud.

Her hands came down hard on my shoulders and I winced from the impact. As her fingers dug into the fabric of her old dress, Nesrin seemed to ponder for a moment. Her eyes searched mine and she took a deep breath, nodding to herself, as if solidifying her decision. "I must do this, Sol; you must understand. I cannot submit myself to a man who might kill me, you see. But you - no one will miss you."

The words, however confused I was, sliced open a wound in my heart. "What are you talking about?"

Nesrin smiled a little sadly. "You will switch places with me and I will get to keep my life."

Panic seized me as her grip on me tightened. "Are you insane–" A slap across my face ripped the rest of my sentence away.

She had a glint of terror in her eyes that I had never seen before. It was gone in an instant. Nesrin cleared her throat and stepped back, smoothing the plain brown folds of fabric. "Whether I am insane or not doesn't matter. You will accept this and you have no choice now - especially now that you do not have a protection charm." She pulled a dagger from the saddle bag and sliced open her palm before I could utter a cry of surprise.

Her bloody hand forcefully gripped mine, her cold fingers intertwined with mine. "Isolde, only daughter of Odessa, life servant of Queen Melantha of Fayharbor. Do you swear to take on the identity of Princess Nesrin, marry the Prince of Faygrave in place of her, and speak not a word of this to a soul for the rest of your living days?"

I suppressed a shiver of dread. "And if I refuse?"

The corner of Nesrin's lips twitched into an amused smile. "You die, of course. Right here, right now." I could overtake her, push her down, or run away. But my eyes kept flickering back to the dagger in her grip. Her eyes told me she was telling the truth and my heart twisted at the thought. I would not doubt she would use it against me. And for whatever it was worth, I did not want to die.

"Fine," I said. Nesrin wasted no time digging the blade of her dagger into my own palm and I hissed from the pain.

Blood oaths were an unpleasant magic to mess with. My mother had always warned me against them and here I was being forced into one.

If my mother knew, her heart would break in two.

I quickly came to the conclusion that Faygrave was always like this. The fog came and went, an eerie wave across the roads at times, but the dark atmosphere continued. It was because of this that by the time we reached our destination I had no idea if the sun had already set or not.

The road we traveled on split in two. One way continued on while the other winded up a large hill ahead. At the very top sat the gloomiest castle I had ever seen in my entire life. Its windows were dark with no sign of life to catch a glimpse of. I could spot thick ivy growing up the sides of the large walls. An enormous iron fence kept us from going any further up the hill, the gates sealed shut. I looked around for a gatekeeper but not a soul was in sight. As Nesrin urged Felix forward though, they opened by themselves. The creak was loud and echoed into the lifeless landscape around us, making me cringe. As we passed through, I watched them slowly close behind us and clang back together.

I snuck a look at Nesrin, who was unusually quiet. Her eyes kept darting around, knuckles white as she gripped the reins. When I had reluctantly asked for the details of her plans earlier she had told me she would get me to the castle of Faygrave, turn me over to the prince, and then leave when all was settled. It was obvious she was scared her plan would not work out.

"I don't need to risk the guards coming after me once I make my escape," she had said when I asked her why even bother making sure I get there.

All things considered, I had felt an odd calm take over me after the initial panic had ceased. I would like to think I had accepted my fate, but I knew it was just more panic in a different form.

"Now is your chance to change your mind," I urged.

"Keep your voice down," she hissed back, shooting me a dark look. Her eyes roamed over my face and the glare flickered to mild panic. "Wait, I forgot." A moment of hope squeezed my lungs and I caught my breath. Had she changed her mind?

When Nesrin's hand closed around my single, thick braid, I knew I would hate this girl for the rest of my life. Her knife flashed. My braid lay limp in her grip, severed from my head. Tears formed in my eyes as I watched her fling the hair into the tall grass around us, the small amount of hope I had going with it. She ruffled the small amount of hair still on my head, styling it with her fingers.

"There, now we match," she said with a satisfied smile. I only just barely kept hold of my sanity.

***

The castle finally loomed before us. The towers reached far into the sky above, disappearing into the dark clouds. A single attendant stood at the bottom of the many steps that led to the enormous double-doored entrance. He was a short, older gentleman dressed in all black, the top of his head clear from any hair.

"The prince is not even here to greet his fiance? How rude," Nesrin muttered under her breath.

I was grateful, however. My frantically beating heart was about to burst from nervousness and if I talked, I was sure to empty the entire contents of my stomach out onto the cobbled path. If my husband-to-be was to forever ignore me, it would be in my best interest.

We dismounted and the man bowed low. As he straightened, I stifled a gasp. His thin, cracked lips had been crudely sewn together. Nesrin was much less discreet than I was. The mute attendant ignored her outburst and merely swept his arm wide to direct us inside. When Nesrin went to step forward and lead us I laid a tentative hand on her arm and cleared my throat. She realized the mistake and grit her teeth. Royalty always led.

I smothered a smile at her anger and made my way towards the doors, lifting my dress as I climbed the stairs. These moments would be the only thing I enjoyed out of this entire ruse - seeing Nesrin play the role of the person who I had been for my entire life, chipping away at all her pride. I had to pretend to be the Princess of Fayharbor, yes, but she also had to be the dutiful maid. From the expression on her face, she already hated it.

Just like the gates before, the large doors opened on their own.

If Fayharbor was the embodiment of sunshine and happiness, Faygrave was its exact opposite.

I stood in the foyer, bright dress and golden hair, feeling extremely out of place. Not only because of the fake personality I wore, but because no castle or home should ever be tortured into having so many dark and dreary colors. There were no windows to be spotted and even if there were it wasn't like there was any sunlight outside that could brighten up the space. Thankfully, every candle in sight seemed to be lit.

We were led to what I presumed would be our rooms by an old woman who had introduced herself as head of the staff. She unceremoniously dropped Nesrin off at a door, saying she would be back for her later. I was dragged off before I could utter another word, far away from the seething princess.

"Ma'am–"

"Here you are," she interrupted as we stopped in front of a set of doors. Before I could open my mouth she had disappeared.

So there I stood, in front of the dark doors, the cold of the drafty hallway seeping through the thin fabric of my dress. My hands shook and I could feel the same tremor start to rack through my body - not from the cold, I knew, but from the anxiety that took over.

Was I really about to be married off to not only a stranger, but one that had so many dark rumors piled on top of him and his estate?

I went to squeeze my necklace for comfort but just like the time before, my fingers grabbed at nothing. Instead, I took a deep breath and gripped the handle of the door before I could change my mind.

A study lay beyond the doors. *This is not my room.* It was dark, lit only by a few candles on the large desk that sat opposite where I stood, but from what I was able to see through the dim light amazed me. Never had I seen so many books in one place. They lined the walls, from floor to ceiling. I couldn't help but run my fingers over their spines as I walked the perimeter of the room. Old books and new alike. Some were near falling apart and some looked like they had never been opened before. No dust coated these books, giving me the impression the owner loved them dearly.

I reached the sole window in the large room. It was tall and narrow, smaller than the width of my body. It was raining now, the droplets battering the glass with fervor. I absentmindedly drew a circle in the foggy glass, seeing nothing beyond but a blurry landscape.

As I went to reach for another book spine, fingers snatched mine into a tight grip. I startled and spun, ripping my hand away. My heart nearly burst from my chest and I immediately opened my mouth to – to what? What was I going to do? I had no idea. The man before me took all thoughts away.

He was tall, very tall, nearly towering over me by two heads. A mess of black hair and even darker eyes is what I was met with. His nose was a little too large for his angular face with a full set of lips that any girl would be jealous over.

Prince Erevos.

I did not know how I knew, but it made sense.

I would have been slightly charmed had he not been glaring at me with such fierceness that had me stumbling back a step. My back pressed against the cold window and I tried to clear my throat. All the formalities I was taught as a child flooded back to me and I dipped into a rushed curtsy. "Your High–"

"Who are you? Who gave you permission to be here?"

I straightened, confused, and repeated my greeting as a question. "Your High–"

"You have touched eighty-seven of my books with your filthy fingers and just about touched another one with condensation, consider me absolutely horrified and offended," he said, his deep voice rumbling through my chest.

I blinked, his words registering slowly. I stared down at my fingers, finding no dirt.

"Are you mute?" He snapped.

A sliver of anger flared through me, chasing away some of the anxiety. I met his glare with a raised eyebrow and clenched jaw. "I am Princess Nesrin. Am I right to assume you are Prince Erevos? Is this how you talk to your betrothed?"

"Ah, so you've arrived," Erevos muttered, dragging his eyes from my dirtied flats to the roughly cut ends of my hair. I felt my cheeks warm in embarrassment. There was no way Nesrin would be able to pull this off. It was a joke to even assume I looked like her, much less a princess.

But the prince merely flicked his wrist and a piece of thick paper appeared clutched in his hand, a quill in the other. He held them both out to me wordlessly.

Determined not to let my surprise show from the sudden display of magic, I squinted at the markings on the paper, my gaze flickering up and down the lines. He was watching me, so I cleared my throat and looked away, head tilted up in defiance. "What is this?"

"Our marriage contract."

I choked on nothing but air and my own saliva as my head whipped back around. "Our what..."

"You just have to sign it."

"Sign it."

"Yes, then we are married," he said, nudging the quill closer.

I was certain I couldn't keep the horror off of my face because the corner of his mouth briefly twitched up. Was that amusement? No, wait, that wasn't important right now. I was terrified at the speed at which this was going. I had made up my mind to go with Nesrin for the time being, yes, but there was no way I could actually marry this crazed man. And here he was oh-so-romantically shoving a contract in my face to sign the deal and be done with it.

"Absolutely not," I forced out, moving away from him.

"Is there a problem? Obviously, you came here knowing we were engaged to be married." One of his perfect eyebrows raised in question.

I grasped for some sort of excuse. "Is this how you tried to woo all of your other previous fiances? How romantic, let's sign a piece of paper and never think of it again."

As Erevos' eyes darkened with anger, I knew I had crossed a line. Whether it was the princess act or my anxiety unraveling my manners, I had no idea what was happening to me.

He flicked his wrist again and both items disappeared. He attempted to smooth back his unruly hair, a muscle in his jaw ticking. "Fine. I understand it may be too fast, I will give you forty-eight hours to adjust and we will revisit it at that time."

The rain continued and the constant pattering against the window of my bedroom suite sounded like a never-ending bad omen. The grandfather clock in the corner of the room announced it was one in the morning and I groaned aloud at the thought of having been in bed for hours without being able to fall asleep.

"I understand it may be too fast," I repeated the prince's words in a mock whisper.

Too fast? That was an understatement. I had literally just met the man.

"I will give you forty-eight hours to adjust."

What did he think two days would accomplish? Unbeknownst to him, the longer I waited the more anxious and unwilling I would become. I let out a short laugh, crossing my arms over the blankets piled on top of me.

"We will revisit it at that time."

If Erevos shoved that piece of paper in my face again I would light it on fire.

With a frustrated grunt, I sat up and rubbed my hands over my face, exhausted. When did I become so angry and frustrated? I had always prided myself on bottling up my emotions and keeping a straight face, even when Nesrin forced all of this on me. One second in the presence of that man and I came unraveled.

The suite that Erevos' staff had placed me in was bigger than anything I had ever stayed in. Not only did I have my own room with an adjoining bath, but a parlor room as well, where I assumed I was supposed to receive all my prestigious guests. A curl of my hair fluttered as I snorted and blew out a breath. As if I had any guests.

My fingers gripped either side of the wardrobe I had been staring intently into for the last ten minutes. It seemed that I had been gifted with all sorts of dresses and corset fittings, hoses and leggings, flats and boots. I wondered for a moment where all of Nesrin's belongings were sent to, unless it was all part of her plan as well to send them elsewhere.

Pursing my lips, I tugged out a green fabric that seemed appealing. It was the plainest piece I could find that did not dip so low in the front that everything would fall out. I paused as I examined the waist of the dress and my heart sank. There was no way I could fit into this. These were definitely prepared for someone several sizes smaller than I.

Not giving up hope, I dug through more of the clothes until I stumbled upon a dark gray dress. It was gorgeous. The silk fabric fell to my ankles in simple folds, hugging my waist with a silken band of ribbon. The elbow-length sleeves were sheer, while the neck a modest scoop. I had never seen anything prettier in my entire life, especially anything that I had worn.

As I was attempting to fix my newly-cut hair in the mirror, glaring at the ends that barely touched my shoulders, a knock sounded at the door, followed by a timid voice. "Your Highness?"

Panic shot through me and I was halfway to the door when I remembered royalty probably wouldn't answer the door. I skidded across the stone floor back to the vanity and cleared my throat. "Enter."

The girl couldn't have been over the age of fifteen. She froze mid-curtsy when she saw me, her eyes going from my feet to the hair I was playing with. "Your Highness has...dressed already?"

My heart dropped as well as the brush I was holding. Oh. Right. I forced a light laugh, startling the poor girl. "I apologize, I was too impatient to wait."

The girl kept her face schooled and I felt my heart warm at the gesture that reminded me so much of myself. She curtsied again and said, "Is your outfit to your liking, Your Highness?"

"Y-Yes? Yes." I said hurriedly.

"Please call for me if you need anything else. His Highness wishes to meet you for tea in the garden at your convenience."

Before I could gather up the courage to ask where the garden was, the girl was gone. I sighed and sat down hard on the bed.

"Off to a fantastic start," I whispered to myself sarcastically.

I was doomed.

It was only after roaming down five hallways and peeking inside a dozen different doors that I came to the horrible conclusion that Nesrin had already left me. I wasn't sure what I had expected. A farewell? Some words of thanks that I knew she'd never actually mean? I wanted to convince myself that anything would have been better than nothing.

After stopping passerby staff for directions twice, I finally opened the ornate, stained glass doors that led to the gardens. My mouth dropped open as the humid heat engulfed me. Whoever had the audacity to call this place a garden should have been slapped across the face. Rather than a garden, I was met with the most beautiful greenhouse. I could just barely see the other side and wondered if it was the size of the castle itself. The ever-present drizzle of rain could be heard pouring down on the hundreds of tinted window panes around me. The ivy that I had seen crawling up the sides of the castle swarmed these glass walls too, casting the room in eerie shadows.

I followed a stone path that wound around hundreds of different types of plants. The common ones like sunflowers, tulips, and roses I could easily point out, but I spotted many more that I couldn't. A flower the size of a man was in the process of slowly devouring a tree planted beside it. A bush sprouted spiky fruit in the brightest shade of violet I had ever seen. There were plants as tall as the ceiling and plants that barely reached the size of my smallest finger.

When I thought the greenhouse couldn't get any bigger, the path climbed up a grassy knoll. Atop sat an enormous weeping willow tree. Its thousands of branchlet arms dragged across the grass and created a sheer curtain. It was in the middle of that circular curtain of leaves that I spotted my fiance.

Dressed in all black, Erevos stood out immensely from his colorful surroundings. It made him more intimidating than he already was. He sat at a small table made for two, sipping from a dainty cup. His eyes flickered to me as I parted the branches to join him and he snapped shut the book he had been reading. "Took you long enough."

I curtsied and sat in the chair opposite. "My apologies, Your Highness, if you had given me a map I might have made it on time."

Erevos watched me with a hawk's gaze, not at all amused. I waited with my hands folded in my lap, having no idea why he summoned me, and instead tried to enjoy the symphony of the insects around us.

"Are your rooms acceptable to your liking?"

I hesitated before answering, caught off guard by the question. "Yes...Your Highness."

His eyebrows drew together. "You may call me Erevos. We are to be married, after all. I'm sure you call your friends of royalty by name, so you may do that with me as well."

"Ah, of course...Erevos." I felt extremely uncomfortable calling anyone by name alone outloud, but it made sense that he would not know that. His name felt awkward on my tongue, like a foreign word I could not pronounce correctly.

Erevos seemed to ever-so-slightly relax after that. He leaned forward, resting his chin on linked hands. "You have questions. I brought you here for an opportunity to ask them."

"Questions," I repeated stupidly.

"Yes. I'm sure by now you have heard all sorts of rumors about me." It was phrased as a statement. He knew about them then.

I decided to tread carefully. "I have heard many things, Your Highness-"

"Erevos," he corrected with a frown.

"-but I'm sure none of it is true," I finished.

Erevos was silent for a moment, narrowed eyes drilling into mine. He flourished a hand through the air as if to say 'carry on'. I heaved a sigh. "Very well. I have heard all of your ex-fiances have mysteriously disappeared."

"Mysteriously?" He laughed low, sending chills up my bare arms.

"Then you admit they disappeared?" I asked, ignoring the urge to break our eye contact.

"They indeed disappeared."

"How?"

"You want me to recount to you every instance in which my fiances disappeared? There are quite a lot of them–"

"Did you kill anyone?" I interrupted. I hardly cared about his past relationships and how they ended. I wanted to know if I was binding myself in matrimony to a murderer.

The corner of his mouth twitched up as if he was hiding a smile as he said, "Yes."

"Oh..."

Erevos really looked like he was trying not to laugh. "*Oh*? That's all you have to say?"

I cleared my throat as sweat broke out underneath my arms. "Thank you for your honesty."

"Well, if we're being honest," he said with a thoughtful gaze to the glass ceiling, "I think I technically killed three."

Such heavy words spoken lightly underneath a beautiful willow tree. As if on cue, a crack of thunder broke out in the skies above and resounded through the greenhouse with a rumble. I swore I could hear the glass rattle. All the while, his dark eyes held mine.

I shoved down the panic that wanted to take control of my emotions and actions. Why was he telling me this? Was he trying to scare me? My gaze flickered to his long fingers tapping against his arm.

"How?"

Erevos looked minutely startled. His fingers stilled. "Excuse me?"

"I will take you up on your offer of endless stories. Tell me how they all disappeared and how three of them were killed by your hands."

He huffed a disbelieving laugh. "Why?"

"Because I don't think you're telling me the full truth. Has no one asked you the details before?"

"To be fair, no one really wants to ask further after I've told them people have died." His smile did not reach his eyes.

"Well I am," I said, raising my chin in a challenge.

Erevos hesitated only a moment before unfolding his long limbs. He began to pace around the base of the tree. "The first left me as one normally would - with harsh words and tears, leaving and never coming back. She disappeared on our way home, I imagine she ran away - she always spoke of another lover." His fingers trailed along the rough bark. "The second drowned in the lake behind the castle. The third attacked me and in self-defense I accidentally killed them. The fourth was the same as the third, unfortunately. The fifth tried to poison me, they obviously failed." He had paced back to his seat but continued to stand, looming over me. "The sixth is sitting here, asking questions she does not want to know the answers to."

I looked up at him, ignoring the jab. "So what you're telling me is that none of it was your fault yet you're taking the blame? Why?"

He seemed fully shocked this time, with a dash of confusion. It was a good look on him. "As if anyone would believe me?"

That I did understand. So I nodded and gave him a small pat on the hand. I don't know why I did it, I just felt...pity. "Well, I believe you." I stood up and smoothed my dress out. "And if it gives you any comfort, I do not plan to poison you."

Erevos gave the dress a once-over, his gaze lingering on the sheer sleeves. "Oh good. Then what is your plan of attack?"

"I hope to annoy you to the point where you actually return me to my mother," I muttered.

"You're doing a poor job."

"Thank you?"

"You're welcome, it was a compliment."

I couldn't help but to laugh and he couldn't hide his smile in return. As I turned to leave, he cleared his throat. I stopped and looked back over my shoulder in question. Erevos was sitting back down, resting his chin on his hand and gazing at me with a look I could not decipher. "Is the collection of clothing in your room not to your taste?"

"Some of the clothes were too small for my size, but I found this dress acceptable..." I let my sentence trail off.

The side of the prince's mouth quirked up in amusement. "Do all from Fayharbor wear nightgowns as dresses? It seems a little...scandalous...but I won't judge."

Warmth crept up my neck and scalded my cheeks. I looked down at the fabric I was wearing with new eyes. Who in the world would wear something this luxurious to bed? Were all royalties this insane? The odd looks the staff had given me on my way here made a little more sense now.

I cleared my throat and curtsied in my nightgown. "Please excuse me, Your Highness."

After changing into more suitable attire, I found myself roaming the halls in search of the crabby head of staff I had met the day before. When she appeared near the kitchens, her ever-present frown deepened at the sight of me.

"Ah, ma'am, would you happen to have seen Prin– er, the girl that arrived with me?" I asked.

"You mean the useless one that ran away? Good riddance with her, I don't know why you kept her around." The woman snapped.

My fears were proven right - Nesrin had taken her chance at escaping.

The woman was still babbling on. "--and I told her we had no place for her here, so she could take care of the geese. Those poor geese didn't even get fed last night."

"Geese..." I repeated with a mumble, not really paying attention. Did this mean that I too could make my escape? The moment the thought appeared, I knew it would never be possible. Nesrin had left under the guise of an unwanted maid, nearly already forgotten. I would cause much more of a ruckus.

The old woman left me to wander around aimlessly once more. I needed to figure out a way to tell Erevos that I was not who he thought I was - but how? The curse forbade me to speak any details.

I slowed to a stop, my heart accelerating suddenly at a thought. "Felix."

The stables were easy to get to - I had seen them outside a window, to the side of the castle. Slipping on the polished tile only a couple times in the soleless flats I wore, I skidded to a halt in front of the doors, breathless. I yanked the handle and nearly ran into a stable boy on the other side.

He yelped and bowed quickly. "My apologies, Your Highness!"

I did away with the niceties, impatient. "Where is the horse I brought with me? The one with the horn?"

The boy faltered. "Your Highness..."

I gently pushed by him, making my way to the stables to see for myself. He trailed behind me, protesting all the way.

My excitement disappeared as quickly as it had come. Felix was in the stall closest to the door and gave a small noise of surprise as the stable door slammed shut behind the boy and I. "What happened?"

"He was like that when we found him this morning," the boy whispered.

Felix's unicorn horn had been completely sheared off, leaving only a sad stump in its place. I placed my hand on his nose with a sigh, feeling none of his thoughts trying to push at me. A Fay unicorn's horn held all its magic.

I had never doubted Nesrin's ability to put her needs first, but I was still disappointed I could not have prevented this. "I'm so sorry, Felix..." I mumbled as he nuzzled my palm.

Back to square one.

My mild concern for escaping this entire situation quickly turned to panic within hours.

Day had slowly turned to night despite the conditions outside showing no sign of the sun's trajectory. I was sitting in front of my vanity while the small girl from before brushed my hair. I had forced myself to wait for her, not wanting to arouse more suspicion. She had made no comment of it while she helped me bathe, dress, and get ready for the evening meal.

Prince Erevos had apparently taken note of my wardrobe comment and filled my closet with all sorts of new clothing that catered to my measurements. I had tried very hard to tamp down the swell of gratitude and relief. There was almost nothing more depressing than a wardrobe filled with clothes too small for me and I doubt he knew how much it meant.

So now I wore a proper dress in a pale shade of sage green. The bateau neckline contrasted with the extreme dip in the back so much that I felt like it was going to slip right off of me. I was also not comfortable showing off skin, but the girl paid my spoken worries no mind when she pulled it out for me to dress in.

"What's your name?" I asked, playing with the long sleeves of my dress. I would rather not mentally refer to her as 'the girl'.

Her thin lips turned into a frown in the mirror I watched her through. Her fingers paused only a second while braiding small portions of my hair. "I'm called Ayanna, Your Highness."

"Ayanna...you didn't tell me I was wearing a nightgown this morning to meet with the Prince," I said. Her fingers completely stilled this time, shocked eyes meeting mine in the mirror.

"Has Your Highness heard of the past fiances?" Her question caught me off-guard but I nodded, wary of the subject change. She continued, "There would have been one our Prince would have left out. Her name has long since been erased from our memories, but the story remains."

My chest felt too tight as her gaze never left mine, my hair forgotten.

Her smile was vicious for a child her age. "It was a woman impersonating a princess from another land. Prince Erevos discovered her lies."

There was not enough oxygen in the room to fill my constricting lungs back up. I didn't dare look away from Ayanna. "What happened to her?"

"The imposter? Oh, she was beheaded of course," Ayanna said with a shrug of her shoulders. "Impersonation is a hefty crime here, you must understand. We've had a horrible history with it."

So yes, I was definitely panicking.

Dinners at Fayharbor were extravagant. Food was always piled higher than your line of sight on the long tables, a small orchestra played stringed instruments in the corner, and everyone was dressed to the brim in colorful lace, satin, and velvet to show off their wealth. While never in attendance, spying through a window gave me as much experience as I needed to know what a proper royal dinner was.

So it was shocking, to say the least, as I sat opposite of Prince Erevos in the gloomiest dining room I had ever seen. Not only was the long table void of heaps and piles of food, but it was void of any people as well. A sad cluster of candles in the middle of the table provided little to no light.

As Erevos sat at one end and a nearby serving gentleman pulled out a chair for me to sit in at the opposite end, it was too far apart to be classified as a casual dinner between two people. But after what Ayanna had told me, the seating arrangement was a relief rather than an annoyance. There was a new pressure now to act my part as Princess Nesrin - death as punishment had never really occurred to me before, as silly as it sounded. In Fayharbor, it had to be a horrid offense to even think of the death penalty rather than throwing someone in the dungeons.

As a bowl of soup was placed in front of me, I picked up one of the many spoons laid out before me with a shaking hand and stirred its murky contents around. Death had a funny way of seizing one's appetite.

The courses were switched out in timed intervals and the servers hesitated each time before taking my untouched food. After I nudged away multiple plates and bowls with pointed, silent looks, they eventually gave up and took them away briskly.

When dinner was blessedly over, a cup of steaming black coffee was placed in front of me along with a variety of sugars and creams. I had calmed my nerves enough that the scent of the darkly roasted beans appealed to my stomach and I picked up the hot cup carefully.

"Leave us," Erevos said, his demanding voice reverberating through the room and my chest. My fingers began to shake again, but I willed them to stay still as I took a hesitant sip. As if nothing bothered me, as if those two, simple words did not shake me to my core.

Silently, everyone in the room took their leave and the doors were snapped shut. There was no rain tonight and for once I wished for it - for something to break the heavy silence. The candles flickered and I finally lifted my gaze to the other end of the table.

Prince Erevos looked every bit the villain people made him out to be. Gone was the gentleness I had glimpsed this morning in the gardens. The dim light cast shadows on his sharp features and did nothing to brighten his dark eyes as he stared at me. My hand betrayed me and shook this time. A few drops darkened the tablecloth. When I set my cup down a little too suddenly, his attention flickered to my hands. I hid them in my lap.

He stood up and I barely contained a flinch as he walked across the large room and grabbed hold of a chair, dragging it towards me. I was sure he could hear the uneven pounding of my heart as he sat beside me in the seat backward, resting his arms on its back. I stared ahead, trying to control my breathing, avoiding his gaze. "Your Highness?" I asked softly, phrasing his title as a question.

"I thought I told you to call me by name," Erevos said coldly.

"E-Erevos," I corrected. I was too scared to try and tease him this time.

"Was the food not to your liking? You did not eat."

Damn. And here I was thinking I had been cleverly hiding my lack of appetite. "I was not hungry, Your– Erevos." My eyes flickered to the fraction of a smile that slid on his lips at hearing his name.

Erevos played with a sugar spoon, stirring the crystals in the tiny jar absentmindedly. "Your demeanor has changed since this morning. What happened?"

Everything. Everything had happened. "Nothing."

He hummed his doubt and silence fell once more between us. I tried to think of something to say, anything, that would distract him from this line of conversation. Clearing my throat, I said, "May I ask a question?" I did not wait for his reply, pushing on. "You have tried for quite some time to arrange a marriage for yourself. Why do you keep pursuing it?"

His hand stilled, the spoon in mid-stir. "What?"

I rushed on, my words coming out in haste. "You just...do not seem like you *want* to get married. Why–"

"Faygrave is cursed," he interrupted. My mouth snapped shut. I had not expected him to reply. Erevos continued, "This land thrives on happiness - the happiness of its rulers' unity, to be exact. Without it, it's–" He waved his hand towards the murky darkness that lay beyond the windows around us, "--dead."

I sat back, shocked. Not only had I not expected an answer, but I also did not expect such an honest one. It made sense now why he was so desperate for marriage. My fingers tightened around the folds of my dress. "What caused the curse?"

Erevos merely shrugged his shoulders once. "Our land has been like this for years."

"Why didn't you tell me this yesterday when we met?"

"Does it matter?" A perfect eyebrow raised in question. "You were sent here by Fayharbor to be wed to me whether you like it or not - whether you are helping this land or not."

I opened and closed my mouth repeatedly, not quite sure which part of that to address first. I chose the former. "Of course it matters. We would be partners working towards a cause rather than..."

"Rather than what? Enemies?"

My cheeks heated and I looked away. "I didn't say that."

"Then what is the opposite of partners?"

I also could not answer that. I ran a hand through my short hair, frowning as I was reminded of the length once more. What a mess we were in. I was forced to pretend to be someone else and here he was having pure enough intentions. My hand froze and my heart stilled. I refused to look at him as I said, "Why do you have to marry a princess? Why not just...grab someone random? Surely that would work."

Erevos did not look worried as he studied the signet ring on his finger. "The land can only benefit from the happiness of lineage with royal blood."

"Ah. Of course."

Surely, I was going to die. Beheaded, actually, by the Prince of Faygrave. I was not royalty and I could not hide it - he would find out one way or another and especially when our wedding ceremony would not produce the revival of his land.

Fantastic.

Great.

If my mother knew, her heart would break in two.

For some horrible reason, Erevos insisted on walking me back to my quarters. "It's late," he had said. So we walked in silence together down the dark and quiet halls. Not for the first time, I wondered where his family was. Of course, there had been rumors - but it seemed a lot of the rumors about this man were twisted lies with just a drop of truth.

"What are you thinking about?"

His voice was soft and caught me off-guard, so I answered without thinking. "I was wondering how lonely it must be to live here by yourself."

I could have sworn his step faltered, but it could have been a trick of the eye, for he still walked in step with me. Erevos answered simply, "I enjoy it."

It was my turn to hum unconvincingly and I received that small smile of his in return.

My room was not far away and soon we reached it. I intended to slip quickly away, but he halted my escape with a hand on my wrist, causing me to startle.

Erevos' attention was on the contact of our skin rather than my face as he said in a low voice, "You have twenty-four hours left."

I had forgotten the ridiculous words he had said just last night and frowned. "You are an odd one, aren't you?"

My teasing did not take effect and there was no hint of amusement on his face. "I could say the same about you."

"Pardon?" I was distracted by his proximity. His fingers were strangely soft around my wrist.

"Such an odd princess," he mumbled, leaning close. I couldn't take my eyes from his lips as he talked. "What kind of princess readies herself in the morning? Or misinterprets a nightgown for a dress?" The words slowly pulled me from my muddled thoughts and he continued, "What sort of royalty addresses other royalty by their title? Or use the wrong silverware at dinner?"

My stomach had dropped by now and I was no longer focused on his touch. My lips parted but no words came out. Fear had taken hold of my vocal cords and I could not answer even if I thought of something clever enough to convince him. Was he always this observant? As pitiful and cliche as it sounded, I was not accustomed to being watched so closely. I was ignored, overlooked.

But Erevos merely smiled. It was a conniving smile - a smile full of promises - or threats? But I guessed they were the same in our situation. He raised my wrist up and pressed his lips to my skin. "Goodnight, Princess Nesrin of Fayharbor."

Did he know?

Of course he knew.

But if so - why not kill me now?

He must not be sure. Was I being tested?

The skin on the back of my hand burned the entire night and I could not fall asleep until dawn. Yet in the face of my impending doom, all I could think was:

How nice it would be if Erevos would call me by my *name.*

Sunshine.

I sat in my bed amongst the blankets and pillows and stared out my windows in utter shock. The past two nights I had left the curtains wide open knowing the sun would not wake me and here it was proving me wrong. Rays of light flooded my borrowed room, soaking it in warmth.

Ayanna knocked and entered, carrying a large tray. "Good morning, Princess. Did you need help dressing this morning?" She set the tray on my bed and lifted the lid. It was laden with every item of breakfast food I could imagine. Coffee, black - just like I had taken it last night - tempted me the most and I took it in between both my palms to relish the warmth. I sipped tentatively. "What is the occasion?"

"His Highness sent it," she said, picking up a small piece of folded parchment from the tray.

My eyes slid from the note to the windows as I said, "Please read it to me."

"It says to meet His Highness at the docks," Ayanna said.

My fingers tightened on the ceramic cup. "I do not need assistance this morning, Ayanna. But I have a favor: Please take this tray back and split it amongst yourselves."

Ayanna's lips parted in surprise. "Princess?"

"I appreciate His Highness' gesture, but I'm afraid I still have no appetite. Please, I do not want the food to go to waste."

The girl seemed hesitant but obeyed, covering the tray back up and leaving the room. When the door clicked shut, I carefully unfolded the note that she had left, staring at the beautiful curves and loops of letters that Erevos had written there.

A shimmering lake was nestled behind the castle, stretching miles in each direction. Dark clouds dotted the skies, but there was still more sunshine than I had seen since arriving in Faygrave. It was beautiful.

Erevos stood at the end of a long pier, hands behind his back. The billowy, dark gray shirt tucked into casual slacks was a stark contrast from the suits and formal attire I had seen him in the past few times. His usually-styled hair was loose, falling over his forehead in the slight breeze. My heart was beating four times for every step I took towards him, my thoughts an absolute scattered mess.

He turned, hands in his pockets. "I had thought I would have to wait here all day." His eyes roamed over the clothing I had chosen for the day and I felt my cheeks warm. I had switched out the dress for high-waisted pants and a button-up blouse. A smile touched his lips and he said with amusement, "We match."

I surveyed the lake, ignoring the warmth in his voice the best I could. "The sun is out. Last night's story of a cursed land sounds a little ridiculous now, I hope you know."

Erevos hummed. "Maybe it senses a growing fondness."

I did not have the chance to reply as he led me to a waiting rowboat. Once he had rowed us out quite a way, he laid the oars down across his lap and surveyed our surroundings. The water beneath us was a murky blue and I could not see how deep the bottom lay. There were no birds, no splash of a fish, no sign of any life. The nerves I had forgotten about started to curl once more in the pit of my stomach. “Why did you bring us out here?”

Erevos’ fingers skimmed the surface of the lake, breaking its odd stillness. “This is a dead lake. No life lives inside it or on its shores. No one comes near it - they’re afraid it is also cursed.”

My mouth was dry and I tried to swallow the rising uneasiness. “That did not answer my question.”

He turned his eyes to me at last and leaned forward, elbows on his knees, fingers interlaced. “No one will hear any conversation from shore. No screams of help or yells of anger.” He paused as fear squeezed my lungs. “But more importantly - no one will hear your secrets, if you so wish to speak of them.”

I faltered. What? My surprise must have shown on my face for he laughed a little.

“Did you think I brought you here to kill you?” Erevos asked with a dark chuckle. “Come now, I thought we were past that.”

“*Past that?* You’re the one who mentioned screaming and yelling,” I mumbled distractedly. There was meaning behind his simple words. He definitely knew I was hiding something, just didn’t know what. I met his curious eyes, my teeth gnawing at my bottom lip. “Even if I could trust you with my secrets, I am...” An odd sensation cut my words off, like a hand gripping my throat. I reached for my throat with my own hand and trailed my fingers over the skin, feeling nothing.

“You are...?” Erevos urged.

I cleared my throat and the pressure weakened. “I am bound to–” A gasp escaped my lips before my airway was completely cut off.

“Nesrin?” The prince leaned forward, fingers touching my wrist.

I struggled to breathe and closed my eyes, focusing hard. The curse must have sensed my want to tell its secret. “I can’t tell you.” I forced out the words and the invisible hand immediately let go. Oxygen blissfully rushed to fill my lungs and the relief had me sagging against the back of the boat. My hand gripped the front of my shirt, the quick beat of my heart reassuring me.

Erevos was staring at me oddly, curiously. My uneven breathing was the only thing breaking the mountains of silence between us. He was studying me like he never had before and if it wasn’t for my near strangulation, I would probably be embarrassed by his rapt attention.

Finally, after what felt like years, he spoke softly. "Do you remember that your forty-eight hours are up by sundown?" I did and nodded my acknowledgment. He continued. "The fate of my land rests solely in my hands, so I hope you understand that I must go through with this marriage arrangement, no matter how much either of us will hate it–"

"You'll hate it?" I asked suddenly, my voice slightly raw.

His eyebrows pulled together in confusion. "Will you not?"

Wouldn't I?

Shouldn't I?

My hesitation confused the both of us. Frustrated I could not speak about the curse, my heart wished it could speak of some sort of honesty. My words were rushed as I said, "If the circumstances were different, I feel like it wouldn't be so bad."

Erevos laughed shortly, no humor to be found. "How romantic."

I blushed. "Says the person who wanted me to sign a contract right when we met."

"Fair," he agreed, dipping his fingers once more into the water.

I tried again, choosing my words very carefully as I mentally tip-toed around the edge of the curse. "Marriage has never been at the top of my list - or any relationship, as a matter of fact. I have worked hard since I was a child and never had the chance to even think about myself. This unfortunate situation has thrown me into a whole new world and I am still adjusting but..." I paused, mulling over the raw honesty I had never voiced. "You are different from what I imagined and from what everyone made you out to be. I can be convinced to help you restore your lands but I would need something from you in return."

Erevos was quiet, arms crossed across his chest. "You do realize you are in no position to bargain, right?"

Thunder rumbled in the distance. Frustrated tears blurred my vision momentarily as a ray of sunshine slid across the lake and engulfed us for a few moments, warming my skin. It lit up the small smile on Erevos' face as he said, "What do you need?"

I took a deep breath, calming my nerves. Our gazes locked and I steeled myself. "I need your help."

The drizzling rain had returned the moment my feet touched the dock. Erevos cursed, putting a hand over his head. As if that would help. He slid his other hand into mine and I jumped from the sudden touch of his skin. A smile teased his lips. "Let's run for it."

As we ran, the drizzle quickly turned to a full torrential downpour and soon we were drenched and dripping with cold rain. Erevos' hold on my hand stayed as he led me through the grounds, inside a door, up a flight of stairs, and through several more doors. I quickly recognized this room to be the office from my first day here. The fireplace was blissfully lit and I went to move towards it, but my hand was tugged back.

"As much as I would like for you to get warm, would you please take your shoes off?" Erevos said as he reached down to take his own boots off.

"Oh, of course, I'm sorry," I said, rushing to slip off the muddy flats. I should have remembered from our first encounter that he liked to keep things clean. As I straightened, I was met with a full view of drenched clothing hugging Erevos' tall frame. My cheeks immediately flared with heat and I couldn't turn away fast enough.

My heart stopped with the realization I probably looked no better. My shirt clung embarrassingly to my body. I turned back to him. "Do you have–"

Erevos raised an eyebrow in question as his fingers swiftly untucked his own shirt. Before I could react, he was pulling it over his head in one go, showing me an enormous amount of pale skin. I turned away with a yelp of surprise and ran into an end table, the heat on my face only increasing. "Y-Your Highness!"

His chuckle was laced with something that did not help the situation *at all.* "You seem flustered."

"Do I?" My voice was high, borderline hysteric. I had successfully made it to the fireplace and refused to look away from the flames. I heard the rustle of more clothing and I tried with all my might to stop the flurry of thoughts and images coursing through me.

Erevos was by my side now and I couldn't help glancing over at him. He had switched to dry slacks but still wore no shirt. I stared instead at our bare feet on the carpet rather than his bare chest. "Your Highness-" He made a noise of frustration and I sighed, correcting myself. So touchy. "Erevos, may I be permitted to go and change clothes? Please?"

"You can borrow mine–"

I looked up at him incredulously, forgetting for only a moment why I was avoiding looking at him. "You think your clothes would fit me? I don't know if I'm offended or flattered."

It was his turn for his cheeks to color. He coughed and looked away, raising his hand to snap his fingers. A neatly folded pile of clothes appeared in his palm and he held them out to me. "They're yours."

I took them, pursing my lips. "You did that before. You have magic?"

Erevos looked embarrassed still. "A little, yes."

Once changed into dry clothes, I made myself comfortable in the chair opposite Erevos, his large desk in between us. The distance between us as well as the shirt that I forced him to wear calmed my nerves immensely, but the thick sheet of parchment lying innocently on the desk did quite the opposite.

Now is the time, I thought, my eyes roaming over the beautiful swirls of letters that I now knew were written by Erevos' hand. My fingers gripped the edge of my chair. My stomach was in so many knots I was sure I was going to throw up. A small part of me still feared the wrath of deceiving the man in front of me, but as I looked up at him through my lashes, I saw the warmth in his own eyes and remembered our promise. We would help each other.

As Erevos handed me a quill and I took it hesitantly. With the tip poised above the marriage contract, I swallowed hard. "You should know everything before I sign this. But it's...complicated."

He was patient, watching me. Where to even start? *How* to even start? I could not risk the curse retaliating against me again. My eyes drifted toward the quill in my hand. A drop of ink had gathered at the white tip and I watched it drip onto the paper below. The black dot spread slowly and my thoughts gathered. "I...cannot read." I bit my tongue to keep *Your Highness* in my mouth. How long would it take to curb that habit?

Erevos did not seem surprised at all. He glanced from me, to the contract, then back to me. "Sorry to disappoint you, but I knew from the beginning you were not Princess Nesrin of Fayharbor."

I could do nothing but stare at him open-mouthed. He smirked and continued. "I was angry at first then I quickly realized you also did not want to be pretending to be someone else, much less my fiance. I only just pieced together this afternoon that you are under some sort of curse to keep you from telling me anything."

I clawed my way through my shock and set the quill down, standing up. "And you were just going to marry me knowing all of this? You said it yourself that the curse on your land will only be appeased from a *royal* wedding."

Erevos tilted his head, his smile slipping. "Today proved all of that wrong."

"Obviously not," I said, waving toward the rain-soaked windows around us.

"There was a moment of sunshine, if you recall."

"That was just a passing storm–"

Erevos leveled a look at me. "There is no such thing as a *passing storm* in Faygrave. It is constant."

I faltered, slowly sitting back in my chair. He leaned forward and laced his fingers together. "Now we just have to find a way for you to tell me your story without actually telling me. Once you are able to get around the curse, it should be broken."

"Why can't I just sign the contract as Nesrin?" I asked.

"It cannot accept any other names other than the one who is signing it." He took a moment to think, seeming to search the room for answers I could not see. I was honestly just grateful he was not sentencing me to death for pretending to be someone else. I wondered if Ayanna's beheading story was another truth riddled with lies.

"There," he said, interrupting my thoughts and pointing to a wardrobe across the room. "Get inside there."

"Excuse me?"

Erevos stood up impatiently and came around the desk. He grabbed my wrist, tugging me out of my chair. "Just trust me, come on."

We stood in front of the wardrobe. He shoved aside all the hanging coats and cleared off a space on the floor. I watched him, utterly confused. When he was finished, he pointed again. "I want you to sit inside here–"

"What?!"

"--and tell the wardrobe what happened," he finished, like it was the most normal thing to say.

I couldn't help but to laugh, which made him frown. I wasn't sure why, but this whole situation was a little...adorable. "I don't think this will work, but if you insist."

"I'm sure the curse says something about you not being able to tell any *living* thing. So sit in there and just...talk."

It was ridiculous.

But as I sat there in the dark, doors closed, and began to speak, I felt no restriction to my airway, no interruption to my words. Since the beginning of this entire situation, I had tried my best to stay strong and not pity myself. I was scared, worried, and so anxious to the point of making myself sick, but I knew none of that would fix anything. And now that I let all the words out, I could feel the curse begin to unwind and slip from where it had bound me together. Relieved, tears slipped down my cheeks and I let myself cry.

I wasn't sure how long I sat there sobbing but the doors of the wardrobe eventually opened, revealing dim light and the prince whom I owed a huge favor. Who would have thought he would be the one to get me out of this mess?

Erevos was holding his hand out to me, worry etched on his features. "Are you okay? Was it too painful?"

I wiped my tears and slipped my hand into his, my heart flip-flopping at his concern. "Your turn now. Let's go break another curse."

"This is ridiculous," Erevos said, borderline sounding like a whining toddler.

"You promised me." I laughed a little, steeling my resolve against the look he gave me.

We were standing at the castle's main doors that were thrown open to the sunshine outside. There was no cloud in sight and it had been that way for days now.

I had signed the contract while still wiping snot from my nose after crawling out of the wardrobe. Given that I could not properly write, it was really just a scribble and an inked thumbprint - but it worked all the same. Such a small gesture and I was immediately wed to Prince Erevos of Faygrave. He had to leave for a day to deal with sorting out all the trouble in Fayharbor and had only just returned. When I had offered to come with, Erevos had absent-mindedly tucked a short strand of hair behind my ear and merely told me I would never have to deal with the likes of them again.

I was a little sad to not be able to explain myself, but I knew Erevos held his own frustrations against Queen Melantha and her beloved daughter. He reassured me his new bride would not be mentioned and he only intended to inform the queen of his daughter's deceit and all the trouble she caused.

We were officially married and yet our relationship was...undefinable. I found that every time I saw him, my heart skipped - every time he reached for my hand, my breath caught. I had never been in love before. Had he? Did he also feel like this? So many unanswered questions, but for now we would celebrate both our curses broken and a new odd sort of friendship taking its place.

So here I stood, outside in the rays of warm sunshine, on the top of the steps of the castle that had been my strange home for the past week. Ayanna squeezed by Erevos through the doorway, putting a suitcase by my feet. I smiled and thanked her. Last night I had packed up all my belongings, which consisted only of the clothing I had been given - the ones that fit, at least.

Erevos frowned at the case, then glanced up at me. "Why do we need to do this?"

"Hush," I said to him, nodding to Ayanna. She pulled the large doors shut with a bang, the noise reverberating through my chest.

I stared up at the castle and looked at it with a new perspective. In the daylight, it seemed much less formidable than when I first saw it. Hiding my smile, I reached out to knock on the door. It opened before I could and Erevos still stood there, his frown even deeper.

"This is ridicu–"

"Like we practiced," I whispered.

He took a deep breath, eyes flicking to the heavens for support. When they landed back on me, I felt my pulse jump. He hadn't styled his hair today and I began to realize it was my preferred look. Erevos' voice was deep as he said, "I'm Prince Erevos of Faygrave. And who might you be?"

I couldn't help the grin that spread across my lips. "My name is Isolde, Your Highness. Please call me Sol."

Erevos smiled then as he heard my name for the first time. He stepped forward, taking my hand in his and bringing it up to his lips. "Sol. Please never call me *Your Highness* ever again."

My heart was going to beat out of my chest, I was sure. To hear him finally say my name was bliss. I blamed the warmth creeping up my neck on the weather.

His lips stayed on my skin, eyes never leaving mine. "Your name means 'sun', did you know?"

I mumbled my affirmation, not really able to do much more. It only made his smile widen as he said, "What a match we are, Sol. The day to my night."

"I HOPE TO ANNOY YOU TO THE POINT WHERE YOU ACTUALLY RETURN ME TO MY MOTHER."

The Nightingale in the Temple

E.A. Williams

In the valley between the three Sister Mountains sat a lake that legend said was as deep as the highest mountain was tall. Long ago a fearless tribe of wandering people settled along its banks, finding the glittering water too beautiful to leave. Slowly they built their lives at the water's edge, growing into a powerful city where merchants would crowd the only road that led to its gate, plying exotic wares from places as far away as the salt sea. Boats carrying noblemen would sail up the river that flowed down from the lake. All of them came to pay tribute to the sultan of the Great City, whose waters fed their people.

Sometimes Andalah would stare up at the clouds that covered the mountain peaks and wonder which was the tallest. The thought would come to her most often in the bleak light of the mid-morning when her brothers, Altair and Akos, began their daily argument over to whom her marriage would be most advantageous. A subject that had only recently become of any interest to her brothers. It was not that they were callous, or perhaps they were, but Andalah did not see it. They were her brothers after all. It was rather that in the years since their mother's death, their father, sultan Ornette, had poured his life's blood into the good works of the city. While the people outside loved him for it, inside the palace walls his family grew apart. So Andalah would stare up at the mountains and wonder how deep the lake must be if she had never seen the top of even the shortest mountain. Eventually, Altair would proclaim his opinion superior by virtue of his status as the first son and heir, to which Akos would storm out of the dining room, a curse and a half-eaten breakfast still steaming at his seat. To which Altair would laugh, his mouth half full of food, and tell Andalah that she would bring them honor when her time came to marry.

Honor was not of particular scarcity in the palace of the Great City, their father was the most powerful man on the continent, save for the Golden City and its warrior prince, a place that Andalah was not convinced was real. Often the stories the old merchants told of the prince and his lands were too outlandish to be believed. Moreover, they could never quite explain how they knew of a land they had never been to, a land beyond the Wild Wood as untamed as its people, and across the Iron Sand, red hot from the merciless sun. They would wave her off and slip a gold coin into the temple offering plate with a smile.

Andalah spent most of her time in the city's temples. They attracted people from every walk of life, from the beggars in their tattered tunics to merchants dripping in silk, the temples welcomed them all. While her mother was alive, Andalah had gone with her each day to pray at the temple steps and offer their hands to do good works. She carried on this way now, going to the temple to serve food to the city's orphans, and tend to the sick, coming home with calloused hands, a consequence of labor her brothers berated her for.

"What man will want a lady with hands as rough as these?" Akos said at dinner, as flames roared in the colossal fireplace behind their father.

The orange and white flames licked the chimney black and Andalah did not answer him.

"Father?" Akos turned to the sultan, framed as he was by the imposing white marble griffins of the fireplace and the blinding light of the flames within.

The sultan's expression was almost entirely in shadow, save for his stiff broad shoulders and his steepled fingers. He was lost in thought tonight, as he had been on many nights since his wife's death. Although tonight it seemed more pointed than the directionless melancholy Andalah had grown used to.

"Father?" Altair grunted, finally catching the sultan's attention. "Akos was speaking."

"I heard him," The sultan acknowledged with a gruff twist of his head towards his younger son. "Worry about your own hands, Akos."

Altair snickered under his breath, poorly hiding his amusement behind a goblet of wine.

"Are you so removed by the cushioned seats of congress that your hands are not as soft as your brother's?" Ornette reprimanded and though Andalah could not see his eyes, she knew they were dark with frustration. "You live in the palace and think yourself above the people who have built it. "

"What is wrong father?" Altair's voice faltered; his amusement was swept away by his father's stern words. "Have Akos and I wronged you in some way?"

The room was still as they waited for the sultan's answer, though Andalah did not need to hear the words. She had heard from the priests of the Southern Temple that the Oracle had refused to bless the last temple her father built. They said it did not fulfill his promise.

The promise was one that sultan Ornette had made to his wife before her death. He would build the most beautiful temple in all the world, for her, to stand immemorial for as long as the city should keep. Since that day he had built three. The first was the Southern Temple which straddled the mouth of the river in a gleaming stone arch that beckoned to weary travelers from the city's gate. Andalah had seen world-worn traders stand in its dazzling hall and stare down as the river ran beneath them, their eyes wide with awe. Yet this did not gain the Oracle's blessing.

The second temple was the Northern Temple which sat at the base of one of the Sister Mountains surrounded by an untamable orchard of cherry trees that bloomed all spring and whose fruit was used to make the wine for all the city's festivals. On the longest day of the year, the sun shone red off the amber walls of the temple and warmed the ground all the way to the shores of the lake. People of the city, rich and poor alike, would bask in its light and forget their social divide in favor of the warmth of its beauty. Still the Oracle withheld their blessing.

The third temple had no name and seemed now like it would never be finished. It sat alone on an uninhabited island in the lake, whose waters were so endlessly deep and wide that the fishermen of the city dared not travel to its center. Masons had toiled for years to build the nameless temple's three twisting spires that mirrored the Sister Mountains. It had taken so long for them to place the final stones that moss had already begun to creep up its walls at the bottom. Even this did not assuage the Oracle's demands.

"There was no blessing," Ornette spoke into his hands, his voice barely louder than the fire. "It is not enough."

"What could ever be enough, father?" Akos asked, his well-known contempt for the temples heavy in his voice. "What can one person know of all the beauty in the world?"

"Exactly," Altair seconded his brother's opinion.

"I made a promise," The sultan opened his hands inviting the scrutiny of all his children. "I am honor bound to fulfill it."

"A promise that the Oracle has made impossible," Akos countered, his dark brows twisting in derision. "Have you not done everything you can to keep your word?"

"What does the Oracle want that you have not given?" Altair asked, sharing a look with his brother that Andalah was left out of.

"The Oracle asks only for one thing." The sultan stared out from the table, his eyes meeting Andalah's with a sad smile that drew his face long. Not for the first time since her mother died, Andalah worried that her father would perish from his broken heart.

"Gold, no doubt," Akos grunted, stabbing his fork into a piece of roasted boar on his plate with a sharp twang when the metal tinges scraped along the porcelain plate.

"Gold, I have, son." Ornette leaned back in his chair, sighing heavily. "The temple is missing a nightingale. I must fill the temple with its song, only then will I have fulfilled my promise."

"A nightingale?" Altair slouched back against his seat, scratching his perfectly groomed goatee. "All the nightingales are dead. No one has seen one since before I was born. The Oracle knows this."

"I do not know if one lies beyond the gates of our city," The sultan answered, the bristles of his graying beard catching in the light. "I have no choice but to look."

"It is a trick," Akos spoke up. "The Oracle wants you to leave the city so they can seize power while you are gone on this ridiculous task. Surely you can see it."

"You will be in charge while I am away. The city will be well tended."

At her father's words, Andalah's stomach tied itself into knots. Without her father here to stop them, Altair and Akos would surely marry her off to some wealthy nobleman who would overlook her rough hands and soft middle for the favor of the palace.

"The congress will demand a sultan to command the city," Altair spoke confidently and concisely in the way that his years addressing the city's congress had taught him to. "If you leave to search for this bird you will have to give up your rule to me."

"Or me," Akos vied for the position.

"I cannot put the burden of the city on your shoulders just yet," The sultan closed his eyes, his thoughts warring on his face.

Over the table Andalah watched as her brothers shared a silent and aggravated conversation of hand gestures, mouthing words she couldn't make out.

"You will go," The sultan sat up, leaning his elbows on the dark wooden table. "You and Akos will go in search of the nightingale. Each of you will take a battalion. Whoever brings it to me first will be named my heir."

A fickle light sparked to life in her brothers' eyes, one Andalah did not like.

"What if they cannot find it, father?" She asked, her voice low and cool like the morning mist.

"In one year if the nightingale cannot be found then I will beseech the Oracle to unbind me from my promise." The despair in her father's voice broke Andalah's heart. "I cannot bring to the temple that which does not exist."

"We'll leave on the start of the next moon cycle," Altair butted in, already planning his quest. "That will be plenty of time to gather men and plan separate routes."

"Yes," Akos agreed.

Her brothers began their conquest before they finished their dinners, both oblivious to the defeated look on their father's face. It wasn't that they were callous Andalah thought, it couldn't be.

Looking back at the city gates Andalah saw the giant arch of the Southern Temple and the torrent waters of the river mouth pouring out from underneath it. The dark stones of its constructions shone inky green like the coiled scales of a massive serpent. She blinked against the glare of the sun and turned her back to the three Sister Mountains that cupped the city between them. A flash of panic pounded in her chest. She adjusted the strap of her bag where it bit into the soft skin of her shoulder.

It was hot under Andalah's disguise and as sweat dripped down her back and under the binding that held her large breasts flat against her chest, she worried that she was making a mistake. She worried that the palace guards had already noticed her absence and sounded the alarm. Even if they had, the palace bells were already ringing, heralding her brothers' departure. The city would not know to look for her for another day. Tucking a stray curl back under the cap that hid her heavy braid, she sped up her pace wanting to keep with the cover of her brothers' caravans for as long as she was able.

The men chatted as they walked along with the wagons, paying no attention to her and so she was able to listen without being observed.

"Akos, himself asked me to join," A tall man with a long-black beard spoke to a man with too many muscles and not enough neck who was almost as short as Andalah. "We are taking the South road, heading to the coast. We will see if nightingales like the sweet flesh of the coffee fruit that grows there, and if not, I am sure that our prince will be consoled by the sweet lips of the women who run the cafes."

The short man snorted his amusement, taking a swig from the wineskin at his side.

"Altair is taking us East," He took another swig. "He has business with a silk merchant in the City of Colors. The markets there are frequented by merchants from all over the continent. If the bird exists, they will have heard tell."

"And if not," The bearded man smirked, tilting his head from side to side in a gesture that made him look smug. "A man could make his fortune in that city."

"Aye," The short man nodded, offering his wineskin to his conversation partner. "Prince Altair is a smart man. Why waste resources going off to look for the nightingale when information could come to us?"

"Akos is clever enough to not waste our time looking for a myth," said the bearded man, taking a long drink. "No one has seen a nightingale in a hundred years. The sultan is a devout man, and his temples bring our city honor, but any man with eyes can see their beauty. The Oracle knows not what they speak, the nightingale is gone."

Andalah tripped over a stone on the road, knocking into the men.

"Careful boy," The taller of the two barked at Andalah and shoved her shoulder hard enough to make her stumble into another man who shoved her back towards the breaded man who tucked her under his arm with a laugh. "Don't look so scared, boy. You've got enough stuffing on you to last the whole trip. Might make it over the Iron Sands with that."

The man patted her cheeks, his face a twist of arrogance and then a vague recognition. Just a flicker of something behind his eyes that had Andalah pulling free of his grip to slink off into the dust and noise of the crowded road, the sweat on her chest having turned cold.

It took the caravans four days to reach the end of the city road, where it split to the East and to the South. Four days of dust, sweat, and blistered feet. Three nights of sleeping with the horses where Andalah would be safe from wandering men. The stench of unwashed bodies barely registered by the time her brother's battalions separated to follow the new roads to the cities of men and trade, to look for the nightingale and possibly their fortunes.

Andalah did not follow. She saw no logic in searching for a creature that had not been seen by the eyes of men in a hundred years, in cities built by them. No, if the nightingale lived, it must be beyond the rule of man. So, Andalah turned Westward, where there was no road, nor promise of safety. The cool breeze of the Wild Wood, it's dark leaves always green no matter the season, swept over Andalah's hot skin. She shivered, adjusting her satchel as she set her shoulders hard against the doubt heavy in her heart. This was as far as she had ever been outside of the city, and she had certainly never gone alone.

There were stories of the woods that were shared in the orphanages of the Great City, legends of the creatures living in its depths. Andalah had listened to a boy half her age tell the other children about a family of tigers that roamed the woods who could speak the common tongue and would burn down half the forest just to bake their bread. Another boy told a story of a tribe of savage women living in the hollowed-out trunks of trees, their skin turned green by moss, who measured their strength by the length of their braided hair. Andalah had liked that one. Her own braid fell to her hips, and she wanted to think that women of the Wild Wood would think she was a warrior.

Inside, the forest was filled with noise; the leaves rustling, the small animals chittering to one another as the stranger moved through their home. Birds called out their songs in long euphonious melodies, none of them the call of the nightingale. This was not what she had expected. The tales of the Wild Wood were always warnings with terrible ends for any traveler naive enough to cross into its dark territory, but here the sunlight dappled against Andalah's skin, and the breeze cooled the sweat her journey set upon her brow.

Turning her back to the sun Andalah made her way deeper into the forest until she heard the gurgling noise of water rushing over stones. She followed the sound to the banks of a river that, unlike the river that flowed from the gates of her father's city, was shallow. Only the occasional ripple disturbed the gentle surface of the stream and Andalah found herself smiling at the serene melody its current played along the smooth rocks of its shore. She followed it for some ways, delighting in the company of birds and small creatures that ventured to the water for nourishment or curiosity.

She stooped to pet the tufted ears of a long weasel sort of animal with a white belly and the kind of keen black eyes that small predators often have, when a shriek from just beyond a bend in the river sent the animal running back into the cover of the foliage. The sounds of something thrashing in the water drew her further along its path where a tree, wider than the fireplace in the great hall of her father's palace, twisted itself far into the river. Half the current caught in the tree's massive roots, where it swirled calmly into a deep pool, shaded entirely by the branches of the ancient cypress.

The shriek rang out again, a furious, violent sound that sent birds soaring from their perches. It was followed by the wet sound of something, or someone struggling in the water. Carefully, Andalah snuck around the trunk of the tree. Though she had yet to encounter any talking tigers or savage women, the sun had yet to set, and her journey was bound to be a long one.

Peeking out from behind a low branch, Andalah saw the slick green skin of something caught in the tree's roots. White water splashed around the creature making it nearly impossible to see clearly, but distress is a universal language that Andalah could not ignore. Shedding her heavy pack and thick leather boots she dove into the pool. In two steady kicks, she was able to take the creature in her arms. Its wriggling doubled as Andalah tried to lift it out of the water. It was of no use. The thing, whatever it was, was scared beyond reason and could not know that she was there to help. It fought with all its waning might against Andalah's grip, tangling its matted hair further into the web of roots that had insnared it.

The creature rolled to its side, preparing to shriek again when its mossy eyes settled on Andalah's. A strange recognition passed over its features, just as the same sort of understanding passed over Andalah's. This was not some pitiable creature caught by the current. This was one of the savage women of the wood, a legend told in whispers by the school children of the Great City. The woman blinked at her before hissing and jerking back, only to be forced under water by the unrelenting current.

"I mean only to help." Andalah shouted, her legs growing tired from keeping them both afloat. "Help. I am trying to help."

The woman's eyes narrowed at her as they both fought to stay above the water, and for a long moment Andalah was sure that the woman would resist again, drowning them both. With wary eyes the woman let herself relax in Andalah's arms. No longer fighting the woman and the water, Andalah could see where the woman's hair was tangled in a branch just below the surface.

Her fingers made quick work of the knots. In a moment they were both free and crawling onto the banks of the river to sit beneath the shade of the tree that was almost their grave.

Coughing, Andalah collapsed onto the muddy bank and let her head fall back. She took several short breaths, the taste of the mossy water fresh in her mouth. After a moment of staring up at the dappled leaf ceiling of the forest, Andalah rolled over onto her side.

The savage woman was crouching, her back against one thick root of the cypress that grew out of the shore. She was studying Andalah with strange green eyes with large dark pupils. Andalah studied her in return. The orphan boy had been right after all, the woman's skin was dappled green and brown like a toad, with grayish lips that were quirked in confusion. Her head tilted to and fro as she watched the princess, whipping a long tangled braid behind her as she did. Out of habit Andalah reached for the hat that had been concealing her own braid, it was gone.

Panic struck her. Without the hat, there was little else that would disguise her as a woman. The bindings around her chest couldn't hide her soft body from suspicious eyes the way the cap implied the shorn hair of a boy. It was such a simple solution and now it was gone. The tightness in her chest pulsed in beat with her heart as Andalah frantically searched the ground. Her fingers dug into the mud and rocks that surrounded her, the strange green woman almost forgotten.

"Dis," The voice was a guttural hiss of a word that had Andalah jerking around to stare at the green woman she had saved from the water.

"Dis," the woman said again, waving a sodden piece of fabric at the princess.

It took a moment for Andalah to recognize it, her hat.

"You found it." Andalah leaped forward unthinkingly and crashed into the tree root when the woman dodged away from her. "Ugh." Andalah shook off the impact and settled herself against the root with a calming breath. "Yes. That," She gestured to the hat. "That is mine. Can I have it back?"

"You want dis?" The green woman looked between the hat and Andalah and then to the long braid that fell over the princess' shoulder. "Why hide?"

"You speak?" Andalah nearly shouted, surprised, not just by the croaking accent with which the woman spoke, but the language that she spoke. The stories that reached the Great City never said the savage women could speak. Then again, the stories that reached the city didn't come from the most reliable sources.

"You speak," The woman parroted back and Andalah worried she had been surprised too soon. "Why not I?"

The common tongue was clunky in her grey mouth, but the words were familiar enough.

"I am sorry. I did not mean to imply that you would not, but I have never been to the Wild Wood. I did not think anyone here would speak as I do." Andalah blushed at her ignorance.

Her shrill embarrassed explanation was met with the slow blinking assessment of the woman as she took in Andalah's wet clothes and bare feet.

"You hide." It was not a question. It was a statement of the facts as the woman saw them. "Why?" She asked again, standing now she made her way over to the bag Andalah had left on the shoreline before jumping in to save her.

"I...I..." Andalah stuttered. Her journey had only just begun, and the disguise was her only protection from the soldiers her father would undoubtedly send to bring her back to the palace, and then she would never find the nightingale. "I'm searching for something. A bird, a nightingale. Have you seen one?"

"No," The woman tossed the wet cap onto the dry riverbank next to the boots and began digging around in Andalah's pack. "You hide from men who hunt this bird?"

"I hide from anyone who would harm me." *Or take me back before I find it*, Andalah finished in her head. "I need to find the bird to keep a promise."

The woman nodded once in a silent understanding, her interest in Andalah's pack waning.

"You follow the water until bends again," As the woman spoke Andalah saw movement in the trees beyond the river's bank, the blinking of half a dozen dark eyes, set in dapple green faces. "Wait there for the tiger, they might know your nightingale."

Andalah glanced down the river towards the place that the woman had pointed to and when she looked back the woman was gone.

The river did not bend that night, or the one after, and as Andalah lay on a bed of moss listening to the sounds of the forest that had so quickly become as comforting to her as the rumble of merchant wagons on the streets of the Great City. A breeze ruffled the long branches of the trees against one another, scratching out an easy rhythm as the animals of the dark chittered back and forth. Songbirds she had never heard before called their haunting music for the moon she could barely see beyond the canopy and Andalah wondered if one of them might be her nightingale.

On the third day in the woods the heat finally broke through the shadows and found her struggling with the heft of her pack. The cloth binding her chest was too tight and with every breath she could feel the creases of the fabric rubbing the soft skin of her breasts raw. It must have been midday by now, though the branches of the ancient cypress that grew over the river were low and scattered most of the sun's light. It shone with a particular harshness that Andalah knew was long past morning.

She paused just as her path beside the water began to curve and threw her pack to the ground. The relief was instantaneous but drew into sharp focus the irritation of her bindings. They had been a good idea, when she was traveling alongside her brother's men. Hiding amongst them as a boy gave her a level of anonymity that her overtly feminine physique would never allow. In those first days the bindings had been her only armor against being dragged back to her father's palace in disgrace, or worse. Now, alone in the Wild Wood, with her hair uncovered and the heat growing by the second, Andalah could not stand another moment trapped inside them, no matter the consequences.

Frantic, she reached beneath the laces of her shirt and pulled at the knot tucked expertly between her breasts. It took her several minutes to find the offending tie, her fingers slipping between the sweaty fold of her chest and belly. The longer it took the hotter she became, panic beginning its lapping roar in her ears as she lost track of her surroundings. Finally triumphant, Andalah yanked the end of her bindings out from under her shirt, uncoiling it one length at a time until she felt the blissful pop of the last loop release her from her sweaty prison.

With a deep breath of relief, she rubbed absently where her skin tingled as blood rushed back into it. That was when she finally heard it. Or perhaps, did not hear it. The song of the woods was no longer populated with the whispers of leaves and calls of curious animals, only the roar remained, one she had thought existed only in the rush of blood in her ears. It was not panic that played this tune, it was something else, something Andalah could not see yet.

A pungent smell greeted her as the wind changed, earthy and charred. Andalah knew immediately what the sound was. Dropping the bindings and abandoning her pack at the river's edge she ran into the forest, where the heat grew thicker. She did not have to go far.

The dense shadows of the lush green vegetation turned darker still with the heavy pall of smoke, forcing Andalah to cover her mouth and nose with her shirt. The flames licked a patch of sky they had cleared for themselves above the canopy. It was by some mercy that Andalah had any idea what to do. When she was small and her mother was still alive, they would visit the house of a city elder who lived high on the cliffs, far from the lake. One day a fire had consumed their stables and with no water to drown it, her mother had shoveled rocks and sand over the flames until they were no more. She had explained to Andalah that fire, like all things, needed breath to survive, to grow, to destroy. It was a lesson she had never found a use for, until today.

Dropping to her knees, Andalah began digging up clumps of wet dirt and throwing it on the flames. Smoke billowed behind her as decomposing leaves and wet soil smoldered before sputtering to a sizzling end. She crawled closer to the flames, her fingernails wrenching into the ground to pull handful after handful into the battle against the fire. Andalah lost herself to the back-breaking rhythm of the work. The heat and noise of the fire her oppressive companion. She knew if she stopped the destruction would spread and the creatures of the forest would be lost.

There was no way to tell how long she had worked with her hands in the soil and the flames at her side. Smoke blocked out the sun, and the light of the flames kept her from stopping well past when her muscles begged her to give up, but eventually the last of the fire choked out with a final angry hiss.

Falling back to sit upon her shins and gaze at the remnants of the wood, Andalah found the charred clearing in which she sat was much larger than she thought. Even as the forest's ever-present breeze blew away that last of the sputtering smoke, she could hardly see to the other side. As the wind picked up, peeling the ash of half-burnt trees into the silent air, Andalah heard a raspy mewl of pain coming from the other side of the clearing. Staggering to her feet, her legs cramped and arms muddy and raw, she made her way toward the noise.

Crossing the burned remains of the forest was quick but hazardous work. Twice she paused to stamp out embers still flickering. There was a body, slumped on its side, breathing in rapid panting heaves, all gray with ash and as Andalah approached, she heard again the raspy mewl that bid her closer in the first place. She studied the body, thinking at first that it was a man, tall and broad, wearing thick fur covered in the debris of the fire, but as the thing took another breath, she could see that it was no man.

"Run," the creature croaked out. "Save yourself."

There was a defeated edge to the creature's voice, a slur of smoke-clogged vocal cords and a mouth that was unused to the common tongue. The thing snarled, a yowling horrible sound, and rolled to face her.

"I said run," it spoke again, eyes wide, the pupils barely visible slits in the wide soot-stained face of a tiger.

"The fire is out," Andalah stopped abruptly, unable to come any closer or move any farther off. She was entranced by the creature in front of her. It was undoubtedly a tiger, even through the ash and dirt she could make out the striped fur and wide toothy muzzle, but its shoulders were set wrong for a beast that walked on four legs, and it wore trousers. Who in all the kingdoms had ever seen a tiger wearing pants, even in the Wild Wood?

"Out?" The tiger asked, closing its eyes in apparent relief. He was set upon by a bout of gagging coughs that wracked his shoulders and he rolled onto his front pressing himself upright.

"I... we," Andalah noticed the dirt covering the tiger's clawed hands and realized that they must have been fighting the fire from different sides. "We choked it out."

With one last hacking cough, he pushed onto his knees and then up onto his hind feet. At his full height, the tiger stood well over a foot taller than her, his thick muscles stretching under his fur. He looked around, twisting at the waist, eyes squinted, trying to get a good look at the extent of the damage when he stumbled, falling into Andalah. The creature was heavier than he looked which said a lot considering how large and muscular he was, but Andalah managed to keep them both upright.

"You need water," When Andalah spoke, the tiger's eyes flicked back and forth in the same way the palace cats' did. It brought a smile to her lips. "And rest I think."

"No," The word came out as more of a meow than a 'no' and Andalah smiled at that too. "I need to make sure the fire is dead."

"It is out," She pulled experimentally on the feline's shoulders, and to Andalah's relief he moved with her, towards the gentle sounds of the river. "I stamped down the last of the embers myself."

She received only a grunt of acceptance from the large cat, but no further disapproval and they made their way to the riverbank in silence.

It was cooler beside the water and when she was certain that they were sufficiently away from the lingering heat Andalah settled the tiger at the water's edge and waded into the shallow water to cool and wash the burns scattered up her arms. Hissing, both in relief and at the stinging of hot flesh meeting cold water. Andalah lowered herself into the river until she sat on the bottom with just her head and tops of her shoulders sticking out. She tilted back and let the current rinse the rest of the grim from her hair. A soft splashing sound had her turning to watch the tiger wading into the water beside her, his steps steady, eyes sharp now that they had time to adjust.

"How does a human make it this far into my woods?" The tiger's voice was still raspy, his jaws and teeth unsuited for the language it now spoke. "Did the guardian's not bar you from this path?"

"Guardians?" Andalah dipped her face beneath the river and scrubbed before sitting up. "The green women?"

The tiger nodded.

"They told me to go this way," She gestured to the bend in the river. "I am looking for something, a nightingale. They said to ask a… to ask you, I guess."

"Ask me to give you a nightingale?" The tiger waded into the river where the current grew stronger and the water deeper. He turned to face Andalah, a trail of ash and dirt flowing behind him. "I do not have a nightingale to give."

"No," She stretched her legs out in front of her, the long day weighing heavy on her spirit. "They thought you might know where I could find one."

"Why should I tell you if I did?" The tiger stalked towards Andalah until it was close enough that she felt the huff of his breath as he watched her. "There is no room for human laws here, no place for little girls looking for pretty birds."

"How do you know the nightingale is pretty?" Andalah squinted up into the tiger's face.

"So, you are as smart as you are brave," the tiger smiled, his black lips pulling up at the corners, revealing a disconcerting number of large sharp teeth.

"You're not as mean as you want me to think," Andalah chimed back, the fresh air giving her a burst of energy. "You didn't start that fire; you were trying to put it out."

"Of course, I didn't start the fire," The tiger rolled his eyes and settled into the shallows of the river next to her with a huff. "Why would a tiger need a fire?"

"To bake your bread," Andalah answered, thinking of the story the boy at the orphanage had told.

"Tigers do not eat bread."

There was a swishing in the water next to Andalah's thigh and she realized with a jerk of shock that it was the tiger's tail, dragging back and forth through the water.

"The Golden City," The tiger spoke again after a moment of silence. "There is a rumor that the warrior prince keeps a songbird as a pet; a nightingale."

"Thank you," Andalah took a deep breath.

"Do not thank me yet," The tiger stood, offering Andalah his hand. "The Golden City lies beyond the Iron Sands and the harpies who live there hunt in its dunes. I wish you luck, little girl. You will need it."

Andalah followed the river until it flowed out of sight, underneath a field of black hollow rocks that marked the end of the forest. She could still hear the rush of water as it flowed underneath her, the wind whipping the red sand into her eyes. Andalah stooped to fill her jug of water before she set her shoulders towards the dunes and marched into the desert.

When the sun began to set Andalah realized the red wasteland she had thought devoid of life was teeming with animals she had never dreamed of, lizards and mice so small and quick she would think they were whispers had she not seen them herself. She paused at the top of a dune, having long since lost sight of the Wild Wood and the river behind her.

Her stomach grumbled its disapproval of the whole situation. In the palace there were no skipped meals, in fact, it was seldom in the Great City that any mouth went without food, let alone the princess. The temples fed the hungry and her father, the sultan, fed the temples. Absent-mindedly rubbing her stomach with a sigh. She had packed food enough for a long journey but looking out at the Iron Sands, she worried if her supplies would get her to the Golden City. There were a few items stuffed in the bottom of her pack she had brought to barter with, but those wouldn't matter if she didn't make it past the desert. The princess dropped her pack on the ground, taking a moment to stretch her aching muscles and sip cautiously at her jug of water. Despite it being mostly full and almost as heavy as the rest of her belongings she was worried it would run out. If she failed to find the nightingale her father would be disappointed, but if she failed to return home at all he would be heartbroken. The sultan would not recover from a loss like that, so even now with a full pack and plenty of water Andalah was careful.

A shadow crossed overhead, small and faint at first, not much more than a flicker of darkness between the princess and the sun.

The next day it came again, a little larger this time accompanied by a screech that echoed across the land. Andalah hitched her pack over her shoulder, squinting up into the sky, the harsh light of the sun burning the impression of a colossal bird soaring high above into her mind. She marched across the peak of the sand dune, her boots sinking well into the fine red powder.

The merchants she spoke with who had been to the Iron Sands always came from the road that wound up through the City of Colors that avoided Wild Wood altogether. No one came from the West, where there was no road. Andalah was wondering if that might be for a reason other than the stories of the wood's inhabitants when the shadow crossed overhead again, larger still. Another screech followed.

Further off the call was returned with equal animosity. A flutter of fear pulsed in Andalah's chest. No one went this way, there were no stories about the predators of the Iron Sands, merchants complained of the mirages and the heat, not being hunted. Laughter bubbled, panicky, and unbidden in Andalah's throat. *What if the Golden City with its warrior prince was nothing but a mirage?* She was already chasing a rumor, why not a fantasy as well?

Her mood was turning dour and the shadow from overhead was clinging to her own. One day turned into another as she put dune after dune behind her. Atop yet another featureless tower of sand, she thought she could see in the distance a bluff of polished red stone jutting up from the earth. She put her hand up to shield her eyes from the glare of the sun, trying to get a look at it. If nothing else, it was something different in the landscape that had been nothing but mountains of sand for miles. As she made her way towards it her boot slipped and Andalah tumbled down the side of the dune. With a crunch, she landed on her back, her bag underneath her.

A groan of pain leaked out as she tried to right herself. The fall had been disorienting. Her head was spinning, and she spit out a mouth full of sand, coughing up even more. It seemed darker at the bottom of the dune than it had at the top. With another gagging cough, Andalah hocked a wet crimson wad of spit and dirt out of her mouth before she stood up fully.

The sound of beating wings was the only warning she had before talons, as long as the dagger in her boot, wrapped around her forearm, jerking her into the sky. She looked up to see a monstrous leathery leg of a harpy with the body and face a woman and the wings and legs of an eagle carrying her into the clouds. Such a creature would have been a shock, a hallucination she could have chalked up to the exhaustion and heat, had she not just come from the Wild Wood with its green women and talking tigers. As such, Andalah did not have time to be shocked or to be carried off course by myths. The harpy screeched, it's cold black eyes looking at her with hunger, and Andalah screamed back, prying at the creature's foot with her free hand.

She struck out, over and over. Another cry tore through the air, and the harpy dipped violently to the side, and Andalah caught sight of another set of wings. A second harpy with the same black eyes as the first glided beneath them. With its human hands, the second harpy reached for Andalah. Kicking out, the princess threw her weight off balance. Without warning, the grip that was holding her released, and she tumbled through the air. She fell ungracefully onto the second harpy, hitting her wing and dragging her, in a jumble of feathers and screams, to the ground.

They landed in a heap, momentarily stunned by the fall. Either the sand was softer than she remembered, or Andalah had not been as high as she thought. When she stood, an inventory of her person revealed no injuries other than a bruise that wrapped around her arm like a cuff where the first harpy had grabbed her. Sensing that the attack was far from over Andalah reached into the scabbard she kept in her boot and drew out a stout dagger.

As the first harpy landed and the second righted itself. Andalah braced for the fight to come. The taller of the beasts lunged at her with a swipe of its claws, and Andalah swiped back with her blade catching the back of its fingers with just enough of the tip to draw a single drop of blood. The harpy hissed, flinching back as the other one pounced. Andalah was ready. She had seen the second harpy finally make it to her feet, advancing on her.

Spinning around, Andalah caught the other one around the neck. For a moment Andalah was sure that she had killed her. A terrible human scream curdled Andalah's blood as the harpy stumbled back, collapsing into the sand in obvious pain. Her body writhed against the red sands as sickening cracking popping sounds accompanied her cries of anguish.

Her enormous brown wings were pulling into her body and the long leathery toes of her eagle feet were rearranging themselves back into something almost human, or at least they would be soon.

Something glinted in the sand, a shiny red pendant whose twin hung around the first harpy's neck. Realization dawned on Andalah. She hadn't cut the harpy's neck; she had cut off her necklace, a charm that it seemed, held the harpy's power. She jumped forward and snipped the second pendant off the other harpy's throat. Catching it, Andalah bent to scoop up the first pendant. Without pausing to see if she was right, Andalah ran, leaving her jug of water and her pack sprawled in the sand with two screaming harpies who were rapidly turning back into humans.

The sun was dropping quickly behind the horizon along with the temperature. Andalah shivered as she marched on. It had been a long time since she left the harpies, long enough for the sun to have set and far enough that she could no longer hear their cries of anguish. She was walking towards the only landmark in the whole of the Iron Sands, the gleaming red cliffs that were now black in the dark, save for a light that shone from a small cave.

As she got closer, Andalah could tell that it was no cave. Caves did not have doors or the smell of cooking stew. Caves did not have stout little women who swept their entrances.

"Hello," Andalah called cautiously to the woman with a wave. "Might I sit by your fire for a moment? I mean you no harm. I only need to rest."

"Oh dear," The woman rushed out to meet her with plump arms.

Andalah did not know how tired she was until those arms wrapped around her with a pleasant softness that belied their strength.

"My girl," The woman spoke with a soft accent, like an owl's call. "How did you get out this far? There are no roads."

"I... I..." Andalah sighed, not wanting to rehash the events of the day or the other days that had come before. "I am looking for the nightingale."

"The nightingale?" The woman tilted her head, taking in Andalah's face with curiosity. "Prince Vireo's nightingale?"

"I only know that I seek the nightingale, not if it is the prince's," Andalah answered. Feeling both worn and hopeful. "Is this prince the one in the Golden City?"

"The very same," The woman smiled. "One of my daughters, Loreley, guards the prince. She has spoken of his nightingale. It will not sing for him."

A spark of hope lit in her chest. The nightingale was real.

"There is a prophecy in the Golden City that reaches even those of us who live in the sands," As the woman spoke Andalah checked over her shoulder for the harpies she had left behind her. "One so old its predictions have been made law. A truth taught to children by their parents for generations."

The woman ushered Andalah inside her home where it was warm and light.

"It says that whoever steals the royal nightingale if it sings for them then they will marry the prince." The woman smiled, mostly to herself, offering Andalah a loaf of bread. "And they will rule the Golden City together."

"Has your daughter not tried to steal it then?" Andalah took the bread.

"Oh no," A chuckle left the woman with an owlish coo. "My girls do not worry about such things. Our kind do not care for marriage."

"Girls?" Andalah chose not to ask what the woman's kind was. It felt rude to pry and given what she had seen so far in this land, it was sure to surprise.

"Yes," The woman went about setting a fourth place at the table. "Yes, two more, Luscinia and Lonan. I am Fukuro and you are Andalah, princess of the Great City between the mountains."

"How?" Andalah was stunned.

"The same way I know my daughters will be late tonight," Fukuro spoke with a calm authority, stretching herself taller than Andalah thought was possible for her short frame. "Where did you get those pendants?"

Fukuro nodded to her hand, where Andalah was still clutching the necklaces she'd stolen from the harpies.

"I took them," She took a step away from Fukuro, her back hitting the stone wall of the little house. "From two harpies who attacked me. I took them and while they were turning into humans I ran. I was afraid."

"Did you harm them?" There was darkness filtering into the woman's eyes that had not been there before.

"No," Andalah was cornered, even if she made it out of the house there was nowhere to hide in the desert. "I do not mean anyone any harm. I only took these so that I might escape."

"Tsk, tsk, tsk," Fukuro flitted away, tottering back to the other side of the kitchen, all together smaller than she had seemed the moment before. "I am sorry for my girls. They have always been rebellious, though that is no excuse for cruelty."

Just as she was about to speak two women burst through the door carrying Andalah's pack and wearing her clothes.

"At least she left us her clothes," The one woman laughed, throwing the pack and water jug onto the floor by the fireplace.

"Boy's clothes," The other taller woman spoke. "I did not know it was a woman until I picked her up."

They giggled uproariously at that until Fukuro coughed.

"Mother," They spoke in unison, dipping their heads in deference.

"I believe you have met our guest," Fukuro wandered over to Andalah as if she had all the time in the world, resting a gentle hand on her shoulder.

"We..." The taller one began to speak before her mother held up a hand to silence her.

"You were being reckless and cruel," Fukuro led Andalah to the table where she pulled out a chair and pushed her into it with a motherly shove. "We do not hunt for sport. There is no glory in it."

"We weren't hunting," The shorter woman sounded petulant.

"Do not lie to me Lonan," Fukuro snipped at her daughter and for the first time Andalah saw the necklace she wore.

"You're a harpy too," Andalah tried to stand up but was immediately plied with a bowl of stew fresh off the fire.

"Of course, my dear," Fukuro cooed again and settled herself at the head of the table, leaving Lonan and Luscinia to get their own bowls of stew. "Only a harpy can make another harpy, and we do like to make more of ourselves.

Now let's talk about how you are going to steal that nightingale." Fukuro smiled at Andalah over her bowl, her eyes as black as coal.

The next night Luscinia and Lonan flew Andalah to Prince Vireo's palace in the Golden City where their sister stood guard. Loreley left a window open high in the tower where the prince slept. Fukuro had warned that the guards only slept for twelve minutes at the stroke of midnight so Andalah would have to be quick and quiet, for Fukuro's daughters would not risk their lives if she were to be caught.

The prince's chamber was at the end of a long corridor and as promised three figures stood guard, Loreley the harpy, a green woman, and a tiger. Andalah waited, tucked behind a wall, in a nook filled with cobwebs. She sat there so long her legs went numb and her back ached, but soon enough the clock bells struck twelve and one by one the guards went to sleep.

As quietly as she could, Andalah crawled out of her hiding spot and crept across the hall to slip inside the prince's chamber. Inside was all dark save for a single candle burning at the prince's bedside that cast a warm circle of light over the bed and a golden cage where a small bird watched her in silence.

Andalah had never seen a creature so unprepossessing, covered in soft brown and white feathers, with a thin beak and beady black eyes. It watched her with a nervous energy that in turn made Andalah nervous. Her hands shook as she reached for the cage.

The nightingale let out one melodious chirp and Andalah jerked her hand away, spinning around, her eyes searching the bedroom for the prince. His head was still upon his pillow, his chest rising and falling in the easy rhythm of sleep. Vireo was a handsome prince, with a strong jaw and skin that had soaked up all of the Golden City's sun. He was the most handsome man Andalah had ever seen. He groaned in his sleep throwing an arm over his eyes and Andalah stumbled back, knocking the single candle to the ground with a thump. It went out. The nightingale chirped again, hopping on its perch in some unknowable delight.

"Shh," She tried to hush the bird as quietly as she could, but the damage was already done. Even in the dark, she could tell the prince was awake. The steady snores of rest had been replaced by a calculated silence and Andalah did not wish to discover why they called Vireo the warrior prince.

Grabbing the nightingale, cage, and all, Andalah raced out of the prince's chambers, past the sleeping guards, and up to the window where Lonan and Luscinia waited for her. They disappeared into the night sky before the prince made it up the tower stairs.

Andalah bid farewell to the harpies at the edge of the Wild Wood, where the river met its end. She followed it back to the bend where the tiger had told her the way, and past the ancient cypress with its swirling pool of roots. When she saw the dappled green faces of the savage women, Andalah was unafraid, but as she came closer to the fork in the road where she had left her brother's caravans Andalah stopped to put back on her bindings and tuck her braid under her cap. It was safer to travel the merchant road into the Great City as a boy, even if the girl beneath had traveled farther than any man.

At the crossroads where the South Road met the East and the Wild Wood loomed like a shadow, Andalah found herself too tired to go any farther and so she stopped to rest, leaning her head against the golden cage. Listening to the gentle chirping of the nightingale until she fell asleep.

When she woke the cage was gone, the smell of horses and men in its wake. The sound of two battalion's worth of men and supplies rumbled up the road toward the city gates. A wound began to open in her heart as jagged and raw as any physical thing. She had come so far and still, she had failed her father. The nightingale would never sing in his temples. He would never keep his promise to her mother. They would both forever be heartbroken. Tears came to her quickly, blurring her vision until she could barely make out the road ahead of her. There was nothing left to do but go home. She had found the nightingale, and someone had taken it. *How had she been so careless?*

Andalah wiped at her eyes and stood, following her brothers home like a scolded hound.

The bells of the Southern Temple were ringing when she passed through the city gates, a celebration of her brothers' return no doubt. She wondered with a disconnected interest if they would ring for her when the sultan saw that she had come home as well.

Then a man with a barrel chest, draped in more silk than any one man needed, a merchant no doubt, grabbed her around the waist and swung her around.

"They found the nightingale!" The merchant cried. "Akos and Altair, they found it. All hail the Sons of Ornette! Did you hear that boy!"

The man swung Andalah around again, laughing.

Another hole began pulling open in her heart right next to the first. Her brothers had stolen the bird from her and now they were going to pass it off as their own triumph. Defeated and weary, Andalah left the main street of the city and wound her way past the palace to a small rickety dock where a holy man held vigil for all travelers to the Great City.

"Blessings on you my sister," The monk's words shocked her, and Andalah jerked away almost expecting to see the face of one of her brothers, meeting instead with the keen eyes of a holy man she knew almost as well as her kin. "You have been missed, princess."

"How?" Andalah was at a loss for words, no one else had seen through her disguise, simple though it was.

"What we do not see with our eyes we feel with our hearts," Monks were always cryptic. "Akos and Altair are with your father at the temple. The Oracle is with them."

"Good." Anger white hot and shameful nipped at Andalah's words.

"It is not a coincidence that you return on the very day your brothers bring back the nightingale, I think." The monk stepped to the side of his boat, making room for Andalah to come onboard.

"It does not matter," Andalah walked to the end of the dock and stepped onto the monk's little craft, barely sturdy enough to hold them both afloat. "I wish to see my father. Please take me to him."

"Of course," The monk made a small bow and pushed off from the dock, steering the small boat towards the three spires of the temple in the middle of the lake, where her brothers were taking credit for her nightingale. "No one has heard it sing yet."

"Hmm?" The journey was catching up to her and Andalah found her thoughts muddling.

"The Oracle said the temple must be filled with the nightingale's song." He was quiet for the rest of the journey and when Andalah stepped onto the temple path he left her with another bow taking his boat back across the lake to stand his vigil at the dock.

Inside the temple was as quiet as the monk. There was no song, only the frustrated breaths of two young men quickly losing their tempers.

Andalah's brother did not look very different than they had when she left them a year ago. Akos had grown a beard and Altair wore his hair long, but other than that the passage of time made no mark on either of them. Andalah did not have to see it to know the year had brought her change. Her cheeks might still be round and her belly soft, but she had walked in places no other person had seen. She was not the girl who had left home.

At the apex of the temple sat her father. Dressed in the deep red robes of his station. The sultan Ornette leaned on his walking stick, beseeching the nightingale with his gaze to sing.

"This is ridiculous," Akos threw his hands up in disgust. "We have brought you your bird Oracle, if it doesn't sing what are we to do about it?"

"Just tell us your price," Altair added, already reaching into the pockets of his silk jacket.

"There is no price," The Oracle began to speak, their voice as discomfiting as it ever was, like a large room echoing with many voices. "Only the song will do."

Andalah began walking towards her father, dragging the cap off her head, and letting her heavy braid fall down her back. It had been too long since she had seen his face and the lines of it had only grown deeper in her absence. Her boots thudded on the stone floor as she drew nearer to them and her brothers spun around, swords drawn.

"Stop where you are," Altair shouted. "This is a private council."

"Peasants are not allowed in this temple," Akos seconded.

Andalah stopped dead, shocked that they did not recognize her, their own sister.

"There are things that the eyes do not see," The Oracle spoke, their eyes meeting Andalah with a knowing smile. "That the heart feels the truth. You have been missed, princess."

"What?" "No." Altair and Akos spoke at once, their disbelief palpable.

"Daughter?" The sultan was on his feet, the nightingale forgotten. "My Andalah, where have you been?"

"I- "Andalah began to speak but did not get the chance to finish as the nightingale began to chirp, hopping happily on its perch.

"There!" Altair pointed at the bird with a shout. "It sang. Now release our father from this silly promise."

Altair crossed between the cage and Andalah as he taunted the Oracle. The nightingale stopped singing. Rage turned his face red, and he stormed the cage bashing his sword flat against its golden bars.

"Stop!" Andalah screamed, throwing herself between her brother and the nightingale. "What has this creature ever done to deserve that?"

"The stupid thing won't sing and release father from this absurd promise," Akos answered for Altair.

"And what have you ever done to deserve its song?" Andalah countered, feeling for the first time the true depth of her brother's selfishness.

"We found it." Altair answered with a sneer.

As they talked, the nightingale began to prance around its cage again, making little sounds.

"Where?" When the sultan spoke, everyone else fell silent except for the nightingale, who twittered out of tune.

"Father?" Altair squinted at his father, confused.

"Where did you find this nightingale?" Ornette walked up to the cage and peered inside where the little brown bird was rubbing its beak against the pads of Andalah's fingers where they curled in between the bars. "Where did you find this bird that loves your sister so?"

"We..." Altair began, looking over his shoulder at his brother for help.

"We found it- "Akos was interrupted by a melody erupting from the cage, so sweet and clear it filled the temple from spire to spire.

"Do not lie to me." The sultan cast a stern eye at his sons. "The nightingale does not sing for you."

"We did not know that the boy we took it from was Andalah," Akos broke first, earning him a withering stare from his older brother. They both looked about, ready to plead their case, when a soldier, red-faced and panting, burst into the altar room.

"Your highness," he gasped. "At the gate..."

He doubled over, his chest heaving with exertion.

"Who is at the gate?" The sultan put a steadying hand on the soldier's shoulder.

"An army." Finally standing straight, the young soldier looked Ornette in the eye and explained. "Prince Vireo of the Golden City has brought his army. He says he wants the one who stole his nightingale."

Andalah was certain there would be more debate about what to do next and where to send their own armies, but she had little interest in measures that would not work. So while the men were distracted, Andalah walked down to the temple steps, where a familiar monk waited with his tiny boat and stepped on board.

"Can you take me to the city gate?" She asked the holy man, resigned.

"All the waters of the city come from this lake. It is the heart of the people." Another cryptic answer.

"Is that a, yes?" Andalah raised an eyebrow in his direction.

"Of course, princess." The monk smiled, already sending them across the lake's placid waters towards the tributaries that would carry them to the city gates.

Andalah reached under her shirt and grabbed the knot of the bindings holding her breasts flat against her chest and pulled. Unwrapping herself seemed easier now; maybe her breasts were smaller, or she was thinner, though Andalah doubted that. It was easier because her fingers were stronger from saving green women, choking out fires, and fighting off harpies. She was stronger, and she would face the armies of the Golden City alone, not disguised as a boy but as herself.

At the gate, their little boat was stopped by the prince's guard, one tiger, one woman, and one harpy whose name Andalah knew but would not speak.

"Tell your prince that I took his nightingale," Andalah announced before they could drag her from the boat. "Tell him it sings for me."

"I know. I heard its melody just before you ran," Prince Vireo's voice matched the rest of him quite nicely, all toasty warm and dark at the edges. "But how can I be sure it was you? It was dark that night."

"It was only dark because I knocked over your candle," Andalah answered, straightening her back in defiance.

"And so, you did," Vireo chuckled.

"What do you want with my father's city?" Andalah drew herself as tall as she could, still having to look up to meet Vireo's stare.

"I want nothing of this city." He took a step closer.

"Then what?" Andalah refused to back away, even as he leaned down to brush a wayward curl behind her ear.

"You see, princess," He let the tip of his nose drag along her cheek. "There is the matter of a prophecy."

"She paused at the top of a dune, having long since lost sight of the Wild Wood and the river behind her."

Lady Knight and the Vixen

Willow Bay

Deep breaths, I tell myself. I shake out the nerves buzzing between my fingertips. Looking up at the overly large wooden doors of the council room, I scoff at the absolutely pompous atmosphere of this place. It's taken me four years to even gain an audience with the jerks. Four years of knight training and studying potions from the most renowned wizards and witches, before they would benevolently decide to hear me out. Boys who have practically just been weened from their mother's breasts would waltz up the steps of this fortress and be shown in immediately. My teeth grind and my hands ball up into fists, nerves now forgotten.

I think about pacing to keep calm but instead, put my ear up to the door in hopes of hearing footsteps approaching. Although I do not hear footsteps, I can make out the muffled sounds of laughter. The scoundrels are having a boon at my expense. That is enough. With an overdue huff, I slam my shoulder into one of the doors. My intention was to open it in one swift indignant motion, but I was stupid to think my luck would allow that. Instead, I am grunting and pushing with all my might to get it to open a mere foot.

"Who needs a door this heavy? What is it made of… lead?"

I grumble to myself. I continued to heave against the door, my shoulder begs for relief, but I ignore it. The last thing I want the council to see is me trying to squeeze my curvy frame between a pair of obnoxiously large and heavy doors. At last, I get the door to open with sufficient space for me to pass through. Sideways and with my stomach sucked in, of course, but I still smirk as I raise myself to my full height and walk toward the council's circle in the middle of the room. I glare daggers at anyone who dares make eye contact with me as I situate myself in the center of the circle. All five members surround me. I know every single one of them. Growing up, they would attend all of my birthdays and my family's holiday celebrations.

"Princess Artemisia, how kind of you to let yourself in."

King Ryliff states in a humorless tone. I am thankful I chose to face him. I would hate to start out the meeting by pinwheeling around. There will be enough of that to come, unfortunately.

"King Ryliff, " I say respectfully, inclining my head. From a young age, my mother taught me never to overplay my hand. And I am sure that I have already irritated everyone here by ignoring the rules of how things are done.

"Impatience is very unbecoming of any young lady, let alone one of such high standing." Queen Emmiline says. Mustering up my most temperate smile, I turn to her.

"Such great insight, Queen Emmiline. I will strive to display patience such as you have throughout your life in the future"

She stiffens at my comment, and her eyes narrow. Oh yes, Queen Emmiline, well known as the woman who helped her aging husband along in death so that she could rule the throne alone. Once she had accomplished that, she bullied her way into her husband's seat on the (at the time) all-male council. She scrutinized me, looking for the hint of sarcasm in my appearance that she could not find in my tone. To her right, King Camber suddenly had a fit of coughing. But I kept my eyes soft and my smile in place.

King Camber was most likely to rule in favor of my quest. He was currently a placeholder for his father's seat, who had taken ill in recent months. He was 10 years my senior at 30 but was still the youngest member of the council and also the most reasonable. I know that Queen Emmiline and King Ryliff will rule against me, but if I got the other two members' votes, then it wouldn't matter.

"Please, Princess Artemisia, explain to us why you are a good fit for the quest of saving Princess Annabella."

King Juliane interjects. I turn to him and give him a thankful nod which he returns. Taking a deep breath, I say the words just as I have practiced a million times.

"Kings and Queens of the council, I come before you today in hopes of being granted access to the ever-growing forest to rescue Princess Annabella. I have trained for four years in various types of combat and also in potions with the intention of traveling through the enchanted forest and gaining access to the princess. I believe, although she is under a sleeping spell only to be broken by a true love's kiss, I will be able to rouse her by way of potions and break the curse."

As I speak, I slowly turn on my heel making eye contact with everyone.

To be expected, King Ryliff and Queen Emmaline look completely unmoved. But the other three members have contemplative expressions on their faces, so I continue.

"I also would like to say that every day that passes, the forest grows, taking over a little bit more of King Juliane and Queen Thianna's land." I am looking directly at Queen Thianna, the newest member of the council, as I say this. She pales slightly but makes eye contact with me, with her brows slightly raised. As if asking if I'm really up for this challenge. In response, I sum up my speech.

"Not only am I more prepared than any other man who has tried his hand at this quest. But I am afraid as time passes and the enchanted forest grows larger, you do not have the luxury of overlooking my request at lifting the curse, simply because I am female."

This last part was a gamble; it could come out as a simple truth or complete disrespect.

"Not only a female Artemisia but, more importantly, a Princess." King Ryliff argues. I shove down the anger that immediately starts to bubble in my stomach.

" And as a Princess, I should be concerned and willing to aid people of my kingdom and of neighboring allied kingdoms. Isn't that right, Father." I challenge, my eyes boring into his. King Juliane Clears his throat, trying to break up a fight that has been ongoing for four years between my father and me.

"I say we vote."

He calmly suggests. The other members nod in agreement, so he continues.

"All in Favor of granting Princess Artemisa a chance at this quest, raise your hand."

My breath catches in my throat, and I force myself to keep my eyes from shutting tight.

I peer around, and my breath comes out in one big whoosh of relief. King Juliane, King Camber, and Queen Thianna are all holding their hands up. My father's face is downright surly when I glance over at him, but it is now out of his hands. King Camber clears his throat, and I turn to him.

"The closest entrance to the Sonfile Castle will be in my kingdom off of the Northeast border. I will have a few of my men escort you to that point and send you with a horse and travel supplies if you need them. Will you be ready for them in a fortnight?"He asks. I smile at him broadly.

"In fact, Sire, I am ready right now. I was hoping to accompany you back to your kingdom so as to not waste time and effort on your part. I have my Horse and supplies ready to do so."I state.

I can hear my father choke, but I do not look his way. If I waited a fortnight, he would surely find a way to stop me from going at all. Although brash of me to ask King Camber to travel back with him, it is my best chance of following through with the quest. If he is surprised, he doesn't show it, he only smiles back at me and says.

"My Lady, you are quite prepared indeed. How could I refuse you when you have put so much preparation and thought into things."

"King Camber, you may be eager to let my daughter throw her life away in an attempt to save her friend and your kingdom, but I am not."

My father seethes. I turn to him. His face is red and he holds himself somewhere between sitting and standing with his hands gripping his chair, knuckles white. Watching him I feel the familiar sting of being underestimated.

"King Camber is simply granting my request, Sire," I say and turn back to King Camber.

"When will you and your Guard be leaving for Raensef?"

"We leave tomorrow morning at dawn. Meet us at the southern bridge if you wish to travel with us."

King Camber relays, both of us ignoring the various sounds coming from my father. I bow to everyone and take my leave. As I walk toward the dumbest doors in existence, I hear fighting ensue behind me. Ignoring it all, I make my way past the doors and start skipping through the council halls. I am finally on my way Annabella.

I bought lodging at an Inn in the southern part of town. They could not provide warm water for a bath, but they offered food and accommodations for Squash my horse. After finishing my dinner, I have a few pints of ale and play a few card games with the innkeeper's daughter. The little troll continues to laugh at me as she wins every round of every game. Her mother's eyes remain wide, and she waits to step in at the first sign of annoyance by me.

"You lose again." The girl says to me, a purely evil grin splitting her face.

"I believe I have had too much ale." I sigh, and she looks at me, and one of her eyebrows rises toward her hairline.

"You were losing before you started to drink."

Before I can come up with a response, her mother hurries over, scolding her and telling her to apologize. Laughing, I excuse myself and head up to my room. I know I won't be able to sleep, but I should try.

Only a few moments after I shut my door behind me I hear heavy footsteps traveling up the hallway. Suddenly my door is being pounded on, and a booming voice comes from the other side.

"Artemisia open this door at once, I have spent half the night looking for you!"

I walk slowly to the door, to show my father I am not scared but also to think of a way to run if need be. Throwing open the door, I try my best to smirk and not grimace at my father's disheveled appearance.

"How can I be of service, Sire?" I ask calmly.

"Do not do this, Arty, please, I beg of you. Do not go off and die because of some childhood guilt."

His words cause my breath to hitch. I expected him to be furious because that side of my father I can handle. But not this. I clear my throat.

"Although your faith in me is lacking. Do not worry I shall save Annabella and return to you intact."

My father hangs his head at my words.

"I know I can not stop you. I have tried to for years and have failed. So please promise me that if it comes between saving your own life or saving Annabella's you will choose to come home." His voice is tight and his eyes remain glued to his feet.

"I promise." An empty promise. We both know I will come back with Annabella or I won't come back at all. But my father looks up at me his eyes glossy and says.

"I will be seeing you soon then." He looks as if he is going to hug me but then thinks better of it and he simply turns and heads back down the hallway in which he came.

"Tell mother to send for more of my favorite tea, I have run out and would like to have some after I return."

My father pauses for a moment nods his head and then continues on until he is out of sight. I gently shut my door and place my forehead against the wood breathing heavily. Asking myself if I should have said goodbye.

"You will save her and return home safely, Art," I whisper to myself. But a very small part of me whispers back.

"Or you will die trying."

I arrived at the southern gate hours before dawn. Sleep had evaded me all night long and eventually, my thoughts drove me out of bed. So I got dressed, paid the innkeeper, and drug Squash out of the stables. Now here my teeth chatter and I curse myself for not staying at the warm inn a bit longer. To pass time I quiz myself on potions and elixirs. Checking and rechecking the contents of my satchel, to soothe my anxiety. The night sky starts to fade into the morning and my stomach is suddenly in knots. What if Camber had told me the wrong gate and is now leaving without me? He could secretly hate me and wish for me to fail even before I start my quest. Maybe because of the history we share. I groan and push all thoughts of the past out of my mind.

Going to recheck my satchel I hear men on horseback approaching. I look up and see King Camber and his guards and suddenly my muscles relax and my mind clears. Camber smiles as he approaches and when he is within distance greets me.

"I am glad to see that you actually showed up. Although I don't know how I could have doubted your stubborn fearlessness even for a moment." I smile back at him, glad that he has dropped all formalities.

"Somehow Camber you always seem to deliver an insult and a compliment at the same time." Camber puts his hand to his heart as he pulls up beside me and Squash.

"I would never insult a lady such as yourself, Artemisia." I swing up into Squash's saddle and snort.

"So much for honest Kings. I believe that is the biggest falsehood I have heard all week."

"Knowing the places you frequent Arty, I find that truly unbelievable." I flush as Camber laughs at his own joke. Then one of his guards calls him over and with a final wink he leads his horse away from me.

Within minutes we are on our way. If my memory serves me right the journey should take about two days if we keep a good pace and three if we take things slowly. I itch to be in the enchanted forest with my quest underway. The thought of it causes me to inadvertently spur Squash forward and drive us to the front of the group. Squash sets himself at the same pace as Lauhlin, Camber's Head of Guard, and he looks over at me and gives a soft smile. The two were inseparable, they had grown up together and for each step, Camber had made to be king Lauhlin had made sure to keep pace and stay right beside him. As a child, I had mused that they were a secret couple, forced to keep their love behind closed doors. What a handsome couple they would make too. Lauhlin with his dark brown hair and blue eyes was a head shorter than Camber but people weren't any less intimidated. His stockier build also meant that he could pummel Camber in any sort of wrestling match or anyone else for that matter. Then there was Camber. Lord have mercy on my nerves, his smile alone kept women begging for his hand in marriage. When combined with his hazel eyes, honey-colored hair, and sharp jaw, he had a couple of men paying interest as well.

I chuckle at my thoughts but then hear Lauhlin clear his throat and I snap out of it.

"I see you still daydream as much as you did a few years ago," He says with a smile but I can hear the warning in his voice. I won't always have a king's guard around for protection.

"I bet she does so even more now. As her life has gotten so boring without us in it." I try not to show my surprise at Camber piping up, he's somehow managed to come up on my left side without me noticing. I really do need to pay more attention.

"Actually, I was just remembering a time when I thought you two were the most attractive couple the world had to offer." At my words I see Lauhlin duck his head, but before I can rib him further, Camber interjects.

"Well, I sure did prove you wrong didn't I Arty?" My cheeks warm but I refuse to be bested.

"I am not sure what you are referring to, Camber."

He tilts his head ever so slightly to the side and responds. "No? Well if you wish to spend tonight in my tent with me I'm sure I could help you remember."

I hear Lauhlin choke as I turn and glare at Camber. He has a bemused expression on his face, obviously enjoying this interaction. But I will not let him shame me.

"No need to repeat another underwhelming venture, that I will soon forget such as I did with the last." At that, Lauhlin looks as though he should like to be anywhere else but beside us, I see him open his mouth probably to excuse himself. But before He can get the words out Camber's voice slices through the air.

"How odd. I don't remember you being underwhelmed with my affections. Rather I can recall quite vividly you demanding more..."

"Enough." I cut him off. He won the battle, and my pride could not take another blow. I turn to him and growl. "I hope you fall off your horse and sustain a head injury."

He looks back at me and I expect a snarky comment but instead am met with a solemn expression. All my anger leaves me and I'm suddenly at a loss for words. Camber quickly changes the subject, and he and Lauhlin carry on as though nothing has happened. It takes me more than a minute to join in with them.

The road to Camber's kingdom is smooth and well-traveled so the hours pass quickly. I try to stay alert but constantly find my mind wandering away from me. It betrays me by thinking of Camber and the past I had with him. A year or so back we had grown close as I was training with a wizard in one of the towns on the outskirts of his castle. He had learned of my presence by word of my father and had invited me to dine with him. I was hesitant to eat with a man who worked closely and often with my father but could not find a polite way to decline. After dinner, he had surprised me by inviting me to drink with him and Lauhlin, not proper by any means. That is exactly why I could not turn him down. He knew this, the cad, just as he knew how to get me to come back time and time again after that night. Camber was no fool, he always seemed to get whatever it was he wished for. I am sure he was shocked when my apprenticeship with the Wizard had ended and I bid him farewell. The feat of pulling one over on the charming King should have given me much satisfaction. But alas, I left Raensef with a heavier heart than I care to admit. I had missed him and Lauhlin often even if I had filled my days with many things to keep myself distracted. Many times my mind tried to go down the path of me staying with him, but I was just a temporary muse to him and I had Annabella to save. So I pushed those thoughts away. But now while traveling with them, the thoughts surge and fight their way to the forefront of my mind.

Soon dusk settles over us, and Lauhlin calls for everyone to dismount and make camp at an outcropping not far from the road. The makeshift camp is assembled quickly and by the time the sky is speckled with stars, everyone is eating and laughing around a large fire. I sit next to a small group of soldiers. We eat together and tell stories of our most treacherous tales. After a few pints of ale the one called Oliver, tells a story of how he had accompanied a barmaid back to her place of dwelling for a night of fun. Only when they had made it back to her room did a man- Oliver found out was her husband- come home as well. Through bouts of laughter, he tells us he barely made it out alive and with everything intact. Similar stories start surfacing from the other soldiers; soon many of us are rolling on the ground with tears of laughter streaming down our faces. That's until Camber abruptly stands beside us, and the laughter dies, replaced by apologies and red faces. The men quickly scurry away and Camber sits down beside me.

"It seems as though I have ruined your fun Arty." There is no apology in his tone.

"You do it so effortlessly, Camber, I'm sure it comes with much practice." I turn to him with a smile to show him there is no real animosity in my words. We sit for a few moments in comfortable silence before he asks.

"Do you think you are ready?" If anyone else had asked, I would bristle, but for him, I answer honestly.

"I don't think I'll ever be truly prepared, but I am as much as I will ever be."

"I can send some of my men with you, if you wish."

I scoff.

"There is no need to wound my pride or waste your men. I will be fine alone."

Camber shakes his head slowly and I wonder if I can steer this conversation in a different direction.

"Everyone knows you are guilty over what happened to Annabella, Arty, but to go to these lengths to rectify it is foolishness."

He is right, but he won't hear me agree.

"Don't be daft, Cam. I am simply saving Annabella for the riches and title that will come with doing so." As I say this I clap him on the shoulder in the overly confident way I've seen countless men do after a bold statement. He laughs, and tension leaves my shoulders that I didn't even know was there.

"I'm off to bed,"

I tell him as I stand up to leave. He nods and replies

"That is wise. One more hard day of riding then we will make camp a safe distance from the forest so as to not wake anything. Tomorrow morning a few of my men and I will accompany you to the edge of the forest and will see you on your way."

I would like to tell him that it is not necessary to escort me but I know it is no use, having heard that tone of voice from him before. He will not be moved. I nod at him once to show I understand and then I head to my bedroll for the night.

The next day of riding passes quickly, I am caught up in thoughts of what is to come and the nightmares that plague my sleep. Even though we make camp a good distance from the forest the men are still restless and on edge. Nervous as to what can come out of the forest. I have heard stories but do not think too long about them it will only hinder me to wear down my nerves before entering the damn thing. Everyone is eager to be moving the next morning but still, each of them wishes me luck and safe travels before I leave with Cam and a few of his men. There are only four of us all together. It is Camber and I and then Lauhlin and Oliver the soldier from a few nights ago. As we make our way to the edge of the forest the mood is heavy and deathly quiet. Part of this is because you want to be as quiet as possible at all times when you are near or in the forest. But also the men with me probably feel as though they are escorting me to my death.

We are ten paces away from the trees when the party stops. My stomach feels heavy, and my breathing grows shallow. It's time for me to break off on my own; I nod to everyone and kick Squash forward. At the edge of the forest, I hear additional hoofbeats approaching. Turning, I find Cam coming up on Squash and me. Confused, I try to ask him what he thinks he is doing, with just my facial expressions. He purposefully ignores my gaze as he catches up and continues into the trees. Mildly alarmed, I urge Squash forward after him. I get as close as I possibly can and whisper.

"What in god's name are you doing, Camber?"

"What does it look like, Arty? I am accompanying you on your adventure."

He whispers back. Rage sweeps over me, and I tamp down the desire to yell. I can't keep the anger out of my voice when I say.

"You are a King; you buffoon. You can not accompany me on my quest. Not to mention that you were not even invited along." He looks back at me with an unbothered expression and in a haughty tone, comments.

"As you just stated, I am a king and can do as I please. Also, who else will sing songs of your bravery and honor after you save the princess? You, unfortunately, can not because your voice is that of a strangled goat. And if you had a sword to your throat, you still could not write two sentences that rhyme"

He does not stop as he talks and I turn back to see the edge of the forest grow further away by the second. Panic grips me.

"Camber, please, I can not be responsible for your safety in this place. If you were not to return I couldn't bear it, I wouldn't be able to look your family in the eye and tell them you lost your life for my cause. You have a kingdom that relies on you; please come to your senses." I am begging, but I do not care at this point. He turns to me with a pained and sad expression.

"As always, Arty, you are more concerned with another's safety when you should focus on your own."

I have no response. The realization that there is no way of stopping him floods through me, making me cold. He would only leave if I came with him, and for all my strength, I don't have enough to give up. Annabella needs me, and for that, I will put anything on the line. Including another's life. The thought makes the cold seep into my bones, and I find myself in disgust at who I have become. We continue on, the silence weighing down my shoulders.

"I am sorry, Cam."

He flinches in his saddle as though he has been struck. To be fair, I do not think he has heard an apology from me in his entire existence. I would most definitely be a little shaken.

"Let us not talk; I do not want to attract anything by the sound of our voices." His clipped response does nothing for my guilt, but I give an affirming nod.

The further we go in the forest, the harder it becomes to see, and the air seems thicker somehow as if trying to suffocate us all on its own. I keep out of my thoughts and focus on my surroundings. That is, until something tackles me and knocks me out of my saddle. While falling, I position myself to roll and grab the knife from my belt. I hit the ground with my shoulder, using my momentum to spin and pull up into a crouch. I hear Cam distantly holler something, but my full attention is on the creature in front of me. Its skin is a sickly green, its face and head misshapen and revolting. Although it only looks to be a quarter of my size, I know not to underestimate it. I lunge at me, a snarl coming from its mouth, if you could call it that. Hitting me with a force much greater than one would assume, the goblin goes for my neck with its razor-sharp teeth. Already anticipating its attack, I smash its jaw upward with my free hand and slash at its belly with my blade. It lets off a gurgled scream and pulls away from me; I feel its blood soak my shirt. Now up from a crouch, I keep my stance loose and fluid, ready for its next attack. The goblin glares at me with its beady eyes, and before it can lunge again, a strong gust of wind overtakes us. It cranes its head as though it is listening to someone speak. As the wind subsides, the goblin snarled at me one last time and scurries off at an inhuman speed. I am left completely bewildered. I feel a hand on my shoulder, and I spin my knife at the ready. But it is only Cam with his hands now raised above his head.

"I yield."

I chuckle at his words and wipe my knife on my pants before putting it back in my belt. Cam hands me a cloth that I quickly soil by wiping as much goblin blood off of me as I can. Once done, I throw the now ruined fabric to the ground and then thank him.

"You seemed to have the situation handled, so I went after Squash, who got spooked," Camber says, handing me the reins to my horse. I don't even thank him but instead, ask the question that is bouncing around my mind.

"Why did it run away?" He shrugs.

"Perhaps it realized it couldn't win the fight." I shake my head; goblins don't think like that. It's kill or be killed. Something scared it, and something scaring a goblin is a very unnerving thought.

"Don't let it get to you. We need to start thinking about setting up camp anyway. We won't be able to make it to the castle by nightfall."

I nod and shove my worries away instead of thinking of the task at hand. Camber and I travel a good while before finding an adequate place to sleep. It's a small area, mostly surrounded by large rocks, so that we won't be visible to absolutely everything in the forest. Still, I put up wards, and a few alarm spells around the camp to give us a warning if anything approaches us. I come back to Cam lying on his bead roll, eating dried fruit and bread. The night is warm enough not to need a fire or a warming spell which is good because both would attract unwanted attention. I've already used as much magic as I'm willing to and my fingers are still crossed that the scent of it is faint enough that it does not catch anything's attention. I throw down my bed roll and lie down next to him, stealing some of his bread. He mutters something about me having my own but then settles back into silence.

"Have you ever regretted a decision as soon as you make it but can't take it back?" Cam asks in a voice barely above a whisper. The weight of his words hit me, and suddenly I'm not hungry any longer. I know he's talking about his decision to accompany me. I don't know what I should say, so I just answer honestly.

"Yes, on a few occasions, actually."

He doesn't say anything, and suddenly I find myself saying every single thought in my mind.

"I'm sorry, Cam: I know I've hurt you in the past, and I know I've hurt you now. It was never my intention. If I had known you would accompany me, I would not have let you and your men escort me to the forest, I swear. I am a fool for the decisions I've made in the past and the ones I continue to make."

I draw in a deep breath at the end of my confession and wait for his response.

"I'm so sorry, Artemisia."

My brow furrows. Why would he be sorry? "If only an apology fixed things, King Camber."

I jump at the sound of a new voice and turn to find its source. Meanwhile, I grab for the knife at my belt and thank the lord I kept my satchel with my potions on me. There is an outline of a woman by one of the rock formations to my left. I face her and say nothing waiting for her to come near. She does not need an invitation and walks a few paces forward to where she is completely visible. Her dress is torn and covered with dirt, but her face is fairy-like and unmistakable.

"Annabella?"

I feel as though my world is collapsing upon itself. My mind fills with so many questions I can't even manage to say one. My jaw hangs open, and I know I stuttering out incomprehensible syllables but can't keep myself from doing so.

"Poor Arty, you have no idea what is happening, do you?"

Annabella says in a mocking voice. I don't know if it is her callous question or her overall rude demeanor, but I readily snap out of my stooper. A smirk overtakes her mouth, and she gets a look in her eye that I hated when we were younger.

"Explain," I demand. Her smile grows wider.

"As you wish, Princess. Let's see where should we start. Oh yes, how about the part where many years ago when you were about to abandon me and go off galavanting? Well, I couldn't very well let that happen; you were my only friend. So I made a deal with an old witch to put my kingdom in an eternal slumber and have a forest surround it that kept you and me together forever."

The galavanting she spoke of was my Father demanding my return from my stay at her kingdom. Every summer, I would come and visit her and stay for a month in the summer. It was the only time we saw each other because her mother was fiercely overprotective and did not let Annabella go beyond the castle walls. As the years wore on, she would beg for more time with me and plead with me not to leave. I had known how lonely she got, so that year I pushed my Father's limits and stayed for the entirety of the season. He was furious and could not be put off any longer. So I finally left.

"But unfortunately, the spell didn't work as fast as I thought it would, and you escaped." Her words sent shivers down my spine.

"I waited years for you to come for me, convinced that you would. But time marched on, and you never came. Every year my forest would grow, eating up more land and killing more people, but you still could not be bothered."

A manic laugh bubbles up from me. "I was training and learning about every type of magic available so that I could come to save you." My words are edged with hysteria. But it is as though she doesn't even hear me as she continues.

"Finally, I reached out to King Camber here with a promise to save his and other kingdoms from my forest and its creatures. He was so desperate he agreed immediately. All he had to do in return was bring you to me."

I whip around to Camber, who I now find standing. He can't even look me in the eye; shame shrouds his features. "I couldn't let my people die, Arty."

Could I blame him? One life for countless saved? It wasn't that hard. But still, betrayal blurred my vision, and tears began to gather at the corners of my eyes. My pride forces me to blink them away. Now is not the time for emotions to overtake me.

"Now that you have completed your end of the deal, you may leave, Camber." I hear Annabella's voice from behind me. With her words, Cam finally looks at me, a question in his gaze.

"I will tell everyone you fought bravely and with great honor," he says, but I don't care about what people think of me, so I reply.

"Just tell my father I am sorry and my family that I love them." He nods and turns to go.

"And take Squash; I have a feeling I won't be needing him."

He doesn't even pause at this, just grabs both horses' reins and walks away. It only takes a minute or so to lose sight of them, and when I do I turn back to Annabella.

"So much work to get me here. Now what?" I ask. She still has got that damn smile on her face.

"I've learned to live well without you, Arty. So I'm afraid I've brought you all this way just to end your life." A wicked laugh bubbles from her lips and fills the space around us. I let her go on for a moment before I speak over it.

"Then do so."

The laughter stops, and a frown mars her perfect face.

"You don't think I will. But I don't want you anymore, Artemisia. Your existence was pathetic, and your death will be as well. Do you want to beg for your life or perhaps try to reason with me?"

I find a comfortable rock to sit on as I contemplate her question.

"No, I don't think so. I've given you enough, and if I am to give you my life, you can not have my pride as well. Lord knows it is the only thing that has stuck by me."

Her face starts to get very red and ugly. I realize that I am probably talking to a woman with the reasoning and emotional range of a child. I can't bring myself to have pity for her, though. I decide if I'm going to die, then I'm at least going to have the last word, so I carry on with my thought.

"Furthermore, I would like to point out that If I am pathetic, then what does that make you? Expending so much effort on my behalf."

That is definitely not what she wants to hear. Her completion is officially that of a beet, I think I see a vein or two bulging on her forehead. She lurches toward me with a dagger in her hand.

From where has she procured it? I have no idea.

"Don't try getting away; this forest belongs to me and bends to my every whim."

"I wouldn't dream of it," I say in a dry tone. I believe that is the last straw because, with a screech, she is upon me, driving the dagger into my stomach. Pain explodes in my abdomen, warning bells going off in my brain, letting me know that something is very wrong. Darkness frosts the edges of my vision. But I lock my gaze with hers. The rage-filled expression melts off of her face as she looks down to find the knife from my belt embedded in her heart. It is my turn to smile, but it hurts. Everything hurts.

"I always said your temper would get the best of you, Bella." She hated that nickname, so it felt right to use it. I felt victory with my final words, which is all one can ask for, I suppose. We fell together onto the forest floor. She was already gone, and I was not too far behind her. The joy of knowing that I had completed my quest brought me warmth as I shuttered a final breath and let go.

"I BELIEVE I HAVE HAD TOO MUCH ALE."

A Witch Called Frog

Monroe Wildrose

In a land where the ground is woven with enchantment, you are lucky if anything is as it seems.

I'll give you three examples:

- A woman who appears to be a doting mother but is, in fact, a heinous sorceress. She wanted only a daughter born to be beautiful and then, when the child was born, hated the angelic child she created.

- A basilica filled with tight-lipped and rigid pious women who turn out to be that little child's greatest treasure. A brood of mothers after her true mother had abandoned her.

- A wafted old witch who lives in a swamp outside of the kingdom is actually a maiden named Cherry, who was cursed by a villain to wallow in the bog.

Now, these are only three things, and only things that happen to have affected me. However, don't let that detract from my original statement.

You are lucky if anything is as it seems.

I had just gone to pull up a horned mushroom from some moss deep in The Wild Wood, and ended up on my rump in a mud puddle after that mushroom turned into a toad.

"You better get! I'll boil you in a stew," I grumbled as the toad stared at me from the log where he perched. He did not move and dared to croak in defiance.

"It's a good thing for you that I don't like the taste of frog." I stood up, feeling the mud seeping through my clothes onto my skin.

I picked up the things that had fallen out of my basket, things I had foraged along the way, and stalked off toward my swamp-side home.

I lived in a small cottage home with lots of flowers growing all around it. For a house in a bog, it was surprisingly homey, and I took extraordinary pride in it. I hopped along with the stones that led to my front door and strode inside. I gave my orange cat a long pet down his back as he arched into my hand, then set my basket of goodies on the table.

Catching my reflection in the spotty mirror, I shot myself a silly face. What I saw in the mirror was an eighteen-year-old girl with butterscotch-colored hair and green eyes, a smattering of freckles cascading over her upturned nose and cheeks. She had ample curves under her forest green dress and practical leather stay. Her stomach was too soft to be considered shapely, but I loved my sonsy shape.

However, because of the curse my mother had placed on me the day before my sixteenth birthday, this is not what other people who happened upon me saw. I supposed it was something more akin to a shriveled old woman with bony fingers and warts—my nose, just a bit too long and pointy.

There was a lack of things to do when one lived in a swamp alone. I took great joy in foraging my food, and I loved to cook. That and talking to the animals of the bog and cultivating my flowers. I also practiced my magic, for one day, I was going to free myself from this dastardly spell.

Not that I minded appearing to be a hobbled old witch. People left me alone to tend to my little life. They were too afraid of the rumors that had sprouted from the truth but now were too lush and overgrown to be recognizable. Once I cast a small spell on a rude boy in the market to make him grow a donkey tail that would disappear in an hour. But the story now was told that I turned a little boy into a donkey and cooked him for supper.

"The most outrageous part of that story, Turnip, is that I would never eat a donkey." I caviled to my cat, who wasn't swayed. "Unimpressed?"

"You'd eat a boy over a donkey?" Was his sharp-toothed response.

"I've never eaten a boy or a donkey, but I assume both would be rather unpleasant."

A knock came at my door just as I was placing a kettle over my hearth to make my afternoon tea. I supposed it to be one of the pious women bringing me my bucket of cherries from their orchard. I adored cherries and could never get enough of them. I loved them so well that the holy women that raised me had named me after the fruit. My mother had given me no name, and Cherry was as good of a name as any.

I opened the door and nearly jumped back from fright. Because the person at the door was no maroon-garbed religious woman but a young man.

And not just any young man but the youngest prince of our kingdom.

"Oh, hello, madam." The raven-haired prince said, pulling his hand back where he had been about to knock a second time.

"What do you want, boy?" I made my voice a little gravelly, as one might imagine an old woman would sound.

"I'm sorry to bother you, good woman, but I seem to have gotten lost in this forest and stumbled upon your home."

To his credit, he only looked a little frightened at my appearance.

"Only a fool would wander into The Wild Wood with no way to get out, Princeling."

"Have we met before?" He tipped his head a little causing a lock of his hair to fall across his forehead.

Prince Fiorello had only gotten more handsome in his age. When I was fifteen, I met him a handful of times. His pale features and high cheekbones contrasted so starkly with his dark eyes and hair that it made him look severe and lovely. Though he had also been the kindest of his three brothers, his looks were deceptive.

Nothing was as it appeared.

"I doubt you would recognize me now, young prince. I've aged since we spoke last."

I almost chuckled at my joke, for when he last met me, I had been heralded the fairest maiden in the land, and he and his brothers had been sent to duel for my hand in marriage. Fiorello had been the only one of the brothers who had asked me if I even wished to become his bride. The other two acted as if it would be my most tremendous honor.

This had been the same day I had been turned into a hag by my pernicious mother.

"I do try to make it a point to remember all the fair women I come across."

"What a treacherous flirt you are to toy with an old woman's emotions." I smiled genuinely. "Come inside, Prince Fiorello, have some tea, and then I shall cast you a routing rock so you may find your way out of the forest. I will also give you a token of protection lest you get eaten by my bog monster."

It was not my bog monster, but we had an uneasy friendship, he and I. It made me sound more powerful to call him mine.

"Are you going to chop me up and put me into your stew for supper?" He asked, and it didn't seem as if he were completely joking.

"I only eat princes on every third full moon. You are safe by a few weeks at least."

"How fortunate," he mused but walked into my modest home without seeming too worried. "Might I get your name?"

"The villagers call me Frog," I said, going to set my kettle of tea on the fireplace.

"Frog?" he asked, horrified as if the thought were absurd. "Why would they call you that?"

"I suppose it's because I look like a witchy human version of a frog." I busied myself about my space, looking for a protection talisman I might use to let the bog monster not eat Prince Fiorello.

"People are quite terrible." He sat himself down on one of my crude wooden stools.

"Some people, not all people. The horrible ones are generally just a bit louder. Aha!" I held up a silver ring I had found lost on the forest floor hanging from a bit of leather cord.

I went over and held it up as the prince opened his hand to receive it. I dropped it into his hand and placed mine over his as I spoke the enchantment over the talisman.

"There, so long as you wear this, the creature in the swamp shall not eat you."

"You've shown me great kindness, however will I repay you?"

"Lessen the tax on your people," I grumbled, and he laughed aloud. It was a wonderful sound.

"I have no control over taxes," he explained to me. "Not yet, anyway. Funny that you would lift the taxes upon the very people that named after you a slimy creature that resides in the muck."

"Very well," I sighed. "I suppose I will have to eat you after all. Maybe just one of your legs."

"How will you prepare it? Salt and pepper? Will you eat it with potatoes?" he inquired, and again I laughed genuinely. There was little cause for laughter when you lived alone.

I found I missed it.

"Probably sauteed in a stew with some onions," I said after my laughter fit subsided.

We were quiet for a bit as I poured the tea into two mugs and set one across the table from him.

"Why do you live in this swamp?" he asked after a time.

"That is a question of a very personal nature, don't you think?" I raised an eyebrow at him.

"I suppose." He nodded into his cup, looking very much chastised.

"Anyway, don't bother yourself with an old froggy crone like me. What is a handsome prince doing in my bog?"

"You find me handsome?" he asked, with a mischievous sparkle in his eye. "Perhaps I shall call upon you for the courting season."

"Oh, hush you, absolute philanderer; you think a bit of flattery and coquettishness will work to save you from me making my prince pie?"

"You tell me?" He smiled again brilliantly, and I leveled him with a stare.

"It is working a bit, but don't press your luck, princeling; this old witch may get peckish yet." I sipped the tea loudly, causing the prince's mouth to tick up in a grin. “What are you doing in The Wild Wood?"

"My father sent my two brothers and me out on an impossible quest." He shrugged. "My brothers went into the great city to seek out magic wielders renowned across the continent."

"And you came to a swamp deep in The Wild Wood?" I asked, slightly confused.

I was confused, in fact, until he met my eye, and a slight glimmer of knowing passed over his face.

"You didn't stumble upon my cottage at all, did you, young one?"

"No, mam, I am sorry to have misled you."

"You hoped that this old bog witch would be as useful to you as the magicians of the great city? That is quite the assumption."

"I went to the people, not the courtiers but the people of the villages surrounding. They all say the same thing."

"What is it they say?"

"They say the magicians in the city are worthless charlatans, and if I wished to encounter a real witch, I needed to go into the Wild Wood and seek the witch called Frog."

I was irritated. Beyond all else in life, I hated to be lied to. While Prince Fiorello had displayed his ability for charm and flirtatiousness, I now felt the need to kick him from my home.

He pushed back his dark hair and gave me an apologetic look. It did nothing to soften the distaste in my mouth.

"I am sorry, Lady," he said, looking a little sheepish. "I did not know if you would allow me in if I started off by saying I was here for a service."

"I certainly would not have let you into my home. But now you have tricked me into offering you company and hospitality. Just because you are a prince does not mean you are owed my kindness. You mustn't take advantage of people this way."

"I apologize deeply; I was not expecting you to be so welcoming."

"You would have felt better about tricking a wicked old witch?" I raised my eyebrows at him.

"No, well..." he hesitated, and I couldn't help the play of a smile that ghosted across my features.

He stopped taking in my expression and looked down into his tea which he rolled around the edges of the cup. *FogGoblin*, he was a handsome sort of man. Perhaps it was because I had been isolated for so long. But then again, I had thought him very handsome once upon a time as well. Back when the last glimpse I had of him was through a stained-glass window. His features colored red; regardless, his smile had been just as devastating.

"Consider me thoroughly chastised, Lady Frog." He stood up and bowed deeply to me. "Since I have obviously behaved with such little civility, I shall take my leave of you."

"Tell me what this impossible challenge is." I reached out and took his cup and mine to a wash basin on my workbench, which was covered in all manner of things. Bundles of dried herbs and a witching bowl for small spells. Teas that I had blended and put into glass canisters.

"I don't wish to burden you," he said, sounding hopeful.

"You've already burdened me. Now, the least you can do is tell me what you've come to get."

He was silent for a bit, looking unnaturally tall in my small cottage.

"My father has tasked me to bring him a yard of the purest fabric. The likes of which are so soft that it can be pulled through the loop of a jeweler's eye."

"What kind of ridiculous request is that?" I growled out, running a palm over my face.

"I think he does not wish to pass down his throne," Fiorello said, shrugging a shoulder. "Either that or he wishes to test our craftiness; I cannot be sure of his motives."

I thought of all the spells I had read, of all the spells I had written. I blinked at the ceiling a few times. I looked over at the prince, who could not be yet twenty-one. There was no guarantee that he would be any better as a ruler than his father was before him. Taxing his people to death and did not care a wit about those who didn't flatter him or line his pockets. Why should I help him take the throne?

"Tell me, princeling, say there was a woman in one of your villages whose husband had died fighting your war. She was left with three children to feed and a babe still on her breast. She could not feed her children, and day after day, the villagers watched as she dwindled to nothing. Feeding her children her own food, the king's guards came to take every bit of money she made washing clothing for taxes."

"Is there such a woman?" His brow furrowed, and his light-hearted eyes filled with concern.

"There are many such women in your future kingdom." I was surprised that bitterness had crept back into my voice. The dry crack of it was like the hopeless faces of the helpless I had seen day after day working in the basilica.

"I do not know," he sighed after a long pause, and my eyes came to meet his. “I wish to tell you I have thought of how to help them, but if I am being honest with you, and I feel as though that is the best course of action, I had not thought of it until just now. I have very little experience outside of the palace. However, I do wish to help, and I am not callous to the needs of my people," he said, and then ended with "All my people."

"Very well, come back tomorrow evening, and I shall have the piece of fabric that you seek."

I shooed him out the door despite his trying to say more and closed the door in his face. I turned to my spell books and let out a deep sigh.

"Are you helping the prince because he's handsome?" Mewled Turnip from where he had been napping on the windowsill.

"Oh hush," I grumbled, going to a rather fat volume with a frayed binding and gold and blue lettering.

"Such handsome hands and long fingers," The wretched beast went on. "Don't tell me you weren't imagining what it would be like for him to pet your patch of fur on top of your silly human head."

"I hope you don't find a single mouse to chase this evening." I retaliated by throwing a small book at him, and he jumped down from the window. I heard him laughing as I tried to will the blush from my cheeks.

My charm must have worked because the next evening, while I was tidying up, there was a knock on my door.

"The monster didn't eat you," I cackled as I let Fiorello into my house once again.

"No, and in fact, it worked so well that I was able to talk to him," He said, ducking beneath my low doorframe.

"Oh?" I blinked in surprise. I spoke to the bog monster, but he never spoke to me. I was a little miffed. That damned creature could understand me after all. I thought of asking him, but I didn’t want to seem too intrigued.

"Tea?" I inquired, pulling the kettle off the fire and motioning to two teacups I had prepared.

The strange truth was that I had gotten ready for the prince for the last couple of hours. I cleaned my home and pulled out my favorite tea that I used sparingly, as the ingredients only came once a year and were nearly impossible to dry. I had even washed my best dress and put it on. What was wrong with me? To his eyes, I was a bedraggled and haggard old witch, and no amount of fluffing could change it. Fine silver cannot make crow more appetizing, as my mother once said. So, while I put on my floral lace-up overlay, I'd rolled my eyes at my reflection.

I had mocked myself, shaking a finger at the stupid girl in the mirror.

You'll never be more than a wrinkled old witch, so you best get used to it. Once a handsome prince comes along, you find yourself wishing for something else, but it can never be. Princes don't fancy hobbled crones.

"I'd love some tea," Fiorello said, sitting on the same stool where he had sat yesterday, knocking me from my self-embarrassed memory.

At least he was awfully polite and kind to wrinkly witches.

"I've made you the softest piece of fabric," I said, setting a brown paper package next to him. "If you touch it, you are sure to soil it, it is so pure, and the magic will allow it to pass through even the smallest of needle holes if your father wishes it."

"Might I see it?" He eyed the brown paper with curiosity in his mischievous eyes.

"Do you not trust me, Princeling?"

"You might call me Fiorello, Lady Frog," he said, chuckling to himself, and I smiled despite myself.

"And you might call me Cherry," I responded without thinking before sucking in a quiet breath.

Unthinking, foolish girl. Only an utter incompetent mushroomed brain...

My chest was tight as I put the kettle back on the hook as casually as I could. Perhaps he wouldn't notice. Surely a prince wouldn't remember a commoner he knew years ago. I was too paranoid. I moved to a bookshelf and tried to appear as if I were browsing titles as I tried to reign in my thundering heart. I controlled my breathing, scolding myself all the while.

"I knew a girl named Cherry once."

I yelped and turned around quickly. While I was regaining my composure, the prince quickly snuck up and was now right behind me. His eyes narrowed as I pressed myself back against the bookshelf, and he stepped in closer, lowering his head to inspect my face.

I couldn't breathe, and all the work I had done to calm my nerves was undone as his pretty lips and sparkling eyes lined up with my own as he searched for answers I could never give him. The only people that knew of my identity were the Pious Women, and they had accepted my fate now much as I had.

"Oh?" I squeaked out. "How strange, such an uncommon name."

"Funny that she had eyes like yours, too," he said, his mouth pulling at a grin as if he already knew something he shouldn't.

"How do you mean?" The question was quiet.

"Green with flecks of golden brown," he answered, his eyes searching for my own.

"Funny you remember her eyes." I moved around him, letting out a breath as I sat on my stool. My hands were shaking as they picked up my cup.

"Well, I had intended to marry her." He moved back to his stool. His eyes bored holes into me as I looked around for anything else in the world to stare at except him.

"Oh?" I asked, sipping my tea and settling on looking into the flames of my fireplace. "Was it her beauty that wooed you?"

"No," he stated, sure, and my eyes flicked to him for a moment for any sign of a lie.

"Was she ugly then?"

"She was as ugly as a golden sunrise over a field of wildflowers, as hideous as a sparkling crown on the head of a powerful queen, as odious as an orchard of cherry trees blossoming in the spring."

He knew.

He knew me.

Had he known before? Damn this prince with his layers of secrets. But it was no matter, for I was no longer Cherry the fair maiden. I was Frog, the swamp witch.

"A regular eyesore then?" I asked.

"Truly." He nodded. "I fell in love with her before she knew who I was. Once I watched a small child fall from a tree where Cherry lived. She ran out to tend to the little one, kicking the tree and lecturing the branches on their careless neglect of the climber." My eyes were trapped by his as he smiled, recalling a memory he thought of often. "Then she cared for the scrape on the child's knee so tenderly, after hurling such filthy insults at a helpless tree, I couldn't help but be enchanted."

I remembered the day. It had been the very day we met for the first time.

"Trees are far from helpless, Fiorello; I learned that from The Wild Wood."

"Might I come to call on you again?" he interjected, and I looked down into my empty cup.

"No."

"No?" he inquired, but he didn't sound surprised, only sad.

"No, you best not. It won't...I can't..." My voice came out strangled and desperate. Desperate for him to understand.

"Very well, Lady Cherry, I shall leave you with my utmost gratitude, and if there is ever a thing you require, you have only to ask it of me." He stood up, bowed, and after we said our formal goodbyes, he set off.

I closed my door, sat against the foot of it, and had a good cry.

Four weeks later, at the same time, a knock came at my door.

I opened the door and was met with dark hair and a charming smile.

"I thought she told you not to come back?" Turnip said from the corner, and I shot the cat a withering look.

The prince looked startled that the cat could speak but recovered rather quickly.

"Lady Cherry, I am sorry to have returned after you requested I did not, but I have another favor of the magical nature to ask."

"What is your blasted father asking for now?" I grumbled, thinking of how much magic it had taken to make the extraordinary fabric.

"He is requesting a dog," he answered, leaning against the doorway of my home.

"A dog?" I questioned, eyebrows raised. "That hardly seems a request of a magical nature. Might I usher you to town where you could purchase a puppy for a few coppers?"

"He wants a small dog." He smiled at me, and my heart skipped in my chest so terribly that I had to turn away from him.

"How small?" I inquired, petting Turnip where he lay sunbathing.

"Small enough to fit in a walnut shell."

"What kind of mucky mud-footed idiot requests such a thing?" I nearly shouted.

I whirled on him, and he raised one shoulder as if he weren't sure how to answer my question.

"Damned bastard king, with these damn requests of nonsensical nature. When you become king Fiorello, you had better never ask such a thing in your entire life. If I hear you are even half as idiotic, I will come out of this cottage to turn you into a frog, do you hear me." I hollered as I gathered things up, throwing them into a satchel.

"I shall indeed remember that very threat as long as I live," he said from where he stood, but he didn't look threatened; he looked amused.

I grumbled some more, and I shoved my sock-clad feet into some boots and headed for the door.

"Turnip, I have to visit The Sisters. I'll be back in a day, don't get into too much trouble." I slammed the door behind me.

"Where are we going?" Fiorello easily kept up with my stomping progression through the wood.

"We are going to see the Holy Women in town. The building sits on the sacred magic ground. If I am to make a dog small enough to fit in a blasted walnut shell, I must perform the magic there, or I'll level all the living things around my cottage."

We walked in silence for what felt like an hour. We were nearly out of the wood when Fiorello stopped. I took a few more steps, but when he didn't resume this pace, I stopped and turned.

"I don't have all day, Princeling," I said, looking him down like a wicked old grandmother calling after one of her rouge grandchildren.

"The Bog Monster wishes to speak to you before you leave The Wilde Wood," he said, tilting his head as if listening to the wind.

"How do you know?" I narrowed my eyes at him.

He pulled the leather cord from around his neck to reveal the token I had enchanted for him.

"He will meet us back a few paces." He turned and headed back into the wood, leaving me staring after him in disbelief.

Once I followed him, cursing all the way, we happened up to a clearing surrounded by white-papered trees that were covered in lilac leaves and smelled of sunshine. They surrounded the small space in a perfect circle, and I was quite sure I had never seen the place before.

"Fiorello, I hate to be the herald of reality, but The Bog Monster lives in the bog."

Deep chortling followed my statement, and I turned to face whatever it was with a wariness building in me. An old man came into the clearing wearing robes of cerulean blue decorated in flowers of golden thread. He hobbled over to us, leaning heavily on a staff of carved grey wood.

I marched forward quickly and stepped in front of Fiorello to protect him.

"You've nothing to fear from me, Cherry, fair maiden of the realm, and a competent enchantress you've grown into as well."

"Who are you?" I called to him warily.

"Child, I am the spirit of the forest or The Bog Monster, as you affectionately call me. I am The Wild Wood."

"Oh," I said, lowering my guard and bowing my head to him. "I am sorry, Forest Spirit; I meant no disrespect to you."

His calm washed over me as a hum of power filled the space around us. The whisper of leaves and rustling of old cracking branches became as loud as a rushing waterfall if one were directly beneath it. It was like that for a few heartbeats before dying down. A scent of damp moss and fresh forest blooms lingered in the air, and I had no doubt this man was who he said he was.

"You've taken care of my forest, little witch. Foraging things in season and respecting life here. You've shown great promise, and you shall be blessed."

"Thank you, Forest Spirit." My head was still bowed, but I felt his old, cracked lips press a kiss just below my hairline. They felt like tree bark against my skin.

"You will always be welcome among my trees, Cherry Enchantress of The Wild Wood, Lady Frog grandmother to my saplings."

I looked up to say something, but the clearing was silent again, and the spirit had gone.

"Thank you for your blessing," I shouted at no one and turned to Fiorello, who was staring at me unabashedly.

"What are you looking at? We have to be going. I don't have time for any more delays." I pushed past him and headed back the way we had come.

Once we reached the parish of the Pious woman, I ushered Fiorello inside, along with the small white dog we had purchased on the way there. Small, but not yet small enough to fit into a walnut shell. I passed several holy women I knew, but I didn't stop to make small talk as they stared after me in disbelief. They were undoubtedly wondering why I was being followed by a dog and a crown prince.

"Cherry!" Mother Holly called after me in a panic, but I had no time to ease her concerns about an animal being allowed in the basilica.

"I'll be right back, Sister!" I called back, not stopping my pace.

I mazed through the stone hallways and to the back of the building, to a small empty room where I had found the magic was the strongest. I made Fiorello stay outside while I unloaded the things I brought into the room.

I cast spell after spell on the four-legged creature, who sat very well-trained in the middle of the room. Once I was pleased with his size and sure I had caused the small thing no internal damage, I emerged holding him in my palm.

"Will it fit in a walnut shell?" Fiorello's eyes were wide as saucers looked at the tiny animal.

"Only one way to find out, I suppose." I stalked out a back door to the orchard beyond.

Most of the trees in the back were cherry trees, but there were two almond trees and one walnut. The walnuts were in perfect season to be rattled from their branches. Luckily, the sisters had already harvested some and cracked them out of their green pods. I sifted through a bucket at the base of the tree to find the biggest one I could. Using magic, I opened it and hollowed it out, taking the tiny dog and placing him gently inside. I put the two shells together and laughed with hysteria as they closed together.

I let him out immediately, placing the walnut shell back in my pocket.

"My father wishes you to present it to him. I told him of your accomplishments, and I'm afraid I've drawn his attention to you," Fiorello explained as he walked around to the front of the parish.

"Fine, but as soon as he has his tiny dog, I am returning to my home in the wood. I don't wish to be bothered with any silly magic request again. I am an incredibly old woman and am too tired and decrepit to be making these kinds of trips."

Fiorello laughed outright at me, and when I turned to glower at him, he only laughed harder. I rolled my eyes as we walked out of town.

The castle was no great walk, but on the edge of town, a carriage met us. The footman got down and tried to help me inside after Fiorello got in, but I chastised them.

"You think because I'm an old woman, I can't get into a carriage on my own." I lectured as he stared at me, confused as I made my way up the steps.

"Have some grace with my poor footman." Fiorello laughed as I sat down hard across from him. "You nearly gave him the tongue-lashing of his life."

I grumbled at them all under my breath as the carriage rumbled down the dirt path up to the palace beyond. During the short ride, I caught Fiorello staring at me several times and became increasingly aware of how his eyes drifted over me. The saltier the glances I threw his way, the more it was apparent that he found my disapproval humorous.

We stopped at the castle gates, and I stomped up the steps, ushered in by several guards who addressed me as 'Lady.'

"I'm not a lady; I'm a witch; take me to your king," I snapped at them as we were led through the palace.

Once we were in the throne room, Fiorello went ahead of me, sweeping his arms in a wide bow before his father. The king looked much like him, only older and fatter.

"Father, I present to you, Lady Frog, Enchantress of The Wild Wood. She made the fabric so pure and soft it could fit through the jeweler's eye. Now she has created the impossible and produced a dog that might fit in a walnut shell."

I didn't bow, didn't bother. I just deposited the dog from my pocket and the walnut shell into the hand of a guard who presented it to the king.

"My youngest son!" The king boomed across the room. " You have finished the last two challenges leagues before your brothers! You have brought me not only a marvel of magic but have produced the fairest woman I have ever beheld."

I scoffed at his words.

Looking around, I realized that everyone was staring at me. I looked down at my hands; to my horror, they were soft and smooth. My nails were perfectly prim and polished. I reached up and pulled a lock of my hair forward, realizing it was the deep golden color it had been years ago.

I stumbled back.

One step, two steps.

How had I not realized I had changed back? When had this happened? I heard Fiorello call my name, but it was distant and muffled as if I were underwater. The panic I could not name rose to my throat, and I turned and ran out of the palace.

I ran until I reached the town and drug myself to the parish, where sister Holly welcomed me with open arms as I cried a mixture of relief and horror.

And when I was done crying, I returned to my home in the bog. I slept in my small bed of straw and cuddled Turnip.

"There's someone in the cottage," Turnip warned me as we approached. I was carrying a basket of chamomile and lemon balm, and he sauntered by me without a care.

"Who is it?" I asked.

"Need you ask?" My cat went on ahead as I dragged my feet.

It had been three days since I ran from the palace. He had been wise to give me a few days on my own. For if he had come before, I might have turned him out.

I came to the door and took a deep breath, for I had no idea what he would ask of me. When I came inside, I saw him seated at his stool, petting Turnip, who purred under his fingers.

"Traitor," I whispered under my breath, but the cat only purred louder.

I went along silently, putting my things away without so much as a glance at Fiorello.

I passed by him to get something on a shelf, and he grabbed me, pulling me to him. I let out a holler of surprise as he turned me so that my face was mere inches from his. His arms were wrapped around me so that I might not escape.

We stared at each other for a while as I reveled in the feeling of his hands on my waist and his eyes complimenting his smile.

"I'm sorry," I whispered, turning my face away from his, but he gently reached up and brought it back so my eyes could meet his.

"You have nothing to apologize for, Cherry; I should have told you as soon as the spirit of the forest lifted your curse." His fingers grazed my cheek, and I leaned into the touch. "I didn't know the right words to say. I thought I would bumble anything I would attempt."

"Next time, I would prefer a bumbled warning over well-executed silence."

"Yes, Enchantress." The name made me blush as he leaned in and hovered just an inch from me. His eyes searched mine, waiting for me to make my decision.

I leaned forward and accepted his lips on mine, soft and promising, a sure and understanding man. Both his hands came up to hold my face to his.

“I'm not ready to marry you." I broke away from him.

"I haven't asked you," he laughed, placing another kiss on my mouth as I pulled away again.

"I still want to live in The Wild Wood awhile," I said again, between kisses.

"Yes, Cherry, Enchantress of The Wild Wood. I shall visit you here as long as you allow. Every day that you let me, your king will come to beg for a moment of your company."

And that is how I became Cherry, Enchantress of The Wild Wood, and Queen of the Kingdom Jestul.

"I SUPPOSED IT WAS SOMETHING MORE AKIN TO A SHRIVELED OLD WOMAN WITH BONY FINGERS AND WARTS"

Lilly's Story

By: Charli M. (9yo)

Once upon a time, Lilly was sitting in her tower and heard a knock on the door. Lilly answered it. It was an old woman and she gave her a poisonous apple and told her to eat it and so she bit into it. Then she fell to the ground and never got up for two years.

When she woke up she saw a handsome prince and they immediately fell in love and lived...

happily
ever
after.

"THEN SHE FELL TO THE GROUND, AND NEVER GOT UP FOR TWO YEARS."

THE DREAM TRIALS

J. Houser

Maribel stood in the hatter's shop, sorting through the available ribbons with her best friend, Celia. Maribel loved fashion, reading, long walks, and learning new things. She and Celia had planned for some time to update their accessories, and the hatter carried an astounding selection.

"I rather like this one," Maribel said, draping a deep plum ribbon over her hand. It complemented her skin tone well.

Celia glanced at the ribbon, shrugging. "I think the buttercup yellow is more fetching."

They may be best friends, but they were night and day. Celia was a tall, thin redhead, covered in freckles. Maribel's complexion was darker, and she had always been shorter and heavier than Celia. They rarely agreed on fashion, but they'd grown up together and shared other interests.

Maribel set the ribbon in her wicker shopping basket to consider. She'd never been a fan of yellow; Celia could choose it for herself if she so desired.

Humming, Maribel ran her finger along the edge of the cut ribbon bin. The precut odds and ends were cheaper, and her mother had reminded her to keep to a strict budget. Smiling, Maribel snatched up a pretty pea-green one with generous length. It had scalloped edges. "Ooh, I like this."

Celia plucked a brand-new spool of bright pink ribbon from a nearby shelf. "Green again? Why not something brighter like this?"

"What's wrong with green?" It had always been Maribel's favorite color. Celia joked that it had to be because the prince's eyes were green, but in all her eighteen years, Maribel had never even met the man. He *did* have green eyes, but her favorite color hadn't been determined by the physical attribute of a man she'd yet to meet.

"Variety," Celia simply stated, depositing the pink spool into her own basket.

Maribel was undeterred. Fretting over someone else's idea of fashion dos and don'ts seemed like a pretty foolish way to spend one's time. She gathered the loose ribbon and put it with the purple one.

"Clouds are rolling in," the hatter's assistant said, staring out the shop windows into the open market.

A gong rang in the distance, and they all paused.

It can't be. The gong resided at the castle, and was only used for special warnings and celebrations.

A heartbeat later, the gong rang again. Maribel and Celia shared a hesitant look. *Please don't let there be a third...* There were no planned celebrations in the kingdom that day, but the people had been put on alert...

The gong rang through the air a third time, then fell silent.

Maribel swallowed.

"She's gone," the hatter's assistant whispered.

"She's gone," Maribel echoed, her chest tight.

Official word had been delivered across the kingdom some weeks ago, warning the citizens to be prepared for the death of the queen. She had been a kind and wise queen. In fact, Maribel had never heard a single person utter anything truly negative about the woman.

Solemnly, Celia set her basket down. "Come on, then."

Maribel perched her basket on the ribbon bin, joining her. The hatter emerged from the back workroom, and followed the girls outside with his assistant. The entire open-air market was lined with citizens now. People filed out of shops and the church at the end of the town square.

It was tradition to pay their respects at the passing of royalty. When the gong rang again, everyone bowed their heads, silent for a full minute.

As the minute began, a rain droplet fell onto Maribel's neck, to the side of her braid. There hadn't even been clouds in the sky a half hour ago. She dutifully kept her head bowed, tears pricking at her eyes as she focused on the loss of their beloved queen.

Another drop moistened Maribel's arm. And a couple more landed in unison on her back.

The gong rang a final time, and everyone stood straight.

The rain picked up quickly, and most people retreated inside.

Maribel and Celia didn't, however. At least a dozen other maidens remained in the open market, also oddly entranced by the rainfall.

Even as the heavens pelted them, they smiled. The rain was warm, iridescent, and otherworldly. There was something almost magical about it. It was like a hug from the beloved queen herself, as a goodbye to her people.

Maribel wasn't accustomed to standing in the open during showers, but it was a beautiful moment she wanted to drink in. She lifted her face to the sky, allowing the rain to spatter her skin, to soak into her hair and clothing, to drain down her neck and legs.

The storm was brief, but Maribel was grateful for the cleansing moment nature had given them during a time of mourning.

Celia giggled, wiping drenched hair out of her eyes. "We should finish our shopping." She hooked her arm through Maribel's, and they reentered the shop.

The hatter had returned to his work in the back. His assistant eyed the girls as they entered. "Why would you choose to get soaked to the bone like that?"

Maribel couldn't stop smiling, despite having been on the brink of tears minutes earlier. "It was wonderful. Couldn't you feel it?"

The assistant rolled their eyes, pointing to the window. "It was something only young maidens were foolish enough to do. Have your parents not taught you better?"

Pursing her lips, Maribel shot Celia a look. Neither of their parents would be pleased to have them waltz into their homes drenched.

"It was special rain," Celia said, defiantly squaring her shoulders.

Heading back to their stool by the counter, the assistant huffed. "Then I hope your purchases make up for me having to mop the floor again today."

Maribel glanced down, guilt washing over her. They'd already dripped all over, a nice puddle forming at their feet. "Oh, I'm sorry."

She was supposed to stop by a few more shops, and hadn't planned on spending her entire allowance at the hatter's, but she generously loaded up her basket and paid for much more ribbon than she needed, emptying her coin pouch to make up for the hassle.

Soggy, the girls strolled toward their homes with their goods, marveling over the rain. "Have you ever felt something like that?" Celia asked.

"No, but it was lovely," Maribel replied.

Celia sidestepped a puddle. "And now we wait to hear more about the prince taking the throne." She grinned. "And taking a bride."

Maribel couldn't help but wrinkle her nose. It felt too early to talk about that. The king and queen had only been able to bear one child—a son—later in life. The king had died two years ago, and the prince was their only heir. The law required him to take the throne within thirty days of his mother's death, and to pick a bride to rule alongside him. Tradition dictated he choose a commoner in the kingdom.

"There are a lot of eligible girls," Maribel said. "And I can't imagine he's excited to start sorting through them all while he's grieving...."

A passing mother nodded at them, and her young boy hopped into a large puddle. The mother gasped. "Daniel!"

Maribel and Celia stifled laughs as the little boy apologized.

"You're not even dreaming *at all* of living in the castle?" Celia asked, wringing her hair again.

They were both of an age to marry, and the prince was only a year older, but the chance of either of them being picked was slim to none. "The castle is probably drafty," Maribel kidded. "And what if he chooses his queen based on stupid criteria? Like which maiden can swim the fastest?"

Celia laughed. "Swimming?"

"Yes. In a lake full of swamp beasts." She grinned wickedly, and Celia laughed again.

"What if it's about favorite colors? What if he *hates* green because he hates his own eyes?" Celia asked comically. "It would be quite the scandal."

Maribel feigned amazement. "What if he chooses based on what he *sees* with his eyes?" She pinched Celia's thin arm. "Maybe he doesn't like scrawny girls...." She poked her own gut. "Or thick ones. Because if that's the case, neither of us will be chosen."

Her own eyes wide, Celia nodded. "Maybe I should start visiting the church more often to find a way to gain his favor... An answer to a prayer...."

Drawing herself back from their moment of levity, Maribel sighed. She had time to plan out her life, and it was futile to chase the unknown desires of a man in power whom she may never even meet. And...

"Let's be respectful." She straightened her posture. "I'm sure he's taking things one day at a time. He's probably not even worried about that until after the funeral." Maribel raised an eyebrow in censure. "And Her Majesty deserves the respect of full mourning."

Celia cocked her head to the side. "True. She'll be missed."

"Yes. No more talk about the prince and some random girl out there...."

After they arrived at their lane and parted ways, Maribel walked into her home and set down her bulging satchel of ribbons.

"Did you fall in the stream on your way back?" Maribel's mother fussed over her on her return.

"I'm fine. It was just the rain."

Her mother frowned, caressing her cheek. "We'll all miss her."

Maribel nodded. The kingdom had lost a treasure today.

"But why in the world did you stay out in the rain? It was only sprinkling during the short observance."

Maribel couldn't resist smiling again. "It was beautiful."

Her mother raised her eyebrows high. "It was only rain. Go change before you catch a cold!"

Maribel did as told. Her mother fussed far too much. She was already eighteen; she didn't need to be told how to take care of herself. As she stripped her clothes in her room, she mused over the rain, though. *Only* rain? It had been beautiful, like nothing Maribel had ever experienced.

When Maribel emerged from her room, her mother stood at the stove stirring split pea soup for their supper. She forced Maribel to sit at the kitchen table and guzzle piping hot bone broth as a precaution to ward off illness. Maribel's younger sister and brother played in the backyard, only joining her and their mother when their father returned from work.

As she retired to bed early that evening, Maribel could have sworn another storm was brewing outside, as the soft pitter-patter of rain lulled her to sleep.

"I love the smell of the earth after fresh rain. Don't you?" Celia commented as they chatted in Maribel's sitting room, sorting through their stash of old and new ribbons.

"You too?" Maribel's mother asked, poking her head in. "Maybe I'm the mad one here...." She proceeded to stroll past the open door.

Celia looked to Maribel, confused.

"I said the same thing this morning, but she swears it didn't rain last night...." And it *was* odd, because there had been no mud, no signs of rain come morning, but Maribel had heard it herself as she'd fallen asleep, and that fresh dewy smell had enlivened her as she rose.

Maribel stacked her ribbon by color and length. Almost half her collection was green; maybe she ought to try more colors after all.

"And then I had the wildest dream...." Celia continued minutes later, massaging her shoulder. "I was crossing under a bridge, and an old beggar asked me for help with carrying something."

Stilling, Maribel listened. The dream was eerie, for she too had had a dream like that the night before.

Celia wrapped a long cream ribbon around her hand. "So, I helped the poor man, but gosh his bag was *heavy*! The strap of the bag dug into my shoulder. I know it was just a dream, but it felt so real." She rubbed her shoulder again.

Wide-eyed, Maribel stared at her. That had almost exactly been her same dream. She'd woken with a sore shoulder; it still ached. "That's mad... I ... had a dream like that too."

"Really?" Celia narrowed her eyes.

"Yes, but Mother said it was just my mattress." Her father's business had been doing poorly lately, and they couldn't afford to replace the lumpy mattress anytime soon.

Brushing off the bizarre coincidence, Celia smiled. "Too weird."

As Maribel went to bed that night, she felt around her mattress. It wasn't the most comfortable, but it wasn't like it was made of rocks. Luckily, the soreness in her shoulder had eased around midday, and she was ready to put the odd shared dream behind her.

After blowing out her candle, she climbed under her quilt, ready for sleep to claim her. Rain sang her to sleep for the second night.

Maribel blinked. She stood in the middle of a busy cobblestone lane. "What the..." How had she gotten there? The midday sun beat down on her, the breeze nonexistent.

She glanced around, trying to piece it together. What did she even remember last? She ought to remember walking somewhere... Though no pain remained in her shoulder, she rubbed it. *The dream.* Could this be another dream? It was so vivid, so real, but her dream the previous night had also started abruptly.

Shoes clicked on the cobblestone, and mumbles of passersby surrounded her, though no one paid her any attention.

Maribel stopped a passing man. "Sir, uh, what day is it?"

"Tuesday, miss." He gave her a single nod and continued walking.

She bit her lip. Tuesday? If her recollection was correct, she'd gone to bed Tuesday night, so this was perhaps a memory from hours before? But she'd spent the whole day with Celia, and hadn't stepped foot in this lane...

Sharp pain stung her toe. "Ah!"

A little boy had randomly stomped on her foot.

"Thadeus!" a woman scolded. She turned to Maribel. "I'm so sorry. He can be unruly sometimes. Are you okay?"

Still in a great deal of pain, Maribel lied. "I'm fine. He's just a little one."

"Thank you," the woman said, exasperated. "Is there anything I can do for you?"

Maribel clenched her teeth, tears pricking at her eyes. How had that small of a child inflicted *so much pain*? "I'm all right."

The boy's mother gave her an apologetic smile, then ran after him, stopping him from wreaking more havoc down the lane.

Blowing out a breath, Maribel stood on one leg. "I need something for my foot...." A cool stream to dip her aching toes in would do wonders.

The next thing she remembered was waking to morning sunlight pouring in through her windows.

She furrowed her brow. *Huh...* Her toe still throbbed. A lumpy mattress couldn't be blamed for a sore toe, could it? She had to have kicked the wooden bed frame during the night, which inspired the dream... That was all—a perfectly reasonable explanation.

After making her bed, she approached the window. No signs of rain again, but that fresh scent filled her lungs. Had she hit herself on the head at some point?

A heartbeat later, a tap on the bedroom door claimed her attention. "Are you up, dear?" her mother asked.

Maribel drew a deep breath. "Yes, I'll be right out." It was the queen's funeral service that day, and they would want to leave the house early to get a good place for the public observance. Maribel chose a forest green dress of a respectable length for the observance, tying her new pea-green ribbon around her waist. The queen had loved bright colors, and had stated her people should reflect hope in their mourning.

Maribel's family joined the throngs who gathered along the path the queen's casket would travel. The queen would be laid to rest at the royal cemetery, but this gave the citizens a chance to offer their last goodbyes.

Her toe still sore, Maribel used the distraction to avoid crying too much about the queen. She'd been devastated at the king's funeral because his death hadn't been anticipated. But she'd always adored the queen, looking up to her as much as she did her own mother. She'd even met the queen once during her years in primary school.

After what must have been a full hour, the crowd to Maribel's right hushed. She stood on her tippy-toes. Seeing past the people in front of her was worth the pain.

Horseshoes clapped on the stone path, the giant regal creatures pulling the queen's flower-laden casket through the street on a lovely cart. Maribel's heart hurt.

The prince's carriage kept pace behind the funeral cart. Facing forward, Prince Jonas wore a solemn look, as would be expected.

After the royal funeral procession had passed, the crowd stirred. Parents with crying children departed, as well as many adults who likely had to get back to work. Maribel's father was one of them. He kissed Maribel and her younger siblings on the head, and his wife on the cheek. "Sorry, but I don't have much choice. Someone needs to tend the shop."

Maribel was the oldest of three, and her little sister was restless.

"Follow the crowds to the services, or return home?" their mother asked.

"Services," Maribel answered, while her two siblings, in unison, voted for home. She couldn't blame them. Funerals could be long and taxing, and it would be a decent walk to and from the official services. "I'll be fine alone. I'd like to go."

Her mother smiled. "Okay. You be careful."

Maribel nodded, trailing the others in the street who chose to follow the funeral procession. Not far down the path, she ran into Celia with her family.

"Is it all right if I join?"

"Of course, dear," Celia's mother replied.

The group walked in near silence for some time. With each footstep, Maribel's toe ached. She leaned against Celia, whispering. "My toe hurts from last night...."

Celia immediately gave her a shocked look. "Yes... Mine too. Another dream?"

Maribel nodded. How could it happen two nights in a row? She'd never shared a dream with someone before, not that it was sharing exactly, since they hadn't seen each other in the dreams. "A little boy stomped on my foot."

It was Celia's turn to nod. "Yes, such a brat."

Shrugging, Maribel hooked her arm around Celia's. "He was just a little child."

Celia rolled her eyes. "Well, call him what you like, but I draw the line at that kind of rude behavior. I gave his mother an earful."

Maribel almost laughed. "It wasn't that bad. And it was only a dream...."

"But was it?"

It had to have been, right? And even if it hadn't been, children could learn...

"What about the rain?" Maribel asked. "I fell asleep to it again, and woke to the fresh air, but there were no signs of it in the morning."

Narrowing her eyes, Celia scratched her temple. "Come to think of it, I fell asleep to it, but I didn't notice that smell in the morning."

Maribel's mind worked. "Do you think—"

Celia's mother softly shushed them.

Embarrassed, Maribel clamped her mouth closed.

After ages of plodding alongside other townspeople, they arrived at the head church. Flowers of every color flooded the area. The clergyman gave a speech, as did esteemed government officials and beloved family members.

Prince Jonas stood last to address the crowd. It wasn't exactly an appropriate time to make the observation, but Maribel couldn't deny he was devastatingly handsome. He had a sharp jawline, neatly trimmed brown hair, and those lovely green eyes. She'd seen him before while attending less-somber public events, and at the king's funeral. He hadn't spoken at his father's funeral, so this was Maribel's first time actually hearing his voice.

He stood at the pulpit, thanking his people for attending. "My mother would be honored to know how many have taken the time to pay their respects." He was elegant, not a hair out of place as he continued his speech. His voice was light and confident, he shared a couple of heartwarming stories that made Maribel tear up. He seemed on the verge of tears as well, and her heart fully went out to him. He was young to take over the kingdom, but he swore to do his best to carry on his parents' legacy.

After he sat, the clergyman said a few last words, then dismissed the people. The crowds shuffled away, including Celia's family, but Celia and Maribel clung to the edges of some bushes to wait for others to pass. They'd walk home together when it wasn't so stifling.

Maribel's eyes were glued to the prince. "He looks so sad." It was the most obvious and least eloquent thing she could have said, but it was true. He stood on the stage yards away, the image of duty as he discussed matters with those in charge of the service.

"I wish they'd explain his selection process," Celia said.

The public knew the required timeframe for him to choose a bride, and the tradition that it had to be a maiden from the kingdom, but not much else had ever been shared about how the royal family selected brides and grooms to join them on the throne. Rumor had it Prince Jonas had briefly courted a neighboring kingdom's princess, and another local maiden at some point, but he didn't seem to have anyone in his sights at the moment.

Shrugging, Maribel replied, "I don't think it really matters how he chooses, does it? As long as they're a good king and queen...."

"I guess..."

Maribel gestured in his direction. "Don't you feel sorry for him, though? He's having to lay his mother to rest, take over the kingdom, and choose to marry a stranger all in a month's time."

Celia scoffed. "No, I don't feel sorry for him. It's probably a lot to deal with, but I refuse to pity a wealthy, powerful, handsome man who gets his pick of the ladies from an entire kingdom."

Annoyed but not wanting a fight, Maribel let it go. Whomever he chose, the girl had a choice in the matter.

"Plus," Celia added, "he's probably been secretly courting someone for ages, and will just pretend he's plucked her from a local town soon."

That had to be jealousy rearing its ugly head. Celia was as interested in the prince as Maribel was, if not more. "Anyway..."

Most attendees had cleared out quickly, but several small children and their parents lined up to greet the prince. He bent and gave the children gracious smiles and handshakes. Maribel's heart melted. She and Celia had been so curious about him over the years. He didn't go out into crowds or give arrogant smiles as one would expect a prince to. He'd always kept to himself during public events. Was it because he was stuffy and full of himself? Maribel would like to think he was kind, and didn't consider himself so much above his people. Generosity to children was a good sign, but that could also just be a politician's move.

"Want to come to my place?" Celia asked. "Spend lunch with us?"

Maribel returned her focus to her friend. "Yes, let's do that."

Maribel quadruple-checked that the skies were clear that night. The moon glowed brightly, no hints of inclement weather on the horizon. After she brushed her teeth, crawled under her quilt, and closed her eyes, rain *somehow* pattered against the window she'd just looked through. She slid a hand to pull back her quilt to go check, but before she could do so, she'd drifted to sleep.

Blinking, she found herself sitting at a study desk, staring at a man who couldn't actually be there. "Mr. Hamon?" He had been one of her teachers years ago, but had fallen ill and since passed.

He gave her a bright smile under his thick white mustache. "Who else would you expect for your test today?"

"I..." She cocked her head. "This *is* a dream, then... Right?"

He simply shrugged. "Does it matter?"

She gaped. "A little? I'm not accustomed to seeing dead people..."

Chuckling, he stacked a few papers on a desk. "No need to fear. It's a simple test."

Wary, she eyed him. "If I don't want to take it?"

"It's your choice."

"And if I fail...?"

The elderly gentleman twisted his lips. "You'll move on with your life."

But I won't move on with my life if I don't *fail?* She shook the cobwebs away in her brain. It was just a silly dream. At least she wouldn't wake with a sore toe or shoulder... "All right. What questions do you have for me?"

They had to have spent hours exchanging questions and answers. He challenged her memory on the most basic of arithmetic, and on the uppermost limits of her science courses and literacy. A good portion of time was dedicated to the geography and history of the world and their kingdom. Maribel was proud of herself for how well it had gone.

She woke in the morning, breathing in the impossibly fresh aroma of rain. This time, her dream had granted her the pain of a headache. Then again, she'd probably just hit her head on a different bedpost, right? Because the idea of physical tokens of pain after strangely lucid dreams was just...

Gnawing on willow bark for the pain later that morning, she met up with Celia to stroll through the nearby woods.

"Need some willow bark?" Maribel offered. "I grabbed another bit for you in case you needed it."

Celia gave her a confused look as she stepped over a large rock in their path. "What for?"

"Headache from the dream last night...."

"That doesn't sound fun. But why would *I* need willow bark for *your* headache?"

A light breeze rustled the leaves in a tree overhead. "I just assumed you had the same dream last night again."

Furrowing her brow, Celia considered. "I don't remember having a dream last night."

"Oh..."

"I honestly can't remember the last time I had a dream."

Maribel halted. "What are you talking about? What about the two prior nights?"

Celia faced her. "What about them? I don't remember any dreams."

Too stunned to speak, Maribel stared at her a moment. "But... The... What about the odd rain at night and in the morning?"

"Are you pulling a joke on me?" Celia smiled. "It hasn't rained since the passing of the queen."

Neither mischief nor guile tainted any of her words.

Maribel rubbed the back of her neck. "I…." What was she supposed to say to that?

"How about we call on Athena while we're in the area?" Celia asked innocently.

"Sure…" Maribel muttered, fully perplexed.

After walking a ways off their path, they reached the homestead of Celia's cousin, Athena. The three of them had spent countless hours together studying, exploring, and chatting.

Athena greeted them with hugs, and welcomed them in. "Tea, anyone?"

Both Maribel and Celia accepted.

"Lovely. I'll put the kettle on."

Since they'd known each other for several years, Maribel felt she could be trusted. "I'm going to help her in the kitchen," she told Celia. Celia was unbothered, still working on a knot in her hat ribbons.

"Thanks for the tea," Maribel cautiously said as she entered the kitchen.

"Of course." Athena smiled, tucking her black curls behind her ear.

Fidgeting with her hands, Maribel second-guessed herself, but she persisted. "Has Celia been acting weird around you the last couple of days?"

Athena shook her head. "Well, I haven't seen her all week. What's wrong?"

Maribel held her tongue, unsure. *She* was the one dreaming of dead and imaginary people, then remembering things wrong. Was she certain she hadn't hit her head recently?

Wincing, Athena rubbed her temple.

Maribel paused. "Headache?"

"Yes. Long night," Athena said dismissively.

Maribel eyed her. Athena was only a couple of years older than she and Celia were. "Any weird dreams lately?"

Squinting, Athena answered. "Yes…"

"A beggar, a little boy, and a—"

"Schoolteacher?"

A squeak escaped Maribel's mouth as she pointed at an equally shocked Athena.

"How would you know that?" Athena asked, all surprise.

"Me too," Maribel whispered.

"Is there a mouse in here?" Celia asked playfully from behind Maribel.

"No. We were just talking about—" Athena started.

Maribel slid a finger to her lips where Celia couldn't see.

Athena did a double take. "Talking about, uh ... the prince. Who else?"

"Save some gossip for me. I'm going to freshen up."

"Will do," Maribel choked out.

Celia's footsteps padded down the hallway.

"Why did you stop me?" Athena whispered. "You said she was acting weird. Doesn't that mean she's having the dreams too?"

Maribel shook her head. "The weird thing is that she *stopped* having them after two nights. Then forgot about them completely, and about the impossible nighttime rain!"

Athena's mind worked. "Yes, the rain."

"Do you know anyone else experiencing this?"

"No. But I could ask...."

"Yes. Let's ask around. But ... carefully. I don't want everyone thinking we're mad or bewitched...."

After a short and awkward visit, Maribel excused herself to walk home alone. Though her headache had subsided, she clung to that excuse. With each footstep along the path, Maribel pondered the unbelievable circumstances. Could magic be at play here? She kept thinking of the rain at the queen's passing. Perhaps it had been cursed, but to what end?

Unable to shake the eerie feeling about the shared dreams, Maribel diverted from her route to pay a couple more homes a visit. She didn't want to alarm anyone, so she'd ask cautiously generic questions about rain and dreams, but nothing specific, then gauge their responses.

She first stopped at the home of her nearest aunt and uncle. Maribel's male cousins seemed utterly disinterested in her questions, and the female cousins were simply confused.

"Has it rained since the queen's death?" Maribel asked.

Her cousins Gwyneth and Eden looked at her strangely as the three of them sat together. She wouldn't normally ask them for a weather report.

"No..." answered Eden, the older of the two. At the time of the queen's death, she and her fiancé had been visiting his family, and had ducked back inside as soon as possible after the gong had released them from the minute of silence for the queen's passing.

"I heard the rain was horrendous," Gwyneth said.

Eden turned on her. "*Heard* the rain was horrendous? You didn't observe the queen's passing?"

"I..." Gwyneth grappled for words. "I didn't hear the gongs," she shyly confessed.

"And what, pray tell, were you doing in the *middle of the day* where you could not hear the castle's gongs?" They lived close enough to hear the on-site gongs, not those used as relays across the kingdom.

The room was thick with tension as Gwyneth swallowed, staring at her hands in her lap.

"Were you with Fasol at the time?"

And *that* was Maribel's cue to excuse herself. Both cousins were older than her, so they could make their own choices, but the impropriety of the situation still punctuated the issue, and she had not come for drama. Fasol was the son of the local baker, and Maribel had noticed he and Gwyneth were rather cozy, but they hadn't announced any plans to wed...

"I just wanted to drop by for a *short* visit." Maribel jabbed a thumb over her shoulder, standing.

"Stay!" Gwyneth insisted.

No thank you. "I, uh... Mother needed me to run an errand. I forgot..."

After excusing herself, she stopped by her friend Hailey's home. Hailey had also had the dreams, and agreed to ask around more.

Over the next several days, Maribel was greeted with the same cycle over and over—vivid dreams, echoes of pain, and the sounds and smells of rain caressing her sleep. A new body part ached each morning, and she lied to her mother every time she asked about Maribel limping or rubbing a sore spot. She blamed it on the old lumpy mattress. Aside from not wanting anyone to think she was mad, she also didn't want to concern anyone until she got to the bottom of it.

Hailey lasted a couple of days longer with the dreams than Celia had before she forgot it all, her memories of the strange coincidence wiped. With Hailey having forgotten everything, Maribel also lost the connection to any friends Hailey had been keeping track of who had also shared the dreams.

On the fourteenth night of dreams, Maribel drifted to sleep, 'waking' in a cave. Only a brightly burning torch lit the large chamber she stood in, foreboding filling her chest, the desire to retreat strong.

She glanced over her shoulder. The path across the chamber continued behind her.

A haunting low rumble bounced off the stone walls. A giant pair of red-orange eyes blinked from the shadows of the path in front of her. They swirled like pools of lava, nothing good in their depths. Maribel could hardly breathe.

A footfall thumped, claws scratching. And another.

Her heart raced.

With another step forward, the creature showed itself—a dragon.

"Oh no..." Maribel whispered, her voice shaky. Her palms became clammy as she eased backward.

Not a single dragon had been spotted in the kingdom in decades, not even in the northern territories. From what she'd been taught, this was a small one, but it was still three times her size, densely muscled, and not easily dismissed.

It scraped another step forward, its growl low. She retreated another footstep, holding her hands up. "Nice dragon?"

Its eyes narrowed as smoke plumed from its slits of nostrils. And far behind Maribel, voices rose, full of panic.

"Come on, we need to get out of here," a woman shouted. Maribel almost agreed, until the woman spoke again. "Hurry, Thadeus, we need to run!"

"Mamma, I'm stuck," the little boy cried.

Maribel's heart froze as the dragon's gaze shifted beyond her. Perhaps it wanted something leaner, something more tender, or more of a buffet.

This is just a dream. It can't hurt you or anyone else.

The little boy cried. "Ouch, Mamma."

"Hold still while I get you loose."

It felt *completely* real.

Maribel wasn't ready to die, nor was she okay with letting innocent people outside the cave be devoured by the beast. But what could she do? She could make a run for the exit behind her, and could hopefully help free the little boy. But dragons were fast and lethal.

She searched the chamber. Rock and more rock, but none on the ground she could pick up and throw. She may be able to make a dash and grab the torch, but were dragons even afraid of fire? They breathed it.

Her searching eyes caught on the faint gleam of metal resting on a rocky ledge beneath the torch. A sword... She was short, and she hadn't been taught to use a sword, but she would try. She would probably fail, but she would try.

With the dragon distracted, sniffing out its prey behind Maribel, she seized the opportunity and sprinted for the sword. As she grasped the handle, the dragon turned to her, ready for its appetizer.

She hefted the sturdy sword, shuffling her feet to place herself between the dragon and the exit. Standing tall, she firmly planted her feet and forced herself to sound much more courageous than she felt at the moment. "No. Stay away!"

Opening its mouth, it displayed dozens of dagger-sharp teeth, and let out a deafening roar.

Maribel fought her instincts to shrink, to run. She stepped forward, pointing the heavy sword at the dragon's chest in warning. Several panicked voices and screams continued to echo behind her.

The beast crept closer, more smoke billowing from its nostrils.

No matter what, she refused to be intimidated, refused to back down. She too, advanced a pace.

Beads of sweat dripped down her neck. The cave was hot, the monster's breath licking against Maribel's skin.

It opened its mouth again, a guttural growl rising as a stream of fire the color of its eyes billowed forth. Maribel charged. Before the blade connected with the dragon's scales, the fire enveloped her.

Gasping, Maribel woke in bed, drenched in sweat. She clawed at her skin, searching for burn marks. There were none. Nonetheless, she ripped off her bedding and stood. Unlatching the window, she yanked it open and sucked in cool, fresh air. The scent of recent rain, despite the bone-dry bushes and grass before her, helped clear the smoke that still lingered in her senses.

It had been *far* too real. Her hands ached as she flexed them. She had gripped the sword like her life depended on it.

Maribel was jittery all morning, especially at breakfast as she choked down scrambled eggs and passed on the blood orange juice her mother offered. She promptly left the house and made her way to Athena's.

Athena invited her into the backyard, where they could have more privacy.

"That was absolutely mad!" Maribel said. "My hands are killing me."

Athena blew out a breath. "Dragons... Wild. But why are your hands hurting? I ... actually don't hurt at all this morning."

Maribel eased herself down on a wooden step of the porch. "From gripping the sword so tightly."

Raising her eyebrows, Athena sat next to her. "You tried to fight it?"

"Yes... Didn't you?"

"I ran away," Athena said.

"Oh." Maribel had known it was a dream at the time, but the lifelike reality had bolstered her determination to save the boy and mother. "That would have been the smart thing to do. I woke covered in sweat."

Athena frowned. "I think I'm done with these dreams."

"Do we even have a choice?"

"Well..." Athena straightened the hem of her skirt. "I mean that when I woke ... I didn't smell the rain."

Maribel's heart dropped. They both knew what that meant. Each young maiden who had shared the dreams followed the same pattern. The first morning they woke without the smell of rain would be the end of the dreams, the end of their memories of it ever happening. Athena would sleep normally that night.

She would be better off, too. Who wanted to lose sleep night after night, only to wake in pain? The girls who forgot could go about their regular lives. All but one of Athena and Maribel's friends who had ever experienced the dreams had already forgotten them.

Maribel hugged Athena. "I don't want to do this alone," she confessed. Perhaps there was a way to stop the dreams, but she honestly wasn't sure she wanted to at the moment. They were intriguing, like a puzzle she yearned to piece together.

Athena pulled back from the hug, giving her a smile. "Figure it out. Tell me someday how it all ends, and I promise to believe you."

Smiling in return, Maribel agreed to do just that.

Two days later, Maribel was alone. Dozens of maidens around her age had shared the dreams, at least as far as she'd known. They had taken part in the adventure and danger and chaos of it, but she was the only girl she knew who still bore the burden.

She visited Athena again and explained it all.

"Wow," Athena said in awe. "That sounds exciting! You're sure this happened to me, too?"

Maribel nodded, and Athena shook her head. "It's honestly a little hard to believe, but I've never known you to tell tales...."

"I promise I'm not making it up."

The teakettle whistled from the kitchen, and Athena held up a finger. "I'll be right back."

Minutes later, she returned with tea for them both. "Thanks for visiting. What's on your mind?"

Maribel furrowed her brow. "Just the dreams...."

Athena smiled, taking a sip. "Dreams? What kind of dreams?"

Her jaw dropping, Maribel struggled for words. "The dreams I just told you about...."

"What do you mean?"

She hadn't only forgotten the dreams; she had forgotten being *told* about the dreams just minutes ago. Maribel's heart grew hollow as she pretended nothing was wrong, as they drank tea and chatted about the decidedly dry summer.

As she ambled home that day, Maribel was stumped. This had to be some kind of curse, right? Something that drove people momentarily mad? Some sort of magic that had tainted the rain at the queen's passing, only unleashing itself on a narrow sliver of the population, in semipredictable ways?

When she arrived home, she finally confessed everything to her mother. Her mother eyed her skeptically, and suggested they see a physician.

They weren't five footsteps from the front porch when Maribel voiced her doubts. "I really don't think a physician can do anything about it...." Magic was rare, and she doubted anyone in these parts possessed it.

Her mother paused, clutching her purse. She blinked. "Well, how severe is your neck pain?"

"Like I said, the pain isn't that bad. It's the dreams and everything else."

Frowning, her mother caressed her cheek. "You've been having nightmares?"

A boulder dropped in Maribel's gut, and she kicked herself for hoping it would have somehow been different with her mother. She had already forgotten the primary reason for the physician's visit.

"Yes, nightmares," Maribel replied weakly.

Her mother nodded, still frowning. "I promise we're saving for a new mattress; hopefully that will help. Let's try some chamomile tea this evening to see if it will do the trick."

"Sure."

They abandoned the trip to the physician.

After eighteen straight nights of these bewildering dreams, Maribel kept chasing the meaning, pondering the purpose during the days as she helped with chores and tried to go about her daily life.

Still fully clueless as to Maribel's plight, Celia dragged her to a couple of shops and then to Athena's for a visit. The usual activities felt so meaningless. Maybe it was simply her loneliness, but Maribel feared there was more at play, that something in her was changing, evolving, emerging in the process.

They wandered the empty pasture behind Athena's home, plucking wildflowers and avoiding the dry old cow chips. "I saw Prince Jonas in his carriage the other day," Athena said, a smile on her lips.

"Any word on his bride?" Celia asked.

Athena shook her head. "No. No one knows. He hasn't said a thing, hasn't been seen with a single girl."

Maribel had been too wrapped up in the mysterious dreams to think of the man. "Maybe he's breaking tradition, and he'll wait a while to take a bride. He's likely still mourning."

Celia arched an eyebrow. "Are you serious? The royal family is blessed to rule. It's tradition and law, and I don't think he would risk breaking either."

Sniffing a fragrant bellflower, Maribel considered. Celia was probably right. And perhaps she should have been thinking about the prince more through this dream ordeal...

This whole thing might be a warning, a premonition about the return of dragons, of society crumbling, of ... who knew what disjointed threat the mess of dreams hinted at. What if Maribel was the last person to still remember, and then her memories vanished like all the others?

It was a bone-chilling thought. And what if it wasn't a premonition? What if it was the beginning of an attack by a neighboring kingdom's sorcerer? There hadn't been war in these parts in centuries, and maybe mankind was due for another.

"How does one get an audience with the prince?" Maribel asked.

Celia and Athena smirked in unison.

"Going to offer yourself as his bride?" Athena kidded.

"If you do, please go in something pink or purple, not green," Celia pleaded.

Exasperated, Maribel rolled her eyes. "I'm not planning on throwing myself at him."

She let it go as they wandered the field and gossiped.

A half hour later, she made an excuse to walk home alone. Celia stayed behind with Athena again.

Kicking pebbles out of her path, Maribel seriously reconsidered the idea of approaching the prince. Her heart sank. If he somehow didn't find her mad, he'd forget with his next breath what she'd told him, just like everyone else. She was a lower-middle-class commoner, too, and may not be granted an audience with him. Though, the queen had been much lower in station than even Maribel when the king had selected her as his bride, so hopefully the prince didn't look down on the poor, not when his mother had once been.

An idea sparked in Maribel's mind as she straightened. Maybe he already knew what was going on, knew about this looming magical threat. Perhaps that was why he hadn't been seen courting any maidens. He was too busy.

She smiled as she recalled how regal he always looked. He would be a good king. He would take care of his people. She would like to meet him someday.

Rubbing her lower back—her current pain of the day from a dream where she'd single-handedly rolled boulders in front of a flooding stream—she convinced herself that if this was indeed some type of threat, the prince was probably already on top of it.

Invisible rain claimed her once again that night. Maribel's eyelids fluttered. Her balance wavered as she took in the scene around her, her heart beating wildly.

She stood atop a small platform floating high above a raging river. She gulped as she glanced over her shoulders. The edge of a canyon loomed far behind her, with no way in sight to reach it.

The only exit from the platform was a narrow stone path directly in front of her, only wide enough to place one foot at a time.

Her short height would probably help with her balance, her lower center of gravity useful as she would work her way across the path, but it was *so* high up here. She was afraid of heights, and the water below was far from welcoming.

She squared her shoulders. These tasks often terrified her, but they also made her feel alive.

Out of nowhere, an invisible hand, soft and warm, large and strong, grasped her left hand. She searched for the owner, but there was none. The hand squeezed hers, bolstering her courage as she took the first step.

She loosed a breath, then placed the next foot forward. Her invisible companion helped improve her balance, step after step, as the torrent writhed far below.

The path was straight, narrow as a balance beam. Each footstep was slow and intentional. Had she been an acrobat, it wouldn't have taken her so long to cross, but she played to her strengths, and that of the imaginary help the dream had provided.

After a painstakingly long time on the beam, she reached the end, her hand still firmly held by ... no one. She stood on another small platform, but had not quite reached the other edge of the canyon. There was no path forward. Only a terrifying gap for her short legs to try to jump across.

Her breath shaky, she kept looking between the edge and the water below.

"I can't swim well," she whispered. With that far of a drop, she likely wouldn't even survive to try swimming if she fell.

The warm hand squeezed again. "You can do this," a voice whispered back. The voice was masculine, kind, and reassuring, from where the man's face might have been had the hand belonged to a real person.

Maribel's heart thundered in her chest. "I..."

"You can do this," the voice whispered again.

"Okay." She sucked in a breath, reminding herself it was only a dream. She wouldn't *actually* die if she fell... Right?

She held the hand tightly. "One... Two..." She crouched. "Three!" She lunged for the edge of the canyon, and the phantom hand released hers right before she landed on the other side on her stomach.

Before she could thank the imaginary hand, she woke in bed to the aroma of fresh rain, a smile on her lips. Her thighs quivered from the exertion of having to balance so carefully for so long. She hadn't even noticed how much they'd burned during the dream, not with the loud river below, not with her focus on the path and the man's hand.

As it was still early morning, she closed her eyes to get more sleep. This time as she nodded off, no rain accompanied her rest, but she kept a smile on her face. She hadn't had a beau for some time. She would like to have a man hold her again, though more than just holding her hand.

Nineteen nights. Nineteen nights in a row had been spent in rain-kissed dreams. Maribel genuinely couldn't tell if she dreaded this pattern continuing, or if she looked forward to it at this point. If it was part of some greater threat, it wasn't a very good one...

She challenged herself to simply enjoy the day and try not to analyze the situation. It was sunny, and she needed to get out of the house.

After breakfast, she called on Celia, and they strolled to the library together. The library was one of the biggest buildings in town.

After an hour of perusing books to borrow, they hefted bags full of novels to take home. Maribel's selections focused on dreams, dragons, and magic. She'd tried to remind herself she was taking a day off from the mystery, so she'd wait until the next day to start reading them.

"Less than two weeks before the coronation—and before we find out who he chose as his bride," Celia said, changing which hand she carried her books with.

Maribel smiled. "I hope he chooses well, and I hope he's happy." If the prince took after his parents, he would be kind and wise, and deserved the best.

As Maribel settled into bed that night, she thought of Prince Jonas, and she mulled over her own life. He was facing a big decision, and stepping into big shoes as he ascended the throne and selected a life partner. Maribel's decisions weren't as weighty as his, but she still needed to sort out her future. She didn't have a deadline for marriage, but she wouldn't turn a man down, providing he was the right one.

Before she knew it, familiar rain rocked her to sleep. Opening her eyes, she was blinded by white. She'd never seen anything like it before.

The room—presuming it *was* a room—had no visible corners, walls, windows, ceiling, or anything. It was just blank whiteness. There were no tasks she could discern. Was she supposed to find a way out?

A knock sounded behind her, and she whipped around. "Hello?"

"Are you dressed?" a male voice asked.

She furrowed her brow. "What?"

"Are you dressed?" he repeated.

She glanced down at her nightgown. "Um... Yes..." It was a little odd to be in her nightgown. The dreams had usually dressed her in something appropriate for the adventure each night.

An ornate wooden door appeared, the golden knob twisting. In strode an elegant man, his hands clasped before him. Not just any man—Prince Jonas.

Maribel's brain stuttered. "I... Hello... Your Highness?" She curtsied.

He gave her a single nod, closing the door behind him. It vanished into the canvas of white. He said nothing, simply observing her.

"I..." She cocked her head. "You're... I mean ... this isn't any different, right? Of course it's not. I mean you're not. I mean..." She tried to calm her racing mind, her rambling. He wasn't actually here. None of the people had *really* been in her dreams.

Her eyes widened. "You're not dead, are you? Because my schoolteacher...."

The prince's lips twitched into a smile. "No, I'm not dead."

"Good. That would be bad. Obviously... Just making sure. But..." She arched an eyebrow. "Would a dream know if the real person inspiring the dream was alive or dead?"

Amusement danced in his eyes, his smile growing wider. "I suppose not for most people...."

"Okay." She blinked, trying to wrap her head around the logic and mystery.

Prince Jonas kept surveying her. "What's your name?"

She pointed to herself. "Me?"

He chuckled. "You're the only other person here."

"Yes, but I'm not accustomed to introducing myself in my own dreams." She swallowed, her mouth dry. Why was he so handsome? "I'm Maribel."

His eyes were the color of freshly shucked peas from the garden, though they sparkled like the night sky. "That's a beautiful name."

She smiled. "Thank you."

"And a nice smile to match." His voice was so smooth. Did he sound like that in real life? She'd only heard a grief-stricken version of him at his mother's funeral.

"Sorry about your mother," she said. It was silly to offer condolences to a figment of her imagination, but it felt right.

As real as anything in the other dreams, his expression was solemn as he nodded. "Thank you. I had good parents." He paused. "What of yours? Tell me about yourself and your family."

At ease and grateful to not be completing an arduous task, she sat on the cool white floor. He followed suit a couple of feet in front of her.

She went on and on, sharing her story. How her parents were kind, her younger siblings fun but annoying, as any siblings should be. He found that comment particularly humorous.

Prince Jonas nodded and took it all in as she explained her family's situation, her childhood, and even talked about her friends. He didn't once grimace or cringe in judgment. Then again, why would he? He was her, after all. He was a figment of her imagination, something a strange magical sleep had created.

Part of her wished he could be more as she bared her soul to him, as he nodded and asked the occasional clarifying question.

She even explained the weird dreams, and he didn't seem to think her mad. He offered a few comments to assure her there was no magical threat at play.

After what had to be hours, she'd caught him up on all the important details. He hadn't shared as much about himself as she had, but she'd loved the tidbits he'd given her. He enjoyed botany, and long hikes with his hound—Wesley—and experimented in the castle's kitchens at times. Everyone in the kingdom knew about Wesley, but the other details must have been something Maribel's imagination made up.

A part of her heart yearned for him to be the real man. He made her comfortable. He felt like a friend. A dashing, handsome, sweet, eligible friend...

She adjusted her seat, making sure her nightgown covered her knees. "I want to know more about you. Or... You know, the real Prince Jonas. Would you *actually* know anything about him? Or since this is a dream, you really only know what I already know?"

Ever calm and smooth, he replied, "I suppose that depends on what you know of the man. You'd like to meet him?"

Her cheeks warmed as she averted her gaze. "I think most maidens in the kingdom would be interested in meeting him."

"I didn't ask about most maidens."

She cleared her throat, locking eyes with him. "Yes. I think that would be exciting, but at least I got this dream."

While she'd fancied him, she'd never once imagined herself baking a cake beside him in the castle's kitchens, or hiking with him and his hound. But now she could, and she'd be terribly sad to remember this conversation with no hopes of it ever coming true.

Prince Jonas drew a deep breath, standing. She stood as well.

He straightened his jacket. Unlike Maribel, he wore full formal clothing, not nightclothes. "I like you, Maribel," he said. "Come find me."

Blinking, she couldn't believe her ears. "What? I... What? Will I get to see the castle in this dream?"

He strode for the wooden door that again appeared before him. Opening it, he turned to her, smiling. "Come find me." Without another word, he passed through the door, and it closed behind him.

She hadn't been able to make out the task of the night, but the only way out was through the door he'd just exited. She grabbed the handle, swinging the door open.

Her eyes shot open as she lay in bed. She soon found her bearings.

Sitting up, she drew a breath, then frowned. *No rain.*

She had to have done something wrong, or the spell or curse or whatever it was had been dispelled. She wanted to go back to figure it out, but there was no door, no white room.

Come find me, his voice whispered in her mind. *Come find me.*

Standing, she wrapped her arm around a bedpost. She couldn't just march up to the castle. She'd never been there, and the madness of a dream didn't permit her entrance to his residence in the middle of the night. Unlike most of the other dreams, she'd woken from this one while it was still pitch-black outside.

Come find me, his lingering beckon whispered, softer than before.

"Where?" she whispered back into the void of her bedroom.

A map bloomed in her mind, a path to a park across town.

Adventure called, and her heart swelled. She was going to be mad enough to answer that call.

She'd been to that park before, though she'd never snuck out in the middle of the night. Nor had these feverish dreams ever called to her when she was awake, but she couldn't resist the challenge.

She glanced at her nightgown and stripped it off, taking a minute to change into a dress. If she was found roaming the streets like a crazed person at all hours, she at least ought to look civilized... Smiling, she plucked up her favorite green ribbon and tied it around her waist, high with a nice bow, so as to match the current fashion. It looked nice against the backdrop of cream fabric. She ran a brush through her hair, then paused.

This couldn't be real. There was absolutely no way the real prince would be at that park in the middle of the night. As she set her brush down, her heart faltered a little. It wasn't real. She was being a fool. She was exhausted from twenty nights straight spent in feverish dreams.

A deep gouge on the wooden vanity claimed her focus, and she ran a finger over it. That scratch had been there as long as she could remember. Had her previous dreams been so vivid? None of them had been set in her present surroundings, in her own home...

Her heart warmed as she recollected Prince Jonas's fetching smile. He wouldn't be at the park. But she would never forgive herself if she didn't check to see.

Not owning a sword, and not being skilled with one—as evidenced by the dragon dream—she instead strapped on the dagger her father had bought her for safety. She may be making questionable choices at the moment, but she wasn't completely daft. Before exiting her room, she scratched out a quick letter to explain where she'd gone.

As she tiptoed down the hallway, only a single floorboard creaked to scold her. She held her breath but made her way out the front door without waking anyone.

The night was cool and clear, the crickets softly singing their song. Maribel beamed. *I'm on my way.*

She didn't trust herself on horseback in the dark, and no public coaches ran the streets at this time of night, so she traveled on foot, aiming for every shortcut she knew. She ran across a bridge, weaved through streets and back roads, and rounded a small pond.

Eventually, the park lay before her, and Maribel hesitated. This was all the mental map—the vision—had shown. It was a fairly large park, too... She surveyed the area. To one side towered a giant tree—a weeping willow—that had been framed within the image.

Her feet tired, she strode for the tree. The trunk was dark under the dense curtain of leaves blocking out the moonlight. As she approached the tree, rustling startled her, and she halted. "Hello?" She cautiously slid a hand to her concealed dagger.

"Maribel," he said. "You came." The voice matched that of Prince Jonas, at least the version she'd just met in her dream.

"Is this ... still a dream?" she asked as a warm rain began to mist above her. She'd never had a dream within a dream, but perhaps that was what this was.

She glanced toward the skies as the rain picked up. Hadn't it been a clear night?

"Come in from the rain," he beckoned.

She did not want to test the thickness of her dress's cream fabric when wet—dream or not. She ducked beneath the willow's branches, and beheld the prince. "Is it really you?"

His smile was swoonworthy. "Yes. Is it really you?"

"Well... Yes." She forgot her manners but quickly recovered, curtsying. "Your Highness."

He folded his arms, leaning against the tree's sturdy trunk. "You don't have to curtsy to me. And you can call me Jonas."

Nervous, she fidgeted with her hands. "I'm not so sure about that. You're the prince. You'll soon be my king." She still wasn't completely sure this was real.

"I'll be offended if you call me by my title."

"Okay... Jonas..." It didn't feel unnatural to utter it.

He grinned. "My name sounds good on your lips."

Her stomach flipped. Everything sounded good so far on *his* lips. She dared to take a step forward. "Did you have a dream that brought you here?" If this was somehow real, how had he known to meet here, in the middle of the night, if he hadn't shared the dream? How had he known her name?

"In a way. I was in *your* dream."

She had so many questions, because he didn't seem fazed by any of this. "Why?"

"Because that's how the selection process works, darling."

Darling? Her heart skipped a beat. And then she put together what he'd said. He couldn't be serious... "When you say 'selection process'...."

Jonas cocked his head. "I think you know."

What did he need to select in the next few days if not a bride? "I'm not queen material!"

He searched her eyes in silence for a moment. "Aren't you? You respected the power and legacy that came before you by observing my mother's passing, by standing in the rain that day. You've completed twenty nights of dreams designed to test you, to find you. With each test, you proved yourself worthy. You were kind, strong, loyal, and brave. Forgiving and clever. Well-educated."

She gaped. She'd told him about the dreams, but not every detail. "There are girls who are smarter, prettier, wiser...."

"But they're not you."

She couldn't believe his casual insistence. "I would have been killed trying to slay a dragon like an idiot!"

He chuckled, a sweet melody to her ears. "Brave, for being willing to risk your life to save others. Clever, for finding the best path to stop the flooding. Kind, by helping a beggar." He rattled off a virtue for each of her tests. "And frankly, darling, no single person can take down a dragon alone with a simple blade. I certainly didn't during my trial."

"But I *knew* I was in a dream, that I wouldn't actually get hurt." She bobbed her head. The dreams had been astonishingly real, and *had* actually hurt her each time, though not much. "You can't choose someone to rule the kingdom with you based on how they act in a dream."

Shifting his weight, Jonas nodded. "Perhaps not in a regular dream. But in an enchanted dream, you are yourself; the most honest and raw version of yourself. For generations, the dream trials have selected correctly. You didn't prepare for them, or put on a face for me, didn't plot or plan to win a prize."

"Isn't that what you just did, though? Put me through twenty nights of tests to show I'm worthy of being your bride? Your prize?"

He winced. "First of all, Maribel, *I* didn't put you through it. The royal family is full of dreamers. As the heavens mourned my mother's passing, as her magic was released into the world, *it* began the process to find you." He paused. "And you weren't alone in your trials. I have also had to face dreams each night."

Maribel furrowed her brow. He *had* just mentioned that he'd faced a dragon during *his* trial... "But you rule by birthright. What do you have to prove?"

"True. Not all our trials were the same. Most were different, in fact. Mine were not to select me, but to refine and prepare me to be a worthy ruler, a good husband, a kind ... father, someday."

She swallowed. *One step at a time...* There were so many maidens out there, and she still couldn't believe it was her he'd called here this night. But it made sense with what she'd witnessed. Several women within her own acquaintance had experienced the first dreams, and the numbers had thinned down each night. "How many girls made it all the way through?"

"You. There is no one else."

She couldn't breathe. "I didn't sign up for it. I… What of your preferences? And mine? And *love*? Maybe I passed a few tests, but shouldn't there be something more?"

Jonas bit his lip. "The magic takes preferences into account. It knows your heart and desires, and mine as well. And you could have ended the dreams at any time. You could have refused to answer the schoolteacher, could have asked others in the dreams how to stop them." He searched her eyes, his expression soft. "And what is love, if not mutual respect, a willingness to work on shared goals, and attraction?"

Attraction? Surely he wanted someone taller, thinner, with straighter teeth, or whose hair didn't frizz in the humidity like hers no doubt was with the rain still pounding down on the leaves and branches above them. "Are you … attracted to me? There are plenty of maidens more beautiful."

His eyes traced her from head to toe, devouring her entirely as a smirk tugged on his lips. "I did get to finally see you in tonight's dream, did I not? I got to know you, and see you. And I asked you to come."

Her heart thundered.

"Do you dislike what you know of me? What you've seen of me?" he asked.

Her knees weakened. "I, uh…" she breathed. No, she didn't at all dislike anything she'd ever learned about him or witnessed. Not a single part of his devastatingly handsome self. "You're … handsome."

He angled his head. "I enjoyed learning about you tonight. But I don't expect an answer right away. My coronation is in a week and a half. We can get to know each other before you decide. I'd like you to spend time with me in my home. You'll have your own room."

She was all nerves. "And if I don't agree to marry you?"

"Then…" His tone held hesitation. "I'll have no choice but to select a maiden at random. I don't imagine I'd be as happy, or that the kingdom would thrive as much, but it's your choice to make. And we wouldn't have to wed right away. We would have a full year. I only have to announce my *intentions*, and *present* you at my coronation."

She had so many questions, so much anxiety. What of her family and friends?

"The public still won't remember the dreams, just like you won't, should you choose to reject the magic's matching. But I'll invite your family to the castle tomorrow, if you like, to discuss the matter."

I might forget this all happened? A frown overtook her lips. She didn't want to forget any of it. As intense as some of the trials had been, and despite how lonely she'd felt at times, she wouldn't trade any of these memories, wouldn't give them up without a fight. And he had been so sweet and charming during the dream just a couple of hours ago, and now as he waited to hear what he hoped for...

Fear. Fear held her back. "I don't know anything about defending a kingdom against a threat. Or proper court manners, or *anything* a queen would need to know."

He smiled confidently. "I was raised for this. I'll teach you."

"I still have nothing to offer but my heart and life. And I want more than to be a checklist wife and mother to heirs."

"Is that what you think my parents' union was like?" His eyebrows knit. "Theirs is the closest, most equal relationship I've ever seen."

She hadn't meant it like that. And she'd never heard anything negative about the pair.

"I would never force you to have my children, Maribel. If it came to it, and we never had children, my cousin would rule after we both pass. And..." He ran a hand through his hair, frustration showing. "You have *a lot* to contribute." He paused, softening. "This is the way it's done. This kingdom was established on the principle of balance. My mother was dirt poor. My father's father before him was also a commoner. The ruling family has *always* selected a commoner. The *magic* has always selected a commoner to help guide the dreamer born with royal blood. You keep us grounded. I've never experienced your life. You could help me understand my own people better. You can see things where my life of privilege may keep me blind. Don't say you have nothing of value to offer."

He was passionate. And she didn't hate a single word that came from his mouth. She swallowed, taking a step forward. "Will you teach me to dance? Because I don't know the right steps for a proper ball."

He smiled once again. "I would love nothing more. But you have to promise me something first...."

"What's that?"

"I take it you're not that shy, from our conversation earlier tonight."

She shrugged. "Not really."

"Then you can teach me that, too. I ... struggle to know how to easily converse with strangers."

It was comical how innocently he'd said it, and also how untrue it was. "You haven't once hesitated to talk with me tonight. You're not shy."

He opened his mouth, but nothing came out for a moment. "I can give official speeches just fine. And I don't have a problem talking to *you*, because I feel like I'm talking to an old friend. Strangers are different."

Her heart melted on the spot. He felt like an old friend as well. An astoundingly attractive one, who she was somehow only a couple of paces from now... "I'll see what I can do."

"So, you'll come home with me?" he asked. "To the castle. Get to know me, and make your decision?"

His lips begged to be kissed. The castle sounded wonderful. Dancing... All of it. Why did she hesitate?

"I'm still nervous," she confessed.

Jonas held out a hand, and she met him in the middle, resting hers in his. His hand was soft and warm, large and strong, familiar as it enveloped hers. In the most gentle, soothing voice, he said, "You can do this."

Her eyes wide, she gasped. How had she not recognized that voice instantly? Or the hand now wrapped around hers? "You were in my dream last night too?"

He smiled brightly. "The first time I got to hear your voice, got to feel you. If I'm honest, that pep talk was half for me, because I'm also not a great swimmer, nor am I fond of heights. But we walked that precarious path together, didn't we?"

He had given her the courage and stability she'd needed to complete it; the boost she'd needed to take a literal leap of faith.

She stared into his handsome green eyes as his thumb stroked the back of her hand. "Let's give this a chance."

Jonas sucked in a breath. "Thank you."

They shared a smile, still standing there. Had she really just accepted the prince's request to court her? To possibly become his bride?

Maribel swallowed again. "How far is it from here to the castle?"

"Not far, considering I have a carriage waiting at the other end of the park." He lifted his free hand, tucking her damp hair behind her ear. "I know I've already asked a lot of you tonight, but will you do me one more favor?"

"What?"

His lips twitched, whether out of mischief or embarrassment she wasn't sure.

"You're breathtaking in that cream dress, but I'm trying to be a proper ruler, not a scoundrel of a prince. And as much as I would like to see through that dress, we shouldn't test the fortitude of the fabric in this rain."

Her cheeks warmed at his bluntness, her heart pounding as much as the rainstorm above.

"You can stop the rain," he said.

Maribel scoffed. "I don't have magic. I can't control the weather."

He drew her in, sliding a hand to her waist, gently holding her chin. "You won't get the dreamer's magic until we wed, but you *can* stop this rain. Only you and I can stop *this* rain, because it was enchanted this whole time for us."

The day of the queen's passing, every night surrounding Maribel's enchanted dreams, and the moment she had arrived at the park and he'd called to her from under this tree...

His eyes held nothing but desire, and it ignited something new in her as she savored his touch. She stretched tall as he leaned forward, their lips grazing in absolute perfection.

And the downpour *instantly* stopped.

She pulled back, shocked. The dark night was still. "We actually did that?"

Laughing, he nodded. "I would never lie to you, darling."

That kiss... "If we... If we kissed again, would it turn back on?"

"No, but we could kiss again if you're worried it will, just to be safe. Just to ensure it doesn't start again and flood the kingdom." He winked.

The butterflies in her stomach took flight anew. He was a magnet she imagined might always draw her in. Standing on tiptoe and wrapping her arms around his neck, she smiled. "If I might be the queen, I feel it's my duty to do everything I can to prevent a natural disaster like that."

A heartbeat later, they savored another kiss, or a dozen... When did one kiss start and another end? It was dizzying as his lips caressed hers time and time again, as every part of her melted in his arms, as her mind turned to putty.

Jonas was the first to pull back, panting. "We should... It's late. Or early... We should get some rest before daylight, don't you think?"

It was the wise thing to do. "Yes." She wanted more in the moment, so much more, more than she'd ever wanted from a man. But she would be wise. "I'll, uh, still have my own room?"

He exuded that same passion, continuing to hold her against him. But like a gentleman, he lifted her hand, kissing it. "For as long as you desire."

Forcing herself to peel away, she straightened her dress, blowing out a cooling breath. "Yes. Let's sleep on this. Separately." She grasped his extended hand, and they emerged from the cover of the tree. Her cheeks warm at what she'd just done, what she'd just agreed to; she was embarrassed, but not ashamed. His hand held hers so naturally. His heart accepted hers so easily.

The carriage driver greeted them and opened the door. Jonas helped Maribel up, then sat beside her on the bench. It was nicer than any coach or carriage she'd been in before. Every part of her wanted to be on Jonas's lap, wanted to be all over him. Never had she connected with someone so deeply, so quickly. She'd only kissed one other beau before, and what she'd just shared with Jonas was nothing like the time she'd let the blacksmith's son stick his tongue down her throat.

There truly was magic in the match. Somehow, she doubted she'd need to take the full week and a half to consider his proposal, but chemistry was only part of the equation. She willed herself to stay on her side of the bench as the carriage jostled forward.

Jonas reached down, rubbing the end of the green ribbon she'd used as a decorative belt. "I like this," he said. "I like green. It reminds me of spring, and all things happy and fresh."

She suppressed a giggle. "It's my favorite color."

His own green gaze settled on her with what she could only describe as bedroom eyes. She took a sharp breath. "So, I want to hear everything about you. Every story, goal, allergy... Everything. Don't leave anything out."

He gave her a toothy smile, resting his hand on her knee. "Where should we start?"

Maribel soaked up everything about Jonas on the ride to the castle. He was sweet, and passionate about his calling as the soon-to-be king. Wesley, the hound, instantly became a new friend upon their arrival. A messenger was dispatched to her home with word of her whereabouts so her family wouldn't worry. Servants didn't hesitate to see to her needs regarding toiletries and a nightgown—a luxurious silky one far above the quality her family could have ever afforded.

The mattress in her chambers was as soft as a cloud, her rest as perfect and still as she'd had before the enchanted rain had taken her on this journey. Just a few hours later, she woke, a little worn from an eventful night, but happy. With a smile on her face, she took in the elegant room.

She blinked, making sure it was real. She was sleeping in the castle, almost engaged to the prince himself. How had that just happened? Her smile widened as she replayed the long conversations they'd held—in the dream, under the tree, and in the carriage. Her heart warmed even more at the memory of the kiss he'd given her as he'd bid her goodnight. Those eyes... Those lips...

Getting out of bed, she readied for the day, excited for the adventure ahead.

The next week was a whirlwind, and Maribel didn't regret a moment of it. Her admiration for Jonas grew by the hour as he held her in his arms for dance lessons to prepare for his coronation, as he taught her what it would mean to be his queen, to be a queen of the people. He invited her family to the castle for a visit, and even Celia. Maribel wasn't able to share the secret of the match, the sacred magic of the dreamers within the royal family, but they were happy for her.

She was a little surprised Celia took the news so well. In the end, Celia's jealousy didn't get the better of her; she was excited to be at the castle, and ecstatic at the prospect of visiting her best friend often for royal gossip and luxurious balls.

The couple explained they'd agreed to keep their courtship a secret until now, and her loved ones were none the wiser, assuming *that* was what she'd really been doing the last few weeks when she'd been running around trying to sort out the mystery of the dreams.

At the end of that week, with just a couple of days left before his coronation, before he had to announce his bride, she accepted, and didn't look back for a moment. They had been matched by the magic, had fought their own dragons, had navigated their own pains and dreams to be worthy of each other, to be worthy of the people they would serve as a team.

Maribel had needed to sort out her life as a new adult, but she hadn't pushed herself yet. Perhaps fate had known all along what her life had been preparing her for...

Maribel strolled through Jonas's chambers, out to his private balcony the night before his coronation, before he presented her publicly as his betrothed. She was still getting used to the heavy ring he'd given her.

She spotted him stargazing on a soft bench. "There you are."

He instantly grinned, scooting to make room for her. She eased down, cuddling up to him.

"Hello, darling."

Why did she love it so much when he called her that? "Sorry it took so long." She'd just been with the tailor for a last-minute fitting for her custom ball gown. "But I'll admit, it's rather nice having someone who fits clothes to your size and shape, and not having to shop around."

"The best for the best," he said.

"Hmm..." She twisted her lips. "That could come across as classist...."

He turned, arching an eyebrow. "Because I think you're amazing, and I plan to spoil you?"

She poked his arm. "Because it could sound like only those in power deserve the finest quality of clothing—the best fabrics, and cuts to properly fit their body."

Jonas cocked his head, considering. "I certainly didn't intend it that way, but I see what you mean... Putting me in my place before we're even wed...." He winked.

Maribel beamed. "Isn't that why you picked me?"

His gaze flickered to her lips, then back to her eyes. "I picked you for many reasons. And I still defend that you're the best, and I intend to give you the best. And I can't wait to see you in that dress tomorrow."

"I'll take it." She snuck a kiss. "Are you nervous about tomorrow?"

He blew out a breath, and they chatted awhile. From the moment he'd walked into her dream, and even before that when he'd held her hand on the precipice, he had felt like a companion to her soul. They would always share moments like this.

It was getting late, and they both ought to go to bed to be fresh for the big day. The attention of thousands would be on them both. But she lingered longer in his arms on that cozy bench, soaking it in.

A smile tugged at her lips. "You know, when we have children...." In their unending hours together, they'd agreed that they both *did* want them down the road. "They'll have the dreamer gift, and they'll be privy to the knowledge of the process...."

"Yes..."

"So, I'll make it a point to let them know their father was a royal pain." She considered the tests she'd had to pass. "You were a pain in the neck, a pain in the backside..." she kidded.

Jonas chuckled, then grazed her ear with his lips. "Okay, but you have to promise me you'll also tell them one other important thing...."

She leaned into his touch. "What's that?"

His whisper was soft and sensual. "Make sure to also tell them I was the man of your dreams."

"THE DREAMS HAD USUALLY DRESSED HER IN SOMETHING APPROPRIATE FOR THE ADVENTURE EACH NIGHT."

Trading Tails

Nickole Storm

I stare at the strange red light as it dances with the music. The deck looks so much like others I'd seen at the bottom of the sea, except now it was alive. The men's arms are slung across each other's shoulders while swaying to music. My eyes dart across their faces until I spot him, his black hair held half up with the rest bouncing around his shoulders as he dances. They run in circles and fall into arched arms, laughing and calling out the chorus together. Suddenly the tune changes, and I duck my head back down as it softens and everyone stops dancing. *Did they see me?* My heart races. I try to move my tail from the rope ladder to quietly slide back into the water, but I'm stuck, the rope forcing into my scales. As the men join together, singing a song I've never heard, I bend over, feeling my stomach smash into itself as I loosen the rope wrapped around my fins and try to get my tail out. Gritting my sharp teeth, I hiss as it finally releases me. My tail flings back beneath me and my arms give out. My splash joins the waves around the ship, as water burns between my fins.

"Happy birthday Prince Caden, happy birthday to you"

I run through these words in my head as I watch the ship sail further away. Suddenly, with a loud bang, the light grows and men are jumping off the ship. There are smaller boats leaving as I rise to the surface, the sound of screams fill my ears.

"Caden, you have to leave him; come on!"

"We need to move. Now!"

"The ship will pull us under when she sinks. Let's go."

"Grab Caden before you join us!"

"He's trying to," cough, "get Smokey," more coughing.

The lights grow higher as the last boat filled with men leaves. I don't see him with them. *They're leaving him behind. They can't!* Coughing and hissing sounds ring from within the small ship. I leap onto the rope once more and pull myself up the heated hull. Now hoarse after inhaling the choking fog his voice joins the crackling of wood.

"It's ok, Smokey, just a little water. Here, I'm going to put you in this, and we'll get out of here."

I reach the deck and see Caden, pulling a door and ripping it from the ship, a small bag next to him moving wildly. A thick brown mist rose from the lights and filled our lungs, and I watch as Caden wheezes trying to drag the door. The misty lights dance their way up to the tall white sails above us, and with a crack, the sail crashes down mere feet from Caden, driving the door towards the edge as the bag on top of it wiggled wildly. The boat begins to split where the pole fell, and I claw my way onto the deck, ignoring the heat from the lights that sizzle near me and the burning from below. "Caden!" I call out, finally reaching him. His eyes meet mine as they start to flutter closed. I help him push the door to the edge and I can feel the mist burning my throat. Caden slumps. We have to get back to the water. Lights burn me as I push the door overboard, then the ever-important bag with claws nearly as sharp as my own.

Grabbing Caden, I use my full weight to pull us into the water with a loud splash and lift him onto the wood as best I can. The ship is sinking fast and we need to leave, so with him halfway onto the door, his head resting a foot from the wild bag, I propel us away from the groaning ship. Every splash of salt water fills me with agony as it flushes the burns on my skin. I push forward in the direction the small boats went until I see land. A large castle rises up from beyond a wall, reminding me of home as the sun begins to fill the sky.

I pull him and the sack to shore and reach a hand to move his hair from his face as his chest rises and falls softly. His tanned skin is covered in dark marks from the ship. A small beard that connects from ear to ear wraps his soft pink lips, the ones that sing so beautifully. Moving closer, my tail rubs against his clothed legs. *That's what truly separates us; he is of land, and I of sea.* Sunlight warms my scales and back as I let my voice rise and sing a song of wishes, no more than a single tune, one note merging with the next until I see his eyes flutter open, and my heart does the same. *Gray, he has gray eyes.*

"Goodbye," I whisper, returning to the water, sand scraping against my wounds. This time I don't look back, he was safe, and I need to see Nessa.

As the old wooden ship appears in the distance, I see the faint glow of Nessa through the open sidings. Her flowy tentacles swish around as she glides from one side of the slow rotting vessel to the other, holding glass vials and shells, some also emitting a faint glow from them. I reach the edge where the door swings ever so slightly with the current and hear humming. The melody fades to an end and two large black eyes with a reflective tint turn to me when I pull open the door with a strangled squeak.

Nessa smiles softly before taking in my state. Her thin, flat head would normally curve in on the top and look as though her eyes were flanked by two large, nearly see-through ears. Now, it flared out in all directions looking as if a giant clam shell surrounded her. Her eyes seemingly widen more as she gasps.

"Marella, what happened?" She drifts closer, inspecting my injuries.

"It's kind of a long story."

"And should I ask your father, or will you tell me yourself? " She pulls back, holding two of her tentacles on either side up and arching them against her others, flaring her glowing forehead at me.

"Please don't tell him," I plead, putting my hands up in front of me in surrender.

"Speak, and I'll decide for myself dear. Did you sneak off to those volcanoes? These burns," she tuts at me, grabbing a shell from a cabinet before softly pushing me back onto the strange, soaked chair. She gently applies cream from it to the wounds on my tail, clearing her throat expectantly.

"Do you remember that voice I told you about?" My gills seal as I await her response. She freezes for a moment before continuing to nurse the wounds, nodding slowly.

"I found him again last night. I saw him," I rush out, my heart pounding in my ears.

"Did, did he do this?" A tone I'd never heard from her, not anger but something worse, like the question itself, was a threat.

"No! He, he was in trouble," I tell her everything from the burning lights to the sandy shore, and those gray eyes like the sky in a storm. I finally end my story and look up at her.

She tilts her head to the side with a sad smile before asking me to sit down again. "That was foolish, child. You know how treacherous they are."

"But he didn't hurt me. It was the light."

"That light was fire, Ella. It burns. Look at what it did to you. You can't go near them; it's dangerous."

"I know, but haven't you ever just wanted more than this life. I mean, I know you've outlived so many of your kind. You've been around since before my dad. You've had children younger than me die of old age. Their music alone makes me feel more alive than anything in my father's kingdom ever has. I just wish," my voice fails me. *Wish what? That I could be with them, my scales drying out and getting more painful splinters for Nessa to extract as she is now.*

"I know what it is to wish, Ella. To want for more than we were given." Her eyes seem to bore into me as she turns, allowing several chips of red-tinted wood to float from her curled tentacle and out of the rounded window to her left. "But sometimes, even if we get what we wish, it isn't what we imagined."

"But can't you imagine it? You've heard their songs before, seen them laugh and dance in the sun as if it were nothing."

"But what if it isn't what you thought? What if he doesn't find you the same way? You'd be up there all alone."

"You didn't see the way he smiles. He willingly risked his life for that sack of claws."

She seems lost in thought for a moment before speaking again."Marella, you're 18 now," she takes a deep pause. "Your father forbade me to tell you stories of this. I've kept many secrets for you over the years. Can I give you one to hold?"

She's never called her stories secrets before.

"Of course."

"When I was young, I was told I would only live to five. Like my kin, I tried to look for ways for us to live longer, to heal whatever failed us. But it was not something I could solve in my lifetime. I saw several other healers like me try to search for things to help not only ourselves but others as well, and when they left us, it seemed we always lost some of what had been gained. Knowledge was taken with their death. I knew if I wanted to truly make a difference, I needed to find a way to last. As a youngling, I was told a tale of a witch in our waters. One who was said to help make wishes come true, for a price, though not all were willing to pay. Sometimes a price leaves you incomplete, though your dreams come alive, they are never as you imagined them fully." As her voice drops she rubs her six tentacles together slowly.

"Nessa." My voice softens as I reach a hand to her,and she stretches out wrapping a tentacle around my fingers with a small smile.

"I had to give up much of myself, but as a reward I am able to live so much longer, to help so many. I got rid of the coral pox years ago, and this burn balm is my own creation." She holds the shell up for a moment, smiling. "What I gave is nothing in comparison to what I gained. Her name is Morfran. You must consider the contract fully, don't make a bargain you don't understand because your eyes are so clouded with desire." She squeezes my hand once more before releasing it, returning the shell to the cabinet behind her.

"She could truly allow me to visit land? To really be with him, to sing and dance as they do?"

"I cannot promise anything. I did not ask for that, but she is powerful, and she helped me, but it will always come with a price, Marella. Think it through and even barter with her if needed."

I could really go on the land with them. I could feel the sun without constantly worrying about holding onto some driftwood or slipping from a rock.

"I'll be careful, please Nessa, tell me how to find her." Nessa turns back to me, raising a tentacle she points out of the open window to our left.

"You will follow the trench. Follow it further than you've ever been allowed, further than when your gut tells you to stop, and at the end lays her home."

"Thank you so much!" I rush forward and fling my arms around her, feeling hers wrap around me in return.

We untie from each other and our eyes meet once more. "Are you sure this is what you want?"

"More than anything, if there's a chance. I have to try."

"I understand my dear, go, be safe. Send word if you can."

"I will Nessa, I promise."

The swim home from Nessa's never felt so beautiful. *I may never get to see these caves and coral again. All of my friends, my family? Father will be so angry, but he would understand, right? Eventually?* I sneak back to my bedroom, writing a note to my father and sister. I tell them not to worry, that I'm following my dreams and will visit when I can. I hide it in my drawer, so no one will find it should I end up returning disappointed.

The next morning, after applying more of Nessa's burn cream, I leave quickly. Following the deepening trench, the water grows colder, even my thick layer of fat can't ward off the icy tickles of every swish of my tail. Light falls away with the world above, my eyesight not dimming in the slightest.

This has to be Morfran's home. The cave before me has pearls embedded into the front edges all around, black, white, blue, and pink, in no particular pattern. As I enter I notice small lights on either side of the cave. *They look familiar but from where?* It's as if a string had grown out from the wall and a small bulb of light lay on its end. I move closer to find where I must have seen this before. My stomach lurches. This was no string. It was skin, blood somehow still pumping through it, through them all, I realize as the small pulse glowers at me; angler fish lights. Looking up I see large claws creeping out of the walls ahead in between the lights. No two claws are the same, each one a different size or shade of red. I count thirteen claws and twenty-two lights.

As I reach the end of the passage it opens into a grand room. Small furniture matching that of Nessa's are scattered about. Faded paintings hang on the stone walls. Small coral and seaweed grow about the room in random places, often cluttering around the furniture that must not have moved in ages. The bumpy exterior blending in with the floor of the ocean leading to it.

"Hello, who do we have here?" A scratchy voice sounds from above, almost screeching in my ear.

I can't believe my eyes, floating above me she leaves a large chair, every inch of it covered in pearls. She's glowing, but not like Nessa's creams, her glow was rising from within her skin. A mound of black hair drifts around her plump face, her luminous eyes and lips green and blue. Her overflowing chest matched mine, but instead of large shells, mere sea stars cover their tops. Her waist was wider than mine, though it could only be from the two large claws hanging from either edge of the beginning of her tail. Four long transparent tentacles swam around her, two at the back, one holds a vial swarming with dark air, the other a pure white shell, and two in-between the claws at her front, attached to her bulging stomach, held wide apart in welcome. Her tail scales seemed to light every few seconds throughout the sides of each one.

I recognize those tentacles, oh Nessa. For a moment, my heart drops, *she gave more than I ever knew.*

"Ahh, a daughter of Merrik I see." She smiles a sharp-toothed grin, less than a foot of space between us. I try to keep the fear off my face and force a smile back. *How does she know me?*

"Yes, Marella. Are you Morfran?" I force fake confidence in my voice.

If I could sing in front of countless subjects at the festival last year, I could speak to one person.

"Of course, you know any other sea witches in this area?" she asks, raising her eyebrows and opening her webbed hands wide. I see the blue light that flows through her tail also glows beneath her scaled arms and as she stretches them apart, strands of it reach between her fingertips trying to connect.

"You harvested lightning?" The words leave me before I can stop them. A cackle rises from her radiant lips. Forcing my hands to stay at my sides proved difficult; it cut into my ears worse than baby dolphin whines.

"In a way I suppose. I help unfortunate people in return for fair payment." She watches me closely, slowly circling , as if waiting for me to figure it out. *But who could give lightning? Another witch? Maybe a creature I haven't met yet?*

When she circles me again, I spot it. A small but thick strand sticks out just between her fins and trails up to the start of her tail, radiating the current as the light flies across her in a pulse. Realization strikes me before more curiosity sets in.

"A lightning eel? But what would they have traded in place of their current?" I feel my eyebrows knit together as I begin to nervously pull at my upper arm, squishing the soft flesh slowly.

"A chance to be something different, isn't that what everyone asks for? Be it cured sickness, a longer life, or a potion of love. It's all the same really. Whether to be truly different or merely appear different in someone's eyes, everyone asks for change. In status, job, hair color, tail color. The usual and unusual all merged into one." She grabs my hands and pulls me to the coral-grown couch, sitting by me.

"Now dear niece, what have you come here for? Did your sister's day not go as she asked?" Her chin doubled as she tilted her head down in question. I feel mine do the same as my jaw opens and shuts as I process the words.

"Niece? My sister? How do you know my sister?" My chest pounds as my mind reels.

What would Cordelia have asked of her? Her face contorts for a moment, and a small shock shoots from her hands into mine, causing me to pull my hands away. It hadn't quite hurt, but it certainly hadn't felt good.

"I thought you knew." She pulls her hand up to a necklace just above her stars.

Why hadn't I noticed it before?

Looking at it closer now, I could see it matched my hair comb. It was my sister's, and before that, my mother's.

"Sorry for the shocker there, both of them I suppose." She drops her hands back down, straightening her shoulders. "Your sister always speaks of you, so I thought she finally decided to tell you about me." An almost sheepish smile forms on her face, the iridescent eyes gleaming at me.

"Tell me what exactly?" *Why wouldn't Cordelia have told me about this?*

"Where to begin, you see your mother told her of me before-" she cuts her sentence and stands as she glances at me before turning and grabbing some bottles off a nearby shelf of rocks. "Well, you know. And she decided to come meet me for herself about a year or so ago. You see, I'm your father's Aunt. His mother's sister." She pauses, bringing over a small tray with some form of food on it, but my stomach tightens so much I can't even look as she sets it on the table before us.

I wrap my arms across my rounded stomach and shake my head slightly. *There's no way, right? She couldn't really be related to me, an evil sea witch? And my sister has known for a year and not said anything? Had she not been wearing her necklace, I would have never considered it.*

"Why did she come here?" My voice was low, throat tightening as I tried to keep my swim snacks from coming up. *What a hypocrite I am, coming here without telling her, and yet I feel so betrayed that she did the same.*

"Well, that would be her story, not mine, but I will say she didn't go looking for a bargain the first time, more to see if it was true, I think."

"But what did she end up bargaining for? What did you take?" I rise from the couch and face her. Her eyes darken as she flicks her tail, jaw set.

"I don't take anything. I bargain, I trade, I ask a fair price before making deals and warn that there are no returns. All who come here are free to decide, not forced. And I will not have the likes of some princess who has no hardships other than being requested to sing at every gathering insult me." Her hair ripples back as if her words would cut it if it came too close. The neon glow around her eyes darkens, and her breathing shallows.

"Then what did she trade?"

"Nothing permanent, but still not for me to tell." Her tone low, voice still crackling on the edges of every other word she speaks.

"How do I know you aren't lying to me?"

"You don't."

"If you are really my aunt, then why haven't I met you? Why doesn't anyone speak of you except mentioning an evil sea witch." I speak slower, my tone matching hers, but seeing her pulse with light I quickly add, "Their words, not mine." raising my webbed hands in surrender.

She tuts, rolling her eyes. "Unsatisfied customers will spread whatever lies they wish in an attempt to cover their bad decisions. After some reached out to my parents when I was younger than you, they tried to lock me away and force my powers out of me. But when I was done being a royal puppet and fought back, they locked me out instead. Forbade anyone to mention me, of course, some still talk, still go looking for magic. Merfolk like your sister and you. I guess it runs in the family." She releases a fractured laugh and a double-lidded wink with her right eye.

My grandparents never did anything like this, at least not that I had heard of. I hadn't known them long, but all the citizens loved them. Their funerals happened when I was young, but there were so many present for the lowering into the volcano that the tides shifted. But here she is, and if what she's saying is true...

I open my mouth, but before I could utter she began again.

"Now, enough about me. Tell me how you got those burns. I assume it has something to do with why you're here instead of preparing for her ceremony." She sits back down, patting the seat next to her. I hadn't realized how far I'd floated away from it, crossing the distance between us. I sit and tell my story again.

"You were very brave to help that man." She slowly pats my arm with a soft smile. "And how is Nessa? You know she never visits. She was quite young; perhaps I scared her away." She rubs the two front tentacles that in the way I've seen Nessa do too many times before.

"She did seem a little weary to tell me of you. Maybe it's from–" The words catch in my throat as I point to the tentacles she was now caressing with her hands.

"Yes, that does tend to happen. It's why I was questioning if I should make a deal with your sister, it was nice to have the company, but I know she will return, just as I hope you will as well." She turns to look at me again. The silence weighs heavy on me. *Would I come back? Will I even be able to?*

"I- it's just..."

"It may interfere with your bargain?" A knowing look in her eyes, and I nod.

"You see, The man I told you about, Caden... I- well it's kind of hard to see him when I need to be underwater."

"I can see how that would put a damper on things. But you came all this way. you must have some bargain to be made for it. What were you planning to ask for?"

"A way to be like them, like him. Oh, I don't know." I flew from the seat and swam in small circles around the table. "Legs are what I'm missing, right? They have them and I don't, so I guess I need a pair." I glance at her, with her crab claws, tentacles, and eel strip. "A pair like theirs, I mean. I guess to lose my tail?"

"So you wish to trade your tail for legs? No, that won't do. You will need to trade something different."

"Then what would I trade? How could I even dream of going on land with this?" I say flipping my tail up and grabbing the ends of the flippers, losing my breath as my stomach squishes further into me shoving my shells painfully into my chest, and my chest into my neck.

"Let's see, what would be a fair bargain for something this big?" She completely ignores my question."All I want from you, in exchange for human legs and maybe even the occasional visit to your dear aunt." Her gaze holds mine as she pauses before telling me the price of my magic trick, the price for a chance with Caden, a chance at happiness. "All I ask for in return is your voice."

My mind, that had spent the last hour racing with new information, came to a standstill. *What did she just say?* My hands made their way to the base of my throat.

"My voice?"

"Yes." Her face unreadable.

"I would never be able to talk again? To sing?"

"Well, we could do it more as a loan then. I give you human legs in exchange for your voice. However, if within one month's time, you get this prince of yours to fall in love and kiss you, of his own volition, you may have your voice returned, and your tail remains mine to call upon when I feel like receiving a visit." She smiles before eating one of the small green balls from the tray.

"And if he doesn't kiss me?"

"Then you return to the sea, your voice remaining mine."

"But, how can I make him fall in love if I can't even speak to him? I've only ever dealt with one suitor before, and Father scared him away before I could learn any courting."

"Yes, I've heard all about that mess from your sister. Now, some of our friends here cannot speak, yet they find their love in their own way. How do they do this?"

Cordelia told her about him scaring off Roman? No, focus Marella. When some of the fish are trying to find a mate, and they can't speak, instead they– "Dance! They do little weird wiggles to catch their eyes!" I shouted confidently, mocking a wiggle mixed with a twirl and falling into a fit of giggles at the image of Caden and I doing that to get each other's attention. A high-pitched laugh joins mine for a few moments before she clears her throat.

"Well, you're half right. Body language makes all the difference, Ella. However, I wouldn't do that wiggle in particular on land, though they do dance to show interest." She slowly shakes her head,laughing as I gather myself.

"But I don't know how to dance."

"Oh, he'll probably love to teach you, especially if he's interested."

A chance, she's giving me a chance.

"Alright, are you ready?" She holds both webbed hands out towards me. Nodding, I join mine with hers. "It was lovely to meet you, my dear. Now this might sting a bit at first, but it won't last long, don't worry." She pulls me in for a squished hug before pushing back to arm's length and lifting her face up. The pulse that flows through her quickens as her eyes begin to glow pure white, mumbling something lowly, too fast to comprehend even if I spoke whatever language she uttered. A fierce shock fliesthrough me, immediately followed by piercing pain, starting in my hands. I look down to see the sheer webs between my joints tearing apart and re-wrapping themselves around each joint they once connected. Purple and black ink flow around them and soon encompasses me entirely before a white glow begins. I'm no longer holding her hands, now surrounded by a vortex of torrents. Everything goes white, and my gills burn. At my waistline, where my scales begin, it feels like someone is tearing them off me before a piercing slice cracks down the length of my tail. I scream out until I can't, I push, but no sound leaves my lips.

Almost as soon as it started, it was over, and replacing the pain was what felt like a cold phlegm coating me. I feel a kiss press to my cheek and hear my own voice say, "Good luck," and I am moving. Water rushes past and I feel the swirl that surrounds me slowly stop after a few minutes and find warm sand pressing into my side as I am laid down, the white glow filtering away to a sunny sky above.

My eyes feel like they are being stabbed by the sunlight itself. Looking at my new strange hands, no longer connecting fingers spread before me. There are no signs of the scales that previously lined my arms, which are now a pale white like the shells that had once covered my now bare breasts. I pull my arms up and cover them as I admire my new legs. They are roughly the same size as my tail, only now split in two. Instead of flowing into another color or being covered in scales all of my skin now matched. My stomach now fell to my thighs lightly, no longer having the support of the water and scales to hold it up. I practice slipping one knee up at a time, the muscles fight to move together, and I have to focus on one leg moving while the other sits still. I'm not sure how long I spend playing with my new legs, but eventually, I manage to pull my eyes away and look across the warm beach. A torn white sail lay hooked on a nearby boulder, the cloth similar to the ones I'd seen humans drape over themselves, and now with no shells on this beach large enough to cover myself, I try to make my way over to it.

A mere ten feet turns out to be a challenge for someone who hasn't used legs before; several times I manage to get to my feet and stand, but when I take a step, both feet move and I faceplant, getting sand in my nose and hair. After a few wobbly steps of learning balance without water, I finally make it to the boulder. Grabbing the sail, I attempt to wrap it around myself. Attempt. It wasn't quite long enough to cover my feet like most of the human clothes I've seen, and it couldn't quite reach around me fully, leaving two or three inches of my side exposed. With no way to keep it up but to hold it in place scrambles my balance routine of holding my hands out while walking. Looking around, I spot seaweed that had washed ashore with me and use it to tie the waist of the material, so I only need to use one hand to hold it over my chest under my armpit.

I see the tops of what looks to be a castle to my left, and I follow the shoreline closer. Soon I notice something coming towards me, like a giant seahorse but with legs longer than me and a deep gray. It seems to speed up and head straight towards me. My heart races as I turn and try to run back the way I came, only to fall to my knees and freeze. *I traded everything away to die the first few hours of having legs.*

"Woah, girl!" A deep voice calls out from on top of the animal and it stops a few feet from me, snorting.

"Are you okay?" the voice asks as two leather boots hit the ground between the animal and me. Suddenly the pounding in my head stops. *That voice, I know that voice.* My eyes slowly trail upwards to the midnight cloth draped over his legs, followed by a loose white material that clings to his upper arms. A short, thick black beard, soft gray eyes, and high cheekbones. His hair is pulled back into a ponytail, and a short crown lies on his brow. *My prince, he found me.* My cheeks rise into my eyesight as a smile flashes to my face.

His face matches mine, and I see my pale cheeks turn coral as he stretches his hands out to me. "Need some help there?"

I nod and reach both hands up, letting his larger ones encompass mine, his forearm muscles jumping as he pulls me back to my feet. I do a small curtsey as I've seen humans aboard the ships do on occasion. I straighten and see shock covering his face, his tanned skin turning bright red as he drops my hands and turns around.

"Madam, your- uh- your dress," he rumbles out.

Looking down, I realize I dropped the edges I was holding when he helped me up and the sail was now only being held at my waist. I would have shrieked in embarrassment if I had the voice to do so. I quickly grab the sides again and hold them tightly in place.

"Are you, erm, decent?" a flustered voice calls. Having no way to respond audibly, I tap him on the shoulder. He turns slowly, eyes traveling the length of me from head to toe as he does.

"What happened to your dress? Wait, is that a sail? Or part of one rather." He looks over my makeshift dress. His stare lingering on the few inches of bare skin traveling the length of me where the fabric was too narrow to cover. I nod my head sheepishly and tuck my hair behind my ears with one hand while firmly grasping the sail with the other.

"Did you get shipwrecked? What happened?" His eyebrows furrow together as he glances out to the horizon, searching for evidence of where I came. I try to force words out, but no sound leaves my throat. I bring my empty hand to it, shaking my head slowly.

"You can't speak?" His eyes widen ever so slightly. "Have you lost your voice?"

He has no idea how perfect a description that is. I nod again. His eyes squint a little as he begins to unroll the fabric balled at his elbow. "Here, I can't very well bring you back dressed like that. The dogs that guard me would be ravenous." After he unrolls both sides he begins to pull it apart from the middle, one section at a time. My gaze follows as he trails down before removing the cloth fully, and hands it to me. Our eyes meet again, and I cover my blush with the fabric, his scent intoxicating.

"That's for you to wear. You'll be able to turn the skirt to cover," his throat bobs, "more, if you have a shirt on. It's no dress but better than a torn sail alone, right?" He laughs a deep chuckle and rubs his hands along some of the baby hairs peeking out from his ponytail. I hold up the shirt with my free hand, trying to find how he wore it.

"Oh, yes, I can see that would be difficult one-handed. Here allow me to assist." I return his shirt. He moves behind me and holds out the sides so I can slide my arm in through the long pieces he wore moments ago. He allows me to put both arms through before stepping in front of me again. I pull the sides of the shirt together as far as I can, my ample chest allowing the edges to just touch.

"If I may?" he asks. Once I nod, he moves forward and grabs the edges together again but slides a small round pearl through a slit just above my chest. When he moves to the next one, he leans slightly closer, and I watch his face as he focuses on the pearls. His cheeks grow even more coral as he moves down. His throat bobs again as he connects the next one, the fabric straining around it. As he moves onto the pearls at my hips, the fabric cannot touch, spreading wide over the sail still tied at my waist where the last pearl was latched. He stands.

"Now, if you turn the sail and retie it, you'll have more privacy."

I nod and reach for the tie as he turns to the bag on the beast and pulls out some rope.

"Here, this should work a little better than seaweed."

I dip my head in thanks and take the rope before he turns. Taking a few steps back, I untie the green vine. Catching the fabric before it can fall, I reposition it. It reaches only halfway down my legs now but can tie to cover my full stomach and thighs under the shirt. I tap him on the shoulder again, and he turns back, assessing my work quickly he releases a low breath. "That will have to do for now. Here, climb on." He steps back from the creature and gestures to a small shelf on its side. I look from him to the shelf, unsure but step forward nonetheless. Setting a foot onto it, I try to lift myself on top, but instead end up on my stomach against the hard contraption on its back. A laugh resounds behind me. "Here, let me help," he speaks before I feel his warm hands on my thighs as he turns me and then grabs my arm and waist and lifts me onto my bottom. My feet dangle over the left side as I face him. He then swings effortlessly behind me, wrapping an arm around my waist. "Hold on tight."

Before my eyebrows have a chance to fully scrunch together, we lurch into motion towards his castle. I hold the arm around me tightly, my head bumping against his warm chest every few leaps.

He whistles, and I hear metal scraping. We fly past the guards before I can register how many there are. We come to a halt within a ship on land that he calls the stables. He jumps down before holding his hands out to me. When I place my hands in his, he moves them onto his bare shoulders and then grabs my waist, lowering me to the floor.

"Reginald, fetch Sarah and tell her to meet me in my drawing room," he calls out.

A small child with red hair comes around the side of the stables and does a low bow. Hereplies, "Right away sire," before running out of the door we just rode in.

"I'll give you over to Sarah for a bit. She'll help you get washed up and give you a fresh dress to wear." Looking down he adds, "And some shoes. Your feet must be hurting. If you'll follow me, I'll take you the back way to the drawing room." He holds a hand out to me, and I take it following close behind him. After a short walk on a stone path, we go through a set of monumental doors. I barely have time to glance at the rich colors that encircle us as he pulls me down several hallways and stairs. Soon we stand before two grand doors, with small carvings of waves and a ship adorning them. He pulls a metal key from his pocket and opens them, leading me into a large room with a stone arch holding fire within it. There is a table with several seats and a few armchairs like Nessa's before it. Royal blue fabrics matching the chairs flow in front of the windows on the wall. A door on the far right wall remains shut. He starts to close the doors behind us, but before he can, a woman in a deep green dress with long brown hair in a braid to her waist knocks.

"Prince Caden, you sent for me?"

"Ah yes," he says, gesturing for her not to enter before stepping outside.

Moments later, they reenter. "My lady, if you will follow me, I will lead you to the guest quarters and get you–"

"The blue sails room should do for her," Caden interrupts.

Her brown eyes widen for a moment, darting between the two of us before continuing, "Yes, and I'll run you a bath and get you a fresh dress." I follow her out of the room, turning back after a few feet to see Caden standing at the doorway, smiling. Two doors down, she opens a room and lets me in. Three armchairs and a small table sit in front of a giant bed with blue cloth covering it. A beige screen stands in the corner next to a tall mirror with a wooden chair before it.

"This is the guest room in the prince's wing. The bathing room is just through here," she leads me past the small stone arch in the wall.

After she helps me bathe, she brings me into the first room once more, wrapping a warm sheet around me. She tells me to dry myself by the fire she lit in the archway she called a fireplace, and that she will return soon with clothing. *Did he tell her I can't speak? She didn't ask anything that required more than a nod.* I wander around the chamber, examining the paintings before I lay on the bed. A small feather escapes a pillow as I revel in the softness until three quick raps sound from the wooden door. I jump back up, stumbling ever so slightly and watch the door creak open slowly. *Is it him?* Sarah greets me instead with a stack of cloth in her hands. She helps me dress before sitting me down in a chair in front of the fire and brushes my hair. Once she decides my hair is finished, she moves me in front of a mirror, and I see myself in a way I never imagined. *I look like one of them, truly like them.* Sleeves of light green that turn slightly darker near the hem match the bodice that hugs my curves nicely before flowing into a wide set skirt that deepens until almost black. My hair is pulled back with a matching green strand.

"Prince Caden has requested you dine with him this evening. Have you ever dined in a great hall before?" she says gently, covering my feet with stiff cloth. I shake my head. *What will dining on land be like? Will I be expected to collect my own dinner?*

"I thought as much, don't be nervous dear. Just remember to work your way from the outside in, and no elbows on the table." She gives my left elbow a slight tap as she leads me to the door and down a set of stairs.

I can hear the music from the ships growing nearer, only now it's softer, slower. Two older men dressed in black open large double doors for us. A long table with water blue cloth is in the middle of the room, small sticks of fire line it. On one edge, plates sit with glinting metal in odd shapes next to them. Strange bowls with plants sit about the dimly lit room. In the far left corner are four men making the music that filled the room and into the hall.

"I'm sorry to have kept you waiting," that deep voice sounds from behind us, and with a nod, Sarah hands my arm to him, curtsies, and leaves the room, closing the doors behind her. I smile softly at him as he leads us to the table edge where the plates lay, pulling out the chair for me. I perch on the edge, and he takes his seat across from me.

"I do hope you like venison," he says as a lady in beige serves us both a thick slab of brown something that smells mouthwatering. I smile at him and nod before looking down at the items around my plate, work your way in. I recognize a knife nearest to the edge and pick it up but am unsure if I need the pronged one next or the almost shell-shaped one. I pause my hand as I reach forward. Glancing up at him I see him holding the pronged one and start for mine, but before I can fully grasp it, my plate is moved away.

"Allow me," his voice rumbles as he begins to saw the venison into small bite-size pieces. "Now, I simply cannot continue to call you my lady alone. What should I call you?" He looks at me with those hypnotic eyes, and I pick at my lower lip with my left hand.

"Maybe we could make a game of it, finding your name, can you give me any hints?"

How can I give a hint? I look around the room, I don't know what half of these things are called, maybe... I use my fingers to thump the table four times *Mar-I-ell-a.*

"Four knocks, like four sounds?"

Kind of, I nod.

"What name has four parts? Can you knock my name?"

Ca-Den. I knock twice.

"Ok, so twice of mine, does it sound similar at all?"

I shake my head. He hands my plate back and begins cutting his own.

"Ok, I'll name some, and stop me if one fits."

Another nod.

"Elizabeth. Penelope. Evangeline. Juliana." The small pause placed between each guess is now interrupted by a longer one as we both take a bite of food. It's a texture I've never experienced before, but I find I love it right away, and as my stomach roars for more, I'm glad the music muffles it.

Placing both elbows on the table and interlacing his fingers, he looks at me. I try to hold his brazen stare, but as my cheeks warm, I match his stance and use my knotted hands to hide my reddening face as best I can. Peeking out between my fingers, I see him smiling. A low chuckle escapes him, where my laugh stays in my silenced throat.

"Lilliana, Izabella" My eyebrows raise, and I lower my hands. *That one's similar.*

"Izabella?" He says with a smile. I shake my head and raise my hands up, holding my first finger and thumb close to each other.

"Ok, so it's close? Maybe part?" My hands flatten, and my lips slightly part as I nod.

"Isa?" A slight pause. "Bella?" I move my hands in a slow circle over each other. "Ella?"

I nod quickly and bounce slightly in my chair, hands clapping. *I can't believe that worked!* His eyes flicker down and back up to mine. "Ella, that is much better than just lady," he says with a chuckle as we continue to eat. Some sides are brought out; mashed potatoes, greens, and carrots, the servers announce. We eat the rest in comfortable silence, only broken by the musicians.

"You enjoy music?" he asks, and I turn to see him leaning his cheek onto one fist, lips halfway crooked up, as he watches me. Sheepishly I nod, realizing I've been ignoring him for the better part of the last few minutes, admiring the performers.

"Shall we dance?" He holds his hand out while standing. *Dance? Just like Morfran said.* I place mine in his, as I stand, hoping the long skirt will cover the fact I don't know what I'm doing. As we move further into the room, near the large floor-to-ceiling windows, he waves to the man holding the instrument with strings and a stick. The man smiles and turns to the other three, and they do a countdown lowly before starting another tune, this one a little faster than the last. Our fingers interlock and he places my other hand on his shoulder, laying his on my waist. Warmth creeps through the fabric and envelopes a good portion of my side. Our eyes lock as he leads us in a circle, I find it's much easier to follow his lead than I had anticipated, and just as I relax in his grip, he flings me into a spin, pulling me back in with the beat of the music. My breathing hitches as he catches me, and I let out a silent giggle looking up at him, my back against his chest. He doesn't miss a beat and continues to follow the music, until I fumble, stumbling over his shoe. My mouth opens to ask if he's ok, to apologize, but of course, nothing comes out. My fingers untwine from his and wave around before landing over my mouth as my eyes race between his foot and face.

"It's ok." He laughs as I regain my breath, one eyebrow lifted to match his smile as one creeps on my face as well. He tries to pull me in for another spin, but I pull away. *I don't want to step on him again.* For a moment his face drops, but soon regains that smile, though not as bright as before.

"I'm sure you're tired, shall I walk you to your room?" He extends an arm towards me, I nod and take it. Too soon, we are back through the halls from before and in front of my door. As I reach for the knob, he gently grabs my hand and pulls it to his lips, pressing a kiss into it. He barely lifts his head from it before speaking, "I'm afraid I cannot ask you to breakfast or lunch, but perhaps you would join me for afternoon tea tomorrow?" Looking down at him from this angle, his eyes seem so much larger, and a few strands of hair drizzle over them. I brush them away with my free hand slowly while nodding.

"Sleep well," he murmurs, and as I open my door, I point at him twice with slight shakes of my head. *You too, my prince.* I worry he doesn't understand at first, but as I start inside my room, I hear him call out, "I'll try."

The smile that lights my face is unlike any other I've worn. I twirl around my room and silently laugh at how red my face is in the mirror. It takes me what feels like hours to finally calm down enough to remove some of the outer layers of the dress and crawl under the blankets to sleep.

The next day I am awoken by a knock at the door before two women dressed similarly to Sarah enter with trays of food and another dress. They help me to dress once more and say they will return later for the dishes before leaving. The door is thumped, and Sarah enters.

"You were requested in the library for tea with Prince Caden soon. Oh goodness, what has happened to your hair?" The smile she wore into the room quickly fades into a frown as she rushes me to the chair once more.

I look in the mirror to see my hair is everywhere. *Underwater it never became much of an issue. A little finger run through, and it was silky, flowing all around, but above the water, it was all tangled up from merely sleeping. In comparison to Sarah's in a neat pile on top of her head, I look like a sea wit- well, like the stories I was told of sea witches at least.* She tuts at me, explaining I must sleep with it braided, and I nod earnestly. If it would stop the painful tugs at my scalp, I'll learn how. It feels as though she's pulling out my hair, like when Nessa's babies decided my hair was a toy last season and nearly took my head off. Soon it was flat and smooth once more. She straightens my dress, and with a final nod of approval, she leads me to another giant entryway. Two large doors, nearly see-through with panes of sea glass in square shapes down them and a half moon at the top. As she opens a door, letting me in, and I stare in awe at the mere size of it, shelves so high they have ladders on them. There's even a balcony above with a large fireplace, cushioned chairs, and tables scattered all around. The two women from this morning follow us in with a tray that holds something with steam rising above it, colorful cups with handles on them, and a small tower with small circles and puffs.

"Put the kettle on the table directly in front Clari, and the cakes Margery," Sarah says in a soft yet commanding voice. "Prince Caden will be arriving soon. Please wait here." And with that, the doors close again. I go to the nearest shelf, filled with rectangles of varying colors. Pulling one off, I open the soft, red-bound thing, the almost woodsy smell that surrounds me is lovely, and I realize this is what Nessa had told me was a book. It is filled with the human language, similar to the shell-carved writings we have at home but their language was so different, more loopy and curved. I couldn't name a single letter of it, but it was beautiful nonetheless.

"Do you enjoy reading?" I jump, quickly closing the book and holding it against my chest as a shock runs through me. *I didn't even hear him come in.* Looking up, I see he now wears a crown, the gold complimenting his deep olive tone well as it holds his hair out of his eyes.. His eyes reflect the red fire, seemingly glowing, and a soft smile gazes back at me.

"I didn't mean to be late, but we ran over in the discussions of the ball next week. Normally the queen would handle such matters, but with none currently, it falls to my father, brother, and I." No queen? His mother is gone too? I place my hand on his arm in what I hope is a comforting manner, looking into his eyes and pulling my lips towards my teeth. I tilt my head. "It's ok, it was six years ago now, but she was wonderful. She would have had the ball planned within a day." He laughs as he walks me to the table where the trays were set. "That's her. Purple suited her well."

As I sit, I look to where he points above the fireplace and see a portrait I missed before. Four people stood in it, a man with a similar facial shape to Caden, but he was blonde, though the same grey eyes stare from below a crown nearly twice the size of Caden's. Next to him was a beautiful woman with deep brown skin and matching eyes, her black hair curled around her in waves, a lighter crown than the king's sat on her brow. In front of them stood two boys. One was clearly Caden when he was younger with the same crown he wore now, but it was crooked sideways as it didn't fit properly yet. He still wore the same smile he has now, and next to him was another boy who must be his brother. He had dark brown hair and brown eyes, a slightly lighter skin tone than Caden, but his face was softer, younger, and more rounded, like his mother's.

As I turn to smile at him, a small furry animal jumps onto the table between us. Making a mewling noise at Caden, its fur, dark grey like stone.

"Smokey, I was wondering when you'd show." Caden laughs while scratching the creature behind its ear. Reaching forward, he grabs a bowl and a small open-mouthed container from the tray and pours out white liquid for Smokey.

"Ella, this is Smokey, my cat. I do hope you don't mind company, he never misses his milk at tea." The cat continued to rumble as he now lapped from the bowl set to the side for him. Smiling, I shake my head, watching the curious creature. "Have you seen a cat before?" Raising my shoulders, I shake my head again, looking away from the cat. "I promise he's quite tame, and resilient, the old man. He survived a shipwreck with me recently. He follows me everywhere and managed to sneak aboard." My eyes widen, not in shock at the wreck but in realization. *This was the creature inside of the sack, the one who clawed me.* I look between the two. "I'm not really sure how we escaped, the men urged me to leave him, but Smokey was a gift from my mother before she passed. She said I could learn a lot by caring for an animal myself, and she was right."

The cat leaves its half-full bowl and rubs against the prince's dark jacket before settling in his lap. "Someone helped us, but it was so hazy from the smoke I couldn't see who. When I awoke on shore, they were gone. But I heard the most beautiful melody that morning, it's one I shall never forget."

I feel myself flush. He *remembers my song. He just can't remember it was me.*

"Though I almost thought it–" He shakes his head and reaches for the steaming container, pouring us both a cup of brown liquid. "How do you take your tea? Milk and sugar? Or just sugar?" He pours the white liquid into his own cup before grabbing two small cubes from a bowl on the table and adding them as well. I reach forward and grab one cube and add it to mine before grabbing the scooping utensil next to my plate and stir it, copying him. "To our interesting meeting," he nods as he raises his cup towards me, I raise mine as well, and he softly clinks his to the side of mine before pulling it to his lips. I take a sip from my cup, a strange flavor that I quite enjoy though I can't place it.

"Oh, macarons! You'll love these." He places an orange and yellow circular puff on my plate and takes more for himself. I take a bite of the yellow first, it was sour yet sweet, the orange one sweet-tart.

"Did you sleep well, Ella?" I nod and hold a hand out to him, head tilting.

"I did, I was wondering if I could show you around a bit today?" I nod again. He continues to ask questions and tell me stories for what felt like moments, but the lights outside the windows had shifted from when we first sat. He did show me around parts of the castle: the portrait hall where his father and mother's portrait hung along with his grandparent's and so on, the main dining room where the king usually dines, the ballroom which was bigger than I had anticipated and had a balcony overlooking the garden, the lower east wing that was his brother's, though we didn't see him, and the entrance to the throne room.

It felt as though we barely spent time together, though, by the lights, it must have been hours when he leads me to my room once more. "Goodnight, Ella, I hope you have pleasant dreams." Another kiss was placed on my hand before he left.

The next morning went the same, food was brought and I was dressed, but this time, I found my way back to the library alone. As I wandered through the shelves of strange words opening several and finding they each had a slightly different smell. Some musty, some woodsy, and some smelled like a far-off storm. As I flip through the pages of a green covered one, the door opens and a boy, maybe 16 or 17 with dark brown hair and eyes, and a thin crown on his head enters. I recognize him from the portrait as Darien, Caden's younger brother.

"You must be Caden's little secret I've been hearing all about." I gave him a small curtsy.

"What's your name?" he asks, eyes traveling slowly from the bottom of my skirts to my eyes. Bringing my hand to my throat, I shake my head, and his eyes seem to almost darken.

"Mute? Leave it to my brother to find a mute and bring it home, though I guess I can't blame him. What with father pushing him to marry now that he's 20, I guess he wanted to have some fun before the ball begins next week."

My brows furrow at what he's implying, but my head tilts in question. He steps closer. "Oh, don't act like you don't know, the ball? All eligible royalty will be there. You think he'll choose a mute over a princess? No matter how voluptuous you may be, he won't make a commoner a queen. He's taking advantage of you." As he stalks closer, I back into the shelf behind me, head shaking. "Oh, he is, but we can get him back for it. Make sure he doesn't have any queen at all." He places an arm on the shelf to my right, now nearly nose to nose. My face scrunches. What *is he asking me?* "If you help me, I can make sure you're properly rewarded." I try to move to the left, but he places his other arm there, blocking me in.

"At least hea-- Ow!" He shouts in pain, grabbing for his leg. I look and see Smokey with his tail flicking. We run for the door as he screams obscenities at us. I follow Smokey to a part of the castle I've never been. Corridors seemingly darker than the others, stopping outside of a door, he meows, rubbing along my ankles, and I pick up the vibrating cat.

Soon the door opens and out walks Caden, he smiles brightly asking, "To what do I owe the pleasure of this surprise?" I hold Smokey up, and he laughs. "If you ever need me, just follow him. He always finds me." He holds out his elbow, and I take it. Smokey jumps up and lays around his shoulders, head between us. He leads us to the main dining hall, where we have lunch before returning to meetings. I almost go back to the library, but fear of running into Darien again leads me to my room instead. Over the next few days, I avoid it except for tea with Caden twice more.

When I wake, a bowl of food has already been placed on the table. Approaching it, I find a singular part of a book, the writing in it wasn't small and organized, but it's definitely the human's looped writing which I can't understand. I eat the sauce like food, it was both bland and sweet with oval shapes in it. I bathe, and as I'm dressing, Sarah knocks and enters.

"You aren't ready yet? My lady, you shouldn't keep the prince waiting." She lectures, helping me to finish, I cock my head to the side and raise an eyebrow.

"Did you not read his invitation? To lunch in the garden?" As she fixes my hair, I grab the writing and hold it out to her. "Yes, that one, did you not notice it before?"

I use both hands to give it to her and point at the lettering. She takes it slowly, brows furrowing. "You-You cannot read it?" I shake my head, avoiding her eyes.

"Oh, my lady, I apologize, would you like me to read it to you?" I nod quickly.

"Dearest Ella, I hope your slumber was as sweet as your smile. Would you join me for lunch in the gardens at noon today? Have Sarah take you to the southwest edge and I can escort you from there. Warmly, Prince Caden. He's a sweet one, isn't he?" She hands it back to me and fluffs my hair slightly before we take off through the castle again.

We come to a door that leads to a deck of rock and waiting next to the stairs I see him, wearing just a fitted black shirt and dark brown pants. When he turns to face me, I see he has ties across his chest that are left open, hair poking through at the V that was left. When I peel my eyes up, he's smirking at me, holding his hand out.

"I've got her from here Sarah. Lady Ella, you look ravishing this afternoon, I hope you're hungry." I take his hand and he leads me between large hedges lined with flowers. "Have you ever been in a maze before?" I shake my head. "They're a lot of fun, but easy to get lost if you don't know your way. Let's see how well I remember, shall we?"

Before I have time to look puzzled, he interlocks our fingers and runs with me in tow, laughing. After several turns, I feel my hand go cold and turn the corner to find myself alone. I follow the path before me until it becomes a fork. One seems to go back the way we came while the other forward, I choose forward, and the hair on my arms prickle. *Where did he go?* I come to another turn and a dead end. As I go to turn around, I feel something begin to worm around my sides and a loud

"Boo!" I jump back and attempt to turn, but I can only partially do so as I am pulled towards a warm rumbling chest "I hope I didn't scare you too bad, Ella, I was never far behind." He looks down at me and smiles. I playfully smack his chest and try to push him away. He laughs, releasing me, all except one arm around my waist. As he leads me back another turn.

"Now, if you ever do get lost in here, just remember to keep one hand on the wall. You will find the way out eventually." As he speaks, he grazes his right hand along the bush next to him. "I used to come in here all the time as a boy. My brother and mother and I would play hide and seek."

I lay my head on his side as we walk, and I listen as he tells me of the times he scared his mom, once by climbing on top of the hedge altogether and pouncing on her. Soon we arrive at a small circular stone pavilion surrounded by colorful flowers, with a blanket and basket inside it. As we begin up the stairs, music rings out from beyond the hedges, somewhere unseen, and I look up at him in surprise, a mock laugh on my lips, not bothering to attempt sound anymore. As we sit, he opens the basket pulling out small sandwiches and some fruit, as well as a small pitcher of water and two glasses.

"Did your family like hide and seek?"

I nod, memories of chasing each other through old shipwrecks and around the reefs near our home rush through me. A soft smile returns to my face. I place my hand on his, and he turns his over gripping mine once more. We sit and listen to the music waft around us as we both eat with one hand alone.

After we finish our food, we find ourselves dancing between the pillars of vines around us to our unseen musicians, I don't misstep nearly as much as last time. He twirls me out, and when I am pulled back in, a soft blue petaled flower is placed behind my ear. He moves my hands to his shoulders, his meeting my waist. Leaning his forehead to mine, we stare into each other's eyes for a long moment. His eyes flicker down for half a second before he straightens back up.

"What's your favorite color?" he whispers gently, his thumb rubbing over my rolled rib. I pluck a leaf from a nearby hedge, holding it up.

"Green? Mine used to be blue, but, I think it's green now, too," He raises his hand to my rounded cheek and thumbs just under my left eye. I lean into it, smiling.

"Ella, would you like to come to the ball next week? I'm sure you've already heard what it's for, and though I cannot ask you to be my date, as I must arrive single, I would very much like for you to come." He takes a slight breath and, before I can even nod, continues. "Unless, of course, you aren't interested. It's fine if I've misundersto–" I grab either side of his head so he will look at me and smile while nodding. *It's cute when he rambles.* He smiles and brings both my hands to his lips, thrice. He leads me back to our wing and says Sarah will be in soon to get measurements for a dress.

Sarah comes in bouncing. "He requested a gown that matches his suit! You know what this means, right? Oh, my lady, your chances are very high, and you've only been here two weeks. It took me three months to get my husband," she continues as she measures me.

The next week passes quickly, I see Caden at least once a day, if for nothing more than tea. I evade his brother completely. Sarah reads me another note from Caden that arrives with some flowers for my room.

Then all at once, it was time. Sarah wakes me early with fruit and a bitter brown drink that she ensures I finish fully. She bathes me and coaches me on how to know who to bow to and not to bow to everyone, or else they would start chattering about me. When we come out of the bathing room, there is another girl, laying the most beautiful dress out on the bed.

It was a deep green that seemed to glow, with a shimmery sheer overlay of gray. It had silver trim along the top of the rounded neckline and sleeves that hung off my arms. There was a corset along my waistline and upper stomach, as they dressed me it tightened just enough to line my waist and lift my chest. Below it, the dress billows out over my stomach. A cape is attached to my shoulders, falling just even with the hem of the dress, skirting the floor in a whisper. Sarah then spends over an hour on my hair, twisting it half up in a braided bun while letting the rest cascade around my shoulders. She paints my eyelids with green and black crème, nearly matching my eyes. She pulls out a crown of green flowers on a vine, "I can't have you being one of the few there without a crown." She sets it on my head and stands back, admiring her work.

"You look amazing, I can only walk you part of the way, but from there, it's just a left and a right." Looking in the mirror, I twirl, and the dress swifts with me, cape following. *I really hope he likes it.* "Oh, I nearly forgot! Here sit, sit." As I sit on the edge of the bed, Sarah grabs a small box from the table and pulls out two flat shoes, both twinkling silver, and puts them on me. "There, now you're ready!" She declares as she opens the door. I take a deep breath and step out.

We walk past the library, back through the royal dining area, now decorated with candles and cloth draped over the walls, flowers everywhere, and many tables lined out, clearly meant for use later. We stop at the edge of the door, and she hands me a note. "Give this to Graham to introduce you. Since we don't know your surname, I just put Lady Ella. Remember to walk down with confidence, he'll be there soon." She closes the note in my hands and squeezes them, "Good luck!" And with a curtsey is gone.

I step into the hall and take a left. There is a blue carpet laid on the hall floor, and at the end of it a door to my right is open. There is a stairwell leading down to a crowd of people and a room of similar décor to the dining hall.

A man in all black stands before me, I hand him the note, and stamping his cane, he calls out, "Lady Ella."

Another man matching him offers his arm and leads me down the vine-wrapped stairs. Over a hundred eyes meet mine, and I smile politely, face heating. At the bottom, the man bows to me and hurries back up the stairs to await the next person to be announced. Beautiful dresses of every color line the floor with mostly black suits sprinkled in. Glinting crowns sit on several heads, but not as many as Sarah had led me to believe. I move to the railing to my left, which is mostly empty, and admire the flowers, trying to keep my breathing even as I wait. Hushed voices sound off around me.

"Too many people know his favorite color is blue. Ugh, I won't even stand out at this point."

"Do you know which entrance song he chose?"

"Oh please, everyone knows it's royal blue he likes. It doesn't matter how shiny she may be, I'll stand out."

"Lady Ella." I turned to find Prince Darien before me, dressed in a blue suit, I give a small curtsey. "I supposed he asked you to come watch him dance with all these girls as a parting gift?" His voice lowers, stepping closer.

I roll my eyes and go to step aside, but he side steps me.

"I'll let you simmer, maybe next we speak, you'll be more accommodating. Just remember I can make sure you can stay here, comfortably, when he tries to toss you aside."

He wouldn't do that, he asked me here because he's chosen me.

"Let's see how his dance schedule goes. You know at my father's ball he refused to dance with anyone but Mother. Do you think Caden will do the same?"

Someone else is announced, but he doesn't glance at Silvia on the stairs behind me. His eyes are menacing until they suddenly flicker to my shoulder, widening in annoyance.

"Don't you dare," he mutters as he steps back, and I hear a familiar hiss as a paw steps onto my shoulder, followed by three more. "I'll let you think on it." He turns away, and I reach up to scratch a purring Smokey behind the ear.

A familiar tune wafts through the instruments on the stage to the left of the balcony entrance, a song I'm sure no one else recognizes. My lullaby. The portion he recalled on repeat, making it flow seamlessly around me.

"Prince Cadan of Curia Kingdom!"

I turn with everyone else to see my prince dressed in a green suit with silver accents, his hair pulled back in a braid crown above it. He looks more regal than I've ever seen him. Back straight and shoulders ever broadened. He descends the stairs slowly and confidently. He smiles as his eyes chase around the room, before landing on me. When he reaches the bottom, everyone lowers in a bow, opening a walkway for him, and he raises a hand. "Please stand, my friends, I welcome you all here tonight. Let the dance begin." He turns and walks to me, holding his hand out and stifling a laugh when I put Smokey back onto the banister before taking his hand. He leads me out to the middle of the now open floor, and the music cuts to the first song we danced to at dinner nearly three weeks ago.

Our fingers intertwine, and he grips my hip as he moves us in the same pattern, eyes never leaving mine. "You look breathtaking, Ella," he whispers in my ear as he dips me. *Has he seen himself? If I'm breathtaking, he's suffocating.* I smile, blushing further as he flings me into another spin. Others have started to pair up and dance alongside us. All too soon, the music starts to die out, and he kisses my hand. "I'm afraid I have to make some rounds, so I won't seem too biased, my dear." We bow to each other, and I return to Smokey.

Picking him up, I turn to watch my prince, dancing with another in a royal blue gown and silver crown. She laughs, and they speak quietly as they spin in the crowd of people. I feel my heart sting, and anger bellows in me. *I thought he meant to talk to people, is it normal to dance with several people? Perhaps this is just how balls go? Though Darien said...* I wait for the song to end and set Smokey back down, who disappears into the crowd of people. Another song starts, and Caden is dancing with a pink dress with no crown. A man with brown hair and brown eyes appears before me wearing all black and is utterly boring in comparison to Caden.

"May I have this dance?" His voice hopeful, a swallow on his throat. I nod and take his hand, allowing him to bring us into the dance floor. We go in circles to the beat, the couples along the floor making a sea of waves. My eyes find Caden's, and we hold each other's gaze, I hear the feet leading mine try to speak to me, but his words fall on closed ears as I see Caden nearing, dropping the pink dress's hand mid-spin.

"May I cut in?" His voice seemed deeper than usual, eyes dark, daring the hand I was already releasing to deny him. We reconnect and join the ocean of dancers again, this time slowly making our way to the right. "I was coming back for you."

Before or after you dance with the whole ball? I look away from him.

"Are you angry with me?"

I'm glad I can't answer. *I'm not sure if it's fair for me to be. Is this just their culture? But if it was, then why can't I also dance with others?* I glance at him and then just watch our connected hands.

"Ella." His voice sounds hurt.

His grip on my waist tightens slightly, and a cool breeze whooshes over us as we stop spinning and exit onto the balcony. "A moment please," he says loudly, and the three couples that stood there bow and return through the door. He leads me to the railing overlooking the garden.

"Ella, look at me," he commands gently. I stare at the maze.

"Ella, please." He softly places his finger and thumb under my chin, gently pulling my face up at him. After a moment, my eyes follow. "Ella, I only danced with others because they came from far away for a chance."

How far did they swim? Did they give up their tails and learn to walk, to dance?

"How would they have felt if they knew they never stood a chance from the moment they entered this kingdom? Knew they had all traveled here for nothing. I've already chosen my queen, and I think I've known that from the moment I found you." His thumb begins to trace along my soft jawline in circles. His eyes flicker down then back again. I place a hand on his chest, and he leans into it.

"I'm merely avoiding starting a war, one nearly broke out when my father chose the first girl he danced with, even though she was from another kingdom." His eyes bore into mine. I can feel his heartbeat quicken under my fingertips. "I have to get back before they start a riot, but you are my choice." He leans forward and places a long kiss on my forehead, his fingers lingering along my chin before he pulls away fully and returns to the dance.

My heart is fluttering, and I turn to face the garden again. My eyes close and I gasp as wind envelopes me, my smile hurting my cheeks. My chest burns, and my throat feels like I'm swallowing a stone for a moment. My eyes open as I hear footsteps approach, I try to reel in my emotions, to slow my heart rate.

"I'm not usually one to say I told you so." Darien. "It must be hard to see him out there with all those others, to know that he tricked you." I wheel around and face him, his hands in his pockets, slowly making his way closer.

"That burning in your belly, the anger that reddens your face." *Quite the opposite, actually.* "I can help, we can get revenge, and I can give you everything he promised."

I force my feet to move, passing by him, but his hand reaches out, stopping me. "Don't walk away from me, Mute." Anger replaces the softness he spoke with before.

I yank my hand from him and run back inside, slowing down once I'm a few feet in. I make my way toward the magician's stage, leaning against the wall. I scan the crowd, avoiding Caden and the yellow dress currently dancing. What feels like too many songs later, the music stops, and King Bastien calls for everyone to enter the dining hall. We all filter into the table-filled area, and I'm told to sit at a table with several others.

"Who do you think he will choose?" a red dress asks quietly. "Do you think he's chosen already? Prince Eric's ball went for nearly a week before he picked Cinthia."

"I don't know, Prudence seems very sure it'll be her."

"Quiet down everyone, Prince Caden has an announcement to make." King Bastien sits at the head of a table at the front of the room. To his right is Caden, then an empty chair, Darien, and another man I don't recognize.

Caden stands, smiling. "Thank you all for coming tonight, you made this a very hard choice for me, but I have found my future queen. Lady Ella, please come forward and take your place next to me."

Gasps sound off, and heads swivel. I stand and squeeze my way between chairs and up to Caden. He takes my hand and looks out to the crowd before us. Applause rings out, even from those who clearly weren't happy. We sit as the music regains.

"I hope I didn't make you wait too long, my dear," he whispers to me. I shake my head and smile. *He chose me, he really chose me, now just one kiss.* My chest warms again, and I place my hands on my stomach before the table as servers pour drinks into our cups.

"My lord." A man leans down and whispers something to Caden, his brows furrow, and he nods.

"I will be right back, my lady," he says, standing, and gives a short bow to the king, who barely notices as he speaks to a gentleman also in a crown at the table in front of us. A few moments later, a man in a blue suit takes Caden's glass from the table. I turn and see the man from the drink table in the ballroom.

"Just making sure the prince has his favorite wine, my lady." He bows and places a new glass on the table, this one fizzing slightly. As I turn back to the table, I see Darien shake his hand, quickly. Something drops, the man scrambles to the floor to pick up a ring with a large red stone in it.

"What are you doing, you Buffoon," Darien whisper yells at the poor man who knocked his ring off his finger.

"Sorry, Prince Darien," the man grumbles out before picking up the ring and leaving through the curtains. *Wait, he didn't give it back?* I turn from where the man left to find Darien eyeing me with a smile plastered on his face.

He pretends to laugh as he speaks lowly, "Keep your mouth shut. Oh, nevermind."

Shut about what? Was he giving that man his ring? But why wo-

My eyes widen in realization as he turns to the main room and laughs at someone's comment. I look between my drink and Caden's, his now settling and nearly identical. His chair pulls out, and Caden sits again, I point to his glass, shaking my head.

"Oh, don't worry, you won't have to have any. Just take a sip of your water instead for the toast." As he says this, plates of food are set before us.

I grab his drink and point to it shaking my head.

"I won't have much either if that's what you worried about," he says, an eyebrow quirking.

I motion behind me to Darien and then to the drink.

"Darien?"

I nod.

"He- He wants my drink?" He looks dumbfounded.

No he put something in it, how can I- I look around the table and settle on the small containers with holes in front of us, I motion to Darien behind me again, and he nods along.

"Darien." I tip a container into his wine. "Put salt in my wine?" he says lowly with a muffled laugh. "Ah, leave it to my brother to force me to drink that in front of the courts. What do you say we get him back?" I tilt my head, waiting. "Watch this."

He stands and goes to the other side of me, goblet in hand, and speaks to the man on the other side of Darien, interrupting their conversation as he sits the goblet next to his brothers as he slings an arm over his shoulder, forcing him to lean further from me. Speaking low to the person on the other side of Darien I watch as Caden slowly takes Darien's glass in hand before returning to his seat, winking at me.

"Let's see how he likes it," he laughs.

A few moments go by, and I feel a splash on my arm. "Oh my, goodness, Lady Ella please forgive me," Darien speaks slowly. I look down to see the goblet in his hand now emptied on my left arm and part of my dress.

"Darien!" Caden says gruffly as he reaches into his breast pocket, retrieving a gray handkerchief. Before he can hand it to me, a searing pain forms on my arm, and I scream out, grasping for the cloth in his hand, I rub my arm.

"It burns," I hear my own voice say, my head torn between the pain and the surprise of having my voice back before we kissed.

"Ella, what's happened? You can speak." He shakes his head and looks at my pulsing arm. "Hold on." He grabs the water glass in front of us and pours it on my arm, the burning recedes slightly. He trades out the cloth for my napkin and dabs at my arm as his voice raises, no longer caring who is in the room.

"Darien. What. Did. You. Put. In. My. Glass." His voice is deeper than I've ever heard it before.

The king stands. "What is the meaning of this?"

"Darien, blue suit, drink, ring." My voice was hoarse and strangled with pain.

"You accuse my own son of treason?"

"Why would she tell me not to drink it if she poisoned it, Father? Ella, we need to get you to the nurse, now." Caden takes my good hand, leading me swiftly away from the hall.

"Guards, lock Prince Darien in his room until we get to the bottom of this."

"Father, no!" Darien calls out as the doors close behind us.

An hour later, after medicine was applied and my arm bandaged, the pain had subsided, Caden and I sat in his drawing room across from each other. I haven't spoken since we left the table. "Ella-"

"Marella," I cut him off, "It's Marella." Our eyes lock.

"Marella." I melt at the way he says it, his voice treating it as if it was a delicacy. "Your voice, when?"

"I'm not sure." The more I speak, the clearer my voice becomes.

"There's so much I want to ask, but I'm not sure where to start." His head shakes a little as he reaches forward, placing a hand along the side of my full chin and neck.

"I have something to show you." I take a deep breath as he rubs along my chin. I sing the lullaby of the sea, both what he had played tonight and what comes after.

His eyes widen, becoming watery, "You, it was you. But how?"

I stop singing after a moment, "There is so much to explain."

His other hand snakes to the roundness of my side. "We have the rest of our lives to go over it." His eyes glance down, and this time he doesn't pull away, he presses his lips to my pillowed ones, and I decide my tale can be told another day. Now it's time for our story to begin, and I kiss him back.

"LIGHT FALLS AWAY WITH THE WORLD ABOVE, MY EYESIGHT NOT DIMMING IN THE SLIGHTEST."

The Fallen Angel and His Lover

Emma Steinbrecher

Nothing burns quite like the acidic gaze of a man promised ownership of a woman—nothing aside from the way a knife would feel dragging across the thin flesh of said man's neck.

The weight of that knife in Gretchen's boot felt heavier than lead as she stared at the monster who all but bought her. He leaned toward her father in conversation, a stray strand of ashy brown hair falling free from his low ponytail. Gretchen winced at the way his mouth moved as he spoke—hot and wet and filled with food. Her nose wrinkled in disgust.

"Gretel." The booming voice jolted her from any murderous thoughts and had her schooling her features to look down at the dark cherry dining table. Her father, King Nero Gandrey, pressed his lips into a thin line, highlighting the wrinkles around his mouth. A chill worked down Gretchen's spine as she waited for whatever storm the king longed to unleash—whatever hell her father desired to call upon.

"Yes, Father?" The weight in Gretchen's boot drew her attention again, burning against the stockings beneath her heavy skirts. There was another sack of abhorrent flesh she'd like to feel the blade pierce through, but despite the way she felt about her father, Gretchen forced a soft smile.

"Prince Lovis was just telling me about your new home." Her father wiped his mouth with a cloth napkin. "Very agreeable climate. How joyful you must be." There was a command woven into the words—a firm order filled with the threat of consequence. She knew her father's consequences all too well—had lived long enough to feel the sting of his hand.

"Oh, yes," Gretchen responded, smiling as she straightened in her chair and tucked a wavey black strand behind her ear. "I hear the castle is quite lovely."

Actually, she had heard awful things about the castle and the foul people that lived there. She had heard enough about their harsh treatments through the pipeline of servant gossip—a pipeline she had access to, thanks to Emily, the maid that stood unmoving in the corner of the room awaiting instruction.

Gretchen threw a small smile in her direction, quickly casting her gaze downward to cover the acknowledgment. Emily would see it, though. She always did.

Her father grunted in satisfaction—ever so pleased at the subservient daughter he presented to the court—and her fiancé. She cringed.

Gretchen reached across her plate to retrieve a bread roll. Her corset was constricting, but she cared very little about its confining presence in the face of good food. Glancing at the clock, and noting that she would only be forced to wear it for another twenty minutes anyway. Then she would retire to her room, hoping her guest would appear tonight as he always did. A smile tugged at her lips. This time, the smile was genuine.

"Do you think you should be eating that much?" a shrill voice asked. Lady Kendrick peered down her thin nose in disgust, her pale skin highlighted with the faintest tint of pink on her lips and cheeks. She wasn't an ugly woman; in fact, she was beautiful. However lovely she looked on the outside, her inside appeared like a rotting corpse. Anger welled in Gretchen's gut at the remark. The demure daughter was the act she played to avoid her father's cruelty, but this wasn't her father, and it wasn't like her to roll over in the face of an insult.

She brought the roll to her lips and let the sarcasm seep into her tone. "I'm trying to secure a nice round ass for my dearest fiancé," Gretchen whispered, her back stiff and her smile smug.

Lady Kendrick huffed. Light from the chandelier reflected off her champagne-colored hair. Her sideways glance skimmed Gretchen's form before she spoke. "Don't you think you already have one?" Her tone was tight.

Gretchen looked the young lady up and down—utterly unamused and desperate to feed her a similar treatment. "It seems you don't know much about pleasing a man." She took a bite of the roll before continuing. "One must provide something to hold on to, of course."

The woman's mouth popped open in shock. "That's repulsive," she hissed.

Gretchen peered just past the woman to Lady Kendrick's new husband as he raised the goblet to his lips. "I'm sure Lord Kendrick would have to disagree with you, madam. Wouldn't you, Wentworth?" Her tone was light and unassuming, but the lord still choked on the wine in his cup. His wife swatted him beneath the table, and the entire encounter brought nothing but satisfaction.

Lightly tanned hands from work in the gardens appeared in front of Gretchen, grabbing her cleared plate as she took the final bite of her roll.

"Best watch your tongue, Gretel," the servant whispered so low it was barely audible. She picked up Gretchen's silverware and placed them on the plate. "That one has fangs."

"Well, my fangs have venom," Gretchen whispered, unable to wipe the smile from her face.

Emily chuckled in response, tapping her once on the shoulder before retreating with her dishes.

King Gandrey shifted at the end of the table. "Quite the engagement party." He pushed the emerald velvet-covered chair back and stood. The golden crown atop his head rested on gray cropped hair. "You're all dismissed."

There was no humor on his face—no humor inside him either; not since mother passed. Gretchen shoved the thought down and stood abruptly before running to the doors. She didn't care that she appeared to be escaping her own engagement party. In reality—*she was.*

Prince Lovis was a valuable political alliance, and her father knew it well. Since Gretchen was an only child, there were no other Gandrey's to marry off—leaving her as the sole bargaining tool the king had. He didn't take that lightly, lavishing her with goods and the best education. None of that made up for his cold resignation, or the fiery discipline he unleashed when the ice of that resignation melted.

The gilded hallway leading from the dining room opened into the grand foyer at the front of the castle. Gretchen's brown boots tapped on the marble flooring as she rushed to the steps. Waiting at the bottom of the staircase was Emily. The servant stopped her by placing two hands on her shoulders. Gretchen got the sense that her friend was fighting the urge to shake her.

"That tongue of yours is going to get you in trouble with that awful man." She was referring to Gretchen's new fiancé, Prince Remington Lovis. Emily's gray eyes glittered with delight despite the warning. She found Gretchen's charming personality amusing.

"Nonsense," Gretchen's own eyes lighted, deep blue sparkling in the dim light of the foyer. "That man has done nothing to earn this tongue. It is off-limits to him, so there is no trouble to be had."

She smiled, and a breathy chuckle left Emily's lips as she caught the princess's meaning.

There was a pause before the servant continued. "You'll have a visitor tonight?" she asked, her smile unwavering.

Gretchen's heart picked up in pace. She placed a hand over her ivory dress, fingers toying with the dusty rose embroidered flowers decorating the gown. "I don't know," she admitted, glancing up the stairs. "I hope so. He does know about the engagement."

Emily's features softened; her hands still firmly placed on Gretchen's shoulders. "I'll keep the servants and guards away." Her friend leaned in, her freckled nose wrinkling. "You know," she offered, "just in case."

Sorrow wound around Gretchen's heart like the vines decorating her dress—twisting and confining—squeezing the organ until it nearly ceased beating. She had been sold to a prince of the north. Tonight, she had been presented as a prized mare to the man—the man hadn't even looked at her. Those vines pulled her under, threatening to take over and suffocate the last bit of hope she had for her freedom. "I'm going to miss you." Gretchen choked out the words as pain sliced through her. It was the truth. She didn't know anyone in the north. Her entire life had been here in the Kingdom of Arendria.

"Maybe Lovis will return you," Emily said with a wan smile. It was a useless attempt to comfort, but the sentiment warmed Gretchen, nonetheless. "That tongue, you know." She winked, and it earned her a breathy chuckle.

"I certainly hope it will serve me well in that regard."

Gretchen leaned forward, kissing her friend on the cheek before bounding up the grand staircase.

If she were to have a visitor tonight, he could arrive any moment, and Gretchen wanted to be sure she didn't miss it.

The fire crackling in the hearth warmed the wooden floors of her room. But even the heat of flames wouldn't stand a chance against the warmth spreading through Gretchen's body as she waited—and waited.

Maybe he wouldn't come.

She stood up, walking to the wardrobe in the corner. There would be no servants coming tonight to help her undress, thanks to Emily, but Gretchen didn't mind.

Removing the thick skirts, and finally, the corset, Gretchen began peeling away the layers of her life until she was in only her undergarments, her long chemise, and the boots she hadn't bothered taking off yet. Grabbing the book off her nightstand and making her way over to the fire, Gretchen gave up hope on him coming at all. She leaned down to unlace one of her brown leather boots, pulling her knife out and resting it on the floor next to her book.

"Interesting choice of footwear."

Fear caught hold of her as she jolted upright in her chair, covering as much of herself as possible. Gretchen knew his voice like the scent of the wind through the palace gardens or the feel of a paintbrush in her hand. She hadn't expected him to come—not this late.

She let the fear dissipate, straightening her spine as much as she could. "Hansel." Her gaze was on the fire, but she could feel his presence as he walked towards her—smell the pine and citrus scent coating the room.

"Gretel."

That voice—rich like soil—would be the death of her.

Gretchen turned to behold the figure in the room with her. His black feathered wings stretched high above his shoulders—chest bare, as it usually was. His deeply tanned skin glowed in the light of the fire, causing heat to bloom in her stomach. She was suddenly and painfully aware of her state of undress, but Hansel didn't seem to mind as he casually ran a hand through dark hair. The angel moved, eclipsing the firelight with his massive form, his brown pants hanging low on his hips. For something so holy, he looked like sin itself.

"What are you doing here?" she asked a bit breathlessly.

He smiled, flashing the dimple on his left cheek. Gretel knew this man, knew him from nights spent talking in her room. The first time he visited her had been almost a year ago. On her nineteenth birthday, he had brought her sweets—though she had no idea how he had gotten ahold of them. Hansel was her little secret—the dream she kept tucked away in the night. Arendria had no magic, only old forgotten stories of the Dark Wood beyond the palace. And she was certain the kingdom's people would flee if they beheld an angel—in the flesh—swooping over the city. Maybe he had brought the candies from the heavens above. She had never gotten the chance to ask.

"I thought I'd visit," he finally answered. "How was the—" She swore she saw him wince. "The engagement party," he finished.

Gretchen blew out a breath, relaxing into the chair. "Boring." She leaned back, looking at the gilded ceiling in her room. The intricate carvings and artwork above were far more interesting than her dinner—and she had grown up observing that same art her entire life. "Hopelessly so."

Hansel raised a brow, and when her gaze flicked to him, his arms were still folded across his broad chest. "And the fiancée?" he inquired.

Despite her best attempts to remain indifferent, Gretchen's nose wrinkled and her stomach churned at the thought of the vile man. While she had kept her features schooled in the face of her father, Hansel was different entirely. Since the first time he had flown in through her balcony, he had cut right through her, baring her emotions to himself.

He had come the night her mother died, and she should have been fearful, but his kindness and her desperation for an ear to listen eradicated any fear, even as the angel swept into her room.

Since that night, it was easy to open up to him. There were no judgmental remarks to ever leave Hansel's lips, only the sweetness of all the stories they had shared. If her fate had been different–her upbringing–she would have liked to marry for love.

Even so, where Hansel was concerned, it was impossible. The heavens held strict rules against it. Hansel has spoken of an angel, long ago being cast from heaven for falling in love with a mortal. It had been gory–brutal. The details of the story stained her mind like the bloodied wings Hansel had described.

"He was repulsive," she finally answered honestly.

"Nonsense." Hansel waved a hand through the air. "I hear he's quite handsome. Prince…." His fingers snapped a few times as if he struggled to recall the prince's name. Gretchen could see from the way one corner of his mouth turned upward that he did, in fact, remember. It had only been a few nights ago that she told him, and she hadn't stopped babbling about the dreaded fiancée since.

"What *was* his name, Gretel? Do help me?"

Gretel peered at him through her lashes, fighting the smile that wanted to break free. Her blue eyes shone in the dim lights, but there was nothing truthful nor innocent about it. "I can't for the life of me remember."

The deep brown of his eyes sparkled, that wicked grin breaking loose and freeing the dimple that made her knees weak. His glittering eyes narrowed. "You liar."

"When have I ever lied to you?" she asked, standing from her chair and kicking her boots off her feet.

Standing in Hansel's presence reminded her of the time they had spent together–the laughter they had shared. Her chest ached at the reality of their situation. She could never be with him, but would instead, be shackled to the prince whose name simply could not be recalled. Fighting the sadness, Gretchen smiled at Hansel, daring him to tell her she was wrong.

He laughed, a deep sound."You've lied to me plenty of times."

"Name one," she challenged.

Hansel held up his hand, rings decorating his fingers and reflecting the firelight as he listed every lie she had ever told him. "You lied that first night when I asked you if you were sad."

"It was a dumb question."

He held up another finger. "You lied about your paintings and told me they were awful."

"Because they are," she asserted. "Art is subjective."

He didn't stop. "You implied that your father hadn't laid a hand on you weeks ago when you told him to go to hell. It was immediately after he presented his plan for your engagement." Hansel leaned in, and Gretchen could smell the mint on his breath. It sent her stomach into knots. "That one infuriated me the most."

"Surely that is all," she said, but the sound was nearly a whisper.

"And you lied to me last night." His eyes hardened, boring into her from where he stood. She didn't need to ask him to elaborate because she knew the exact lie he was speaking about. This one, however, she would deny. Gretchen would present the falsehood as truth until she believed it herself.

"I meant what I said," she asserted. "I have come to terms with my marriage. I will be able to find happiness in the arrangement since I have no romantic feelings to compare anything to."

Something flashed across his face. "You lied," he whispered.

"I didn't."

"You have no romantic feelings to compare to?"

Gretchen couldn't tell if it was truly a question. It felt more like an accusation. She opened her mouth to confirm her statement, but her lips snapped shut. Her heart was pounding an erratic rhythm in her chest. Whatever he was implying–they could never have it.

She knew exactly what it meant for them—for her. This was one truth she could not confess. It was dangerous and cruel, but the feelings were there regardless. She didn't remember the exact moment it had happened. Through many of her sleepless nights, they had built a friendship–a friendship and more. Those feelings needed to remain hidden.

At least—hidden as best she could manage.

"Answer me."

Gretchen hadn't realized how long she had been staring at him, lost in thought, and tracing his features with her gaze. She longed to memorize him entirely. There would be no forgetting him when the time came to move to the north, and that thought sent pain ripping through her chest.

If she had been born to a different fate, maybe she could have had something different. Maybe she could have had love.

"It's forbidden," she whispered. It was the only answer she could offer him.

Hansel stepped forward, practically shaking. "It is." His voice was low as he crowded her space.

Gretchen nodded slowly; blue eyes wide.

"But if it weren't," he continued, "what truth would you tell me?"

During that night, the night he had told her the story of the angel Julien, Gretchen had sworn that she would prevent herself from feeling for Hansel, though she certainly knew it would be a challenge, for feelings already existed.

The angel's wings had been broken and bleeding in the story. He was cast from heaven for taking a human lover–poisoned with foxglove and left to die by a river. *The river ran red.* Hansel had said *long after the angel stopped breathing.*

Gretchen's heart clenched as she looked up into Hansel's eyes. After all the time they'd spent together—the secrets they'd shared—she couldn't imagine giving him that same fate.

"I can't—" She fought for words. "I can't tell you."

"Why not?"

"I—" A tear dripped down her cheek slowly, staining her skin with the depth of her emotion.

Hansel traced the moisture with his gaze until he brought his hand up to the side of her face, brushing the sorrow from her flesh.

"It is possible," she began slowly. "That I've thought about you more than I care to admit." She reached up to place her own hand over his. "That when you touch me like this, my entire world implodes, and I cannot think straight." Gretchen bit her lip, nerves racing through her veins. "If it weren't forbidden, I may be tempted to confess that I feel for you." Her gaze met his once more. "Deeply."

"And if we had a choice?" he asked, his thumb gently tracing circles over her cheek.

"If we had a choice," she began, "then I would run."

"Where would you run to, Gretel?"

She took a deep breath, closing her eyes and leaning into his touch. "Anywhere with you," she whispered. "I wish I had a choice in my own fate."

"For one night, maybe you can."

Hansel didn't hesitate. As his lips pressed to hers, memories flung like weapons in her mind, tearing at the seams of her resolve. If she were to choose one thing for herself, this would be the last time she could do it.

The room grew warmer–his motions hungrier, and Gretchen couldn't help but encourage him to keep going. Not when she knew the life that was about to be taken from her.

Rules be damned, Hansel laid her gently on the bed, kissing away her tears as he showed her a glimpse of what they would never have–the life she so desperately wanted. She gave him everything, her body–her soul, confident that they would soon part ways by morning.

Sleep was a fleeting ghost.

Gretchen stirred beneath the lush, golden-colored blankets as the fire dimmed in the hearth. She reached a hand to the other side of her bed, feeling the place where Hansel had slept before exiting by the balcony. Those balcony doors were still open, a gentle breeze coming in with the looming dawn. Stars still flickered in the night sky beyond the gardens, but soon the sun would rise to replace the night and leave her with only the memories of his hands sliding over her skin.

Looking out the window, Gretchen imagined Hansel up in the heavens, tending to his duties in a palace not much different from her own.

There was another world up there in the sky—one with kings, queens, and magic—nothing like the heavens she had heard about as a child. It was Hansel's stories that taught her of the secret place where other kingdoms reside. And as she trailed her finger over her bottom lip, still swollen from kissing, she imagined a reality where he could have taken her there to escape the doomed marriage set to become her reality in a few days.

Those kinds of stories were for fairytales, though.

Sadness twisted in her gut at the parting look he gave her before stretching his dark, feathered wings and flying out the window. Gretchen knew then that it would be the final time she saw him. She would become a wife, but maybe the choice she made for herself in the night and the depths of her affection would work as a salve, healing the hatred she harbored for Prince Lovis.

Sighing, she threw off the blankets and floated to the balcony to gaze at the night sky. Millions of stars decorated the navy expanse. Gretchen thought that if she squinted hard enough, she could peer into one of the lights, and see black wings stretched wide. No such thing occurred—no matter how hard she strained to see him—he was gone.

Light glittered from one of the pinpoints, flickering and falling fast. Gretchen gasped, watching as the shooting star descended rapidly. "Wishes are for children," she whispered, but it didn't stop her heart from pleading for a different fate.

The star continued falling, burning hot and bright. Her brows furrowed as it closed the distance between the sky and the earth, becoming larger and falling faster.

Her heart was beating a wild rhythm in her chest when she realized that the star wouldn't stop until it landed in the gardens just outside the palace. Placing her hands on the stone balcony's edge, Gretchen leaned out to get a closer look. Fear was racing through her veins, her hands trembling.

The light flared and the wind whipped her unbound hair, ruffling the thin chemise she wore—the only piece of clothing she had donned after Hansel left.

It wasn't until Gretchen saw black wings that she realized the light wasn't a star at all.

Without thinking, she ran back into the bedroom, pulling on brown pants and shoving her chemise into them. She laced up her boots, tucking her knife into the side, and ran back to the balcony to throw her leg over the ledge.

Thick vines tangled up the stone castle, creating the perfect ladder for her descent. Thorns scratched and stabbed into her hands, catching on her chemise and staining the fabric with small flecks of blood. It didn't stop her before she jumped to the ground and sprinted through the gardens to the angel lying next to a bush of roses.

"Hansel!" she yelled, gasping for breath.

Her boots kicked up gravel on the garden path, pounding the earth until she was close enough to kneel and shake him. One wing was torn, fresh blood pooling onto the ground. Gretchen wiped her cheeks frantically. Her hands trembled as she carefully tried to turn him over to see his face. Hansel groaned when his injured wing shifted.

"I'm sorry," she whispered. "I'm so, so sorry."

Sobs threatened to break free. He was bleeding and broken—an ancient story come to life. It was her reckless actions that caused this—her selfish entitlement.

"Foxglove." Hansel's voice was gravelly and low, straining to fight whatever pain he was in. "Foxglove," he repeated.

Her brows furrowed. "Foxglove?" She didn't know what he was saying.

Hansel leaned over before retching. His vomit mixed with his crimson blood.

Something clicked in her brain, washing away the hazy confusion there just moments before. "Foxglove!" she yelled. Gretchen touched his cheek as his eyes met hers. "I'll be back," she swore. "I promise."

Running through the palace to the servants' quarters, Gretchen couldn't calm her stirring thoughts. There was no room for guilt here—no room for sadness. She could only focus on each footstep propelling her down the long hallway.

"Emily!" She was pounding on the door, heedless of the other staff sleeping.

When the door clicked open, Emily was tying an old robe around her waist and yawning. Her eyes widened when she discovered Gretchen's distress.

"Gretel," she asked, "What is it?" Her voice was low as she stepped into the hallway.

"Foxglove. Do we have the antidote in the healer's chamber? Is it still there?"

Gretchen closed the wooden door behind her. Her voice was still hushed, seriousness burning in her gaze. "Has someone been poisoned?" she questioned.

"Hansel. He—" Gretchen couldn't finish the sentence. She had to keep herself steady and focus her mind on a solution.

Emily seemed to understand. "Follow me."

The servant moved quickly, rushing down the spiral staircase into the healer's chambers beneath the castle. When they passed the stone archway, they were greeted with shelves of herbs inside various jars. The old room was damp and disorganized, with papers scattered along one wooden table at the center.

Emily began rifling through the shelves, inspecting labels, and observing the contents of each jar. While she moved, Gretel searched for the kit the palace healer used for stitching wounds. She found it beneath the table in a small metal box and grabbed it. She didn't know much about stitching wings, but doubting her abilities wasn't an option.

"If it's foxglove, we should have the antidote somewhere. Digoxin—" Emily paused for a moment. "Something like that. There was more to it." As she scoured the shelves, Gretchen clenched her hands. Her nails dug into her palms, but the pain provided something to think of aside from the bleeding angel in the garden.

"It's my fault," she whispered, barely able to combat the guilt creeping steadily.

"Oh, hush," Emily chided. "Save whatever you're feeling for another time." Her eyes lit up at the small vial in her hand. "Here." She looked back at the shelf, taking a handful of vials and shoving them in her pockets before turning to the exit. Gretchen followed her out of the palace and back into the garden where Hansel was still lying on the ground, covered in his own vomit and blood.

Emily cursed under her breath before kneeling to administer one of the vials. "He should feel better in the next hour but will need more." When she finished, she stood up, her expression pained. "Gretel, how will you hide a sick *angel* in the palace? Especially with your wedding so soon. We don't live in the Dark Wood. You could hardly explain his presence."

"I know, I—"

She needed to think. There had been very little thinking after the moment Emily had opened the door.

Gretchen looked out past the gardens to the stables, her breath coming out in harsh pants as ideas swarmed in her mind before taking shape. *We don't live in the Dark Wood.*

"We'll leave," she presented.

"What?" Emily's jaw hung open; a crease etched on her brow when Gretchen looked at her closest friend. If she stayed, she would lose everything and gain Lovis. If she left—she at least had Hansel.

"I will get my horse, and we can leave. Go off into the Dark Wood and just—*leave.*"

"And once you're in the forest where the kingdom has little control? Then where will you go"

Gretchen looked back at Hansel, his eyes closed, thick lashes kissing his cheeks. "I don't know," she whispered. "We will go somewhere far from Lovis and my father."

When she looked back at Emily again, she could tell her friend understood her seriousness. Gretchen may have been her father's object to pass as a political bargaining tool, but she was stubborn—willful. The silence stretched on.

"You're sure?" Emily's eyes blazed, and Gretchen clutched the small box she had tighter. She would get him onto a horse and take him somewhere to stitch up his wing.

There was no time to ponder the consequences of her actions. Gretchen knew two things with great certainty. The first was that she loved Hansel—it had happened slowly—in the same way the sun rises in the morning. The second was that every time she thought of the life awaiting her and that horrid prince sleeping somewhere in the palace, she was filled with burning rage. The knife in her boot burned her flesh, calling to the hatred she felt for the man she had been sold to—the hatred for her own father.

The future she had waiting for her was nothing of value. It was manipulation and courtiers, gowns, and artificial smiles. One could only last so long under such conditions.

Gretchen knew her answer—she owed it to Hansel. This was her fault anyway.

"I'm sure," she declared.

Morning light drifted through the leafy green of the trees as dew coated the brush below, giving way to a calmness that contrasted the last five hours of Gretchen's life.

She rode through the forest with Hansel behind her, leaning against her and fading in and out of consciousness. She had been fearful that his hulking form would topple to the ground, but so far, he had kept himself upright, his arms wrapped around her waist—clinging.

She had stopped early on to stitch the wound on his wing, hoping the rough sewing would be enough for him to heal. She knew the basics of first aid but hadn't a clue about wings. It wasn't every day someone stitched up the wings of an angel. Even so, as the black horse huffed, hot breath mixing with the golden morning light, she couldn't stop her mind from drifting back to that moment—from hearing his screams in her ear.

The worst part was now that she had time to think about her decision, fear finally worked through her veins and settled like lead in her gut. While she was entirely sure of her feelings for Hansel, he had made his choices with the thought of her leaving. What if running away with him—what if taking him into the Dark Wood was a mistake? Was she forcing herself upon him?

The sound of a stream carving its path through the trees drew her attention, and she spurred her mount toward the sound, hoping to find a safe place to rest and combat the stinging in her eyes. Whether that was from tears or lack of sleep, she did not know. But she sincerely hated to cry.

"Hansel," she whispered, though she wasn't sure why. Maybe it was the peace of the misty forest she couldn't bear to disturb—or maybe she was just tired. "Hansel, you have to get up. I cannot get you off this horse by myself."

He stirred behind her, a groan leaving his lips as he straightened. She would need to give him another vial soon to continue combatting the poison. At least the vomiting had ceased.

"Can you get down?" she asked.

"You smell like hope." He slouched against her with his chin resting on her shoulder. Hot breath ruffled her hair when he spoke. "Like lemongrass and oranges. It almost makes me believe the world isn't falling apart."

She couldn't dwell on what he said—deciding to shove feelings aside before throwing her leg over the horse's neck and dismounting. Gretchen fought to steady Hansel and helped him slide off the back of the horse.

He swayed on his feet before crumpling to the ground. Gretchen did her best to help him fall gently. She was no fragile woman, strong beneath soft curves, but his sheer size alone was enough to have her grunting against the force.

After untacking the horse and eating some of the food Emily had packed, Gretchen gave Hansel another vial—deciding to rest her head on a log beside the stream.

Sleep was no longer a ghost—but a trustworthy companion joining her when she felt alone.

When she awoke, Hansel was still sleeping soundly in the dirt. His breathing had steadied—bare chest rising and falling gently.

Gretchen shucked off her boots and clothes, folding them on a rock by the stream. The cold-water bit at her skin and stung as it washed over the cuts littering her body. For a moment, she thought about how quickly she climbed down the side of that castle—headless of the thorns stabbing her flesh. It had been worth it. Looking back at Hansel, she wondered if he would believe it was worth it too.

After scrubbing her body clean, Gretchen pulled on her pants, boots, and white chemise. Her hair was damp against the thin fabric while she looked deeper into the Dark Wood. She wasn't sure how exactly it had gotten its name. In the light of the early afternoon, the wood didn't seem dark at all. When she was a child, her mother used to tell her stories of the forest outside of the castle. It seemed to stretch on forever—filled with magic and creatures. Those were just stories, though.

Mostly.

"Gretel?"

Gretchen stood quickly, spinning to see Hansel sitting up on the ground. His skin was less pale, eyes brighter than before.

"Here." She flipped open the leather of their pack, grabbing the vile shoved at the bottom and handing it to him. "This should be the last one." He took it from her, fingers warm against her skin. "Drink."

A soft whinny danced through the trees as their mount found a new patch of grass to graze on. She watched Hansel bring the vial to his lips slowly, his eyes never leaving hers. The movement of his throat when he swallowed sent heat to her cheeks. She coughed, turning to get food out of the pack as well. Her stomach was hollow, and she was certain his had to be, after all his retching.

"This food won't last us long." Gretchen handed him a piece of bread. "We will have enough for a few days. I don't know much about the Dark Wood aside from the stories my mother told. I know people live within—somewhere. I'm sure we could find someplace to stay."

Hansel placed his hands on the dirt, moving to stand. He grunted, and his wings shifted at his back. That was another problem when it came to finding somewhere, even within the wood. Someone could see his wings—know that he wasn't human. Though the chances of that being a problem were slim based on the stories.

"Please don't," she murmured, moving swiftly to help him rise.

His deep brown eyes bore into hers. In them were all the memories of their late-night talks—the things they had shared. Despite it all, that seed of doubt began to grow. What if he didn't want this? Would he be angry that she ran away with him? She couldn't bear to marry that man.

Hansel was still looking at her, making her thoughts spin faster.

"What?" she whispered.

His gaze flicked over her, assessing and mapping out her features. He had seen it all before. That was why they were in this situation. But it still had her gut churning. "I don't regret my choice if that's what you're wondering. I also saved your life, and I understand if you don't want to be with me forever. That was free of charge, of course." She smiled, drawing on the familiar ease of banter. Her smile soon dropped. "I don't know, I saw an opportunity to leave. I wasn't thinking."

"Gretel." His tone had softened, a warm thumb pressing to her chin gently and forcing her gaze to his once more. She didn't know what he would say.

It almost makes me believe the world isn't falling apart.

One side of his mouth turned up, revealing the dimple on his cheek. "Your shirt is soaked through."

Looking down, she noted that her wet hair had bled through her chemise, making it entirely see-through. She huffed a laugh and tried to cover her body with her arms.

Hansel swayed a bit before running a knuckle along her jawline. She closed her eyes at the touch.

"Gods above," he breathed, "you're beautiful. If I weren't so injured—"

Her eyes shot open, warmth washing over her body before it was soon replaced with frustration. "That's all you have to say?"

"No," he whispered, bringing his lips to her forehead and kissing her gently before rearing back. "Tell me your worries."

It was something she had done before on the darkest of nights. Gretchen had confessed all her thoughts to Hansel, revealing herself one story at a time. It had been easy then, but now, with him standing before her, the doubt seemed to seal her lips closed. The question of *what if* was too much to carry.

He pressed on. "Tell me what you're worried about, and I will work to calm your fears."

Gretchen couldn't resist the invitation. She had to know if what she had done was a mistake.

"Is this—" She nodded toward the stitched wing at his back. "As well as the poison . . . Is it because of me?"

His expression darkened, brows lowering. Hansel didn't look away and didn't move his hands from where they now rested on her shoulders. "I do not blame you," he began. "None of this is your fault, Gretel. I may have been cast out because of what we did, but it was *my* choice." He licked his lip. "I wanted it."

"And do you wish to be with me?" she asked, hating how desperate she sounded. This was the question haunting her as they paraded through the forest. She abandoned her life in an instant. Where would she go if he refused her?

Hansel leaned in, placing another gentle kiss on her lips. They were warm against hers, sparking something hot inside her. When they broke apart, he whispered, "For as long as you'll have me."

Relief washed over her. It was sweet like warm tea and honey on a rainy evening. A final question danced on her tongue.

"Do you love me?" Embarrassment washed over her.

Hansel's hand rose to cup her cheek, the dimple popping out with his smile. His eyes were warm.

"Now that," he began, tilting her head up slightly. "I thought *that* was obvious."

Hansel had fully healed, insisting that he guide them through the Dark Wood the following morning—claiming there were places deep within the forest where they could go. Long forgotten towns, witches, and more. Those who wouldn't balk at his appearance.

Gone was the golden light filtering through the trees at the beginning of their journey. Instead, they were surrounded by a gray mist that seemed to coat the limbs in sorrow. Gretchen realized now, how the forest had gotten its name. The Dark Wood was somewhat of a mystery—a place for stories and tales. It stretched from the north of the palace onward, and she knew very little about its inhabitants. Gretchen's father seemed to leave the forest alone when it came to his rule. With the eerie feeling that overtook her, she began to wonder what they would face.

"You're certain?" Gretchen questioned. She could feel Hansel at her back, one arm wrapped around her waist to hold her steady atop their horse. His other hand clutched the reins. "You're certain there will be places that will think nothing of what you are?"

"What I am?" He was smiling now, his lips so close she could feel it. "You make me sound like a monster." Hansel huffed a laugh, his breath causing her to shiver as he pulled her closer. "I understand your concern, Gretel, but honestly. Is my appearance that frightening? You didn't seem to mind just over a day ago."

Gretchen allowed herself to lean back against him, her head resting on his solid chest. "The wings are a bit much. Difficult to position when I place you on your back." A smug smirk appeared on her face as she closed her eyes, allowing the gentle motion to quiet her mind. Hansel chuckled before the silence stretched between them, begging her to lose herself to sleep.

When she awoke again, the light had faded through the trees. Her brow furrowed.

"It's only early in the afternoon," Hansel said as if reading her thoughts. "There's a reason they call it the Dark Wood. I'm sure we are getting close to something."

"And how do you know?"

Hansel leaned in, his lips ghosting over the shell of her ear when he whispered. "Magic."

Their horse stopped, hoof scraping against the ground as hot breath exited his nostrils. Gretchen felt a sudden spike of fear. The tired branches stretched out above her, black and looming like death.

Gretchen cleared her throat. "It's hard to believe we are headed into anything good, Hansel."

"Look."

Gretchen looked to where he was pointing and saw an opening beyond the trees. In the clearing was a white cottage wrapped in ivy with thick smoke billowing from the chimney. A massive greenhouse sat to the left with misty glass and abundant life pressing against each window. Just beyond the cottage was a pool with pale blue water shimmering beneath the warm glow of the now vibrant sun.

"How does this place exist," she breathed. "Everything was so dark just moments ago."

"I told you." Hansel swung out of the saddle, bringing the reins over the horse's head to lead him forward. "Magic."

"So, what you're saying—" Gretchen looked back to the greenhouse, her eyes fixed on the massive structure. Something like fear gripped her, but she ignored it. "You're saying that this place won't mind the bird wings."

"They are not *bird* wings," he chided. "But no, I don't believe they will notice at all. Look there." Hansel nodded to the wooden door at the center of the building. Carved on the door was a five-pointed star, a circle cast around it. "Seems we've stumbled upon a witch's cottage."

"A witch?"

The horse halted, and Gretchen dismounted, stretching to will the stiffness out of her limbs.

"I suppose so," Hansel answered. "There's also a sign that indicates a bed and breakfast."

Gretchen nodded, following him up to the door and leaving their horse to graze on the grass of the small meadow. The sun felt warm against her skin and made the feathers on Hansel's black wings shine silver when they caught the right angle.

The stone steps leading to the door were jagged and worn, causing Gretchen to take care not to stumble. For a moment, she feared what would happen as soon as the door opened. Where once her life was carefully constructed around her future marriage to prince Lovis, she was now uncertain and floating. Like seeds scattered to the wind, Gretchen was forced to now trust the hospitality of a stranger—a witch of the Dark Wood. It never occurred to her that deciding a path for herself, even in haste, could feel so hopelessly out of control.

Hansel's hand rested on her lower back, steadying her as he turned to knock on the door. Stories were woven on the wooden surface, spoken with every stray mark or splatter of mud. It wasn't the stories that caught Gretchen's eye, but the five-pointed star etched just above the center—a reminder that she was no longer in the world of court politics and strict lessons.

Before he had a chance to knock, the door swung open to reveal a tall young woman, willowy in her frame. Her white hair cascaded down her back in an intricate braid decorated with dark black pearls and woven with green ribbon. Her crystal blue eyes regarded the new guests as she smoothed down the long black dress before tightening the moss-colored sweater around her waist.

There was something unsettling in her smile. Her pink lips stretched across pale skin like a strained piece of thread waiting to snap.

"Welcome." Her voice had a musical quality to it, as if it were designed to lure sailors from their ships and drown them in the ocean.

Gretchen shifted, leaning into Hansel and allowing him to speak on their behalf. "We saw the sign," Hansel stated. "We were hoping for a place to stay."

"Of course." The witch turned on her heel, moving into the antiquated home. Dried herbs hung from the ceiling, and smoke danced through the air, making the entryway appear dusty. Hansel and Gretel were left to stand on the wooden floor as the witch disappeared.

"You're sure about this?" Gretel's brows were furrowed, her heart fluttering in her chest. She could feel the heavy weight of her knife tucked safely in her boot. Even so, Gretel knew that angels descended from the heavens and conversed with princesses. She now knew witches lived deep within the Dark Wood. What was a knife in the face of magic she didn't understand?

Hansel grunted. "I'm not certain about anything." He turned to look at her, brown eyes shining with understanding. "Say the word, Gretel." His voice was low. "Say the word, and we will be gone."

It was her fault. Even after what he had said in the woods, she couldn't stop the guilt that threatened her. Straightening her spine, Gretchen nodded once, hoping that her expression didn't give away her fear. "No, we can stay. You need to rest more. We can't be wandering through the forest forever."

The rattling of steaming teacups on a tray drew Gretchen's eyes back to the pale woman appearing from the hallway.

"Follow me," the witch said. "We will discuss the terms of your stay."

To the left was a parlor outfitted with shades of red and gold. A fire crackled in the hearth. Gretchen sat next to Hansel on the couch, the witch in the chair across from them pouring tea into cups now resting on a short wooden table.

"We don't get many visitors here in the Dark Wood." The witch sat back, smiling behind the pale blue cup. "Please." She gestured to the tray. "Help yourselves."

Her hospitality helped settle Gretchen's nerves.

Hansel's wings draped over the side of the couch, forcing him to sit at an angle. Gretchen noticed the dark circles hanging beneath his eyes, and the sallow complexion of his skin. The day's journey must have worn on him.

"I'm sure visitors are quite rare," Gretchen spoke. She allowed the courtly mask to overtake her face—the one she used to appease her father. "We would appreciate a room for the night. Should you have one available, of course."

"Of course."

"The terms?" Hansel asked.

"Ah, yes." She set the teacup down on the tray. "We have a pond perfect for swimming. Breakfast will be provided in the morning. There is also our greenhouse. I highly encourage you to take a walk-through and look at the artwork. It's quite magical." Her blue eyes were almost wistful. "Might I ask where you're coming from? It's not often I see a woman traveling through the Dark Wood accompanied by an angel." One brow flicked up. "An angel who appears to be injured."

"It was an accident," Hansel interceded.

"I'm sure." The witch didn't look convinced. She regarded Hansel carefully with her cold presence. Ice coated Gretchen's veins. "An accident of love?" she concluded. "How romantic."

Gretchen cleared her throat and shifted uncomfortably. "We would love to see the greenhouse."

That caused an almost predatory smile to stretch across the woman's face. "Yes. I will get your rooms ready." The witch stood up, leaving the tray on the table. "The angel and his lover can take their tea, then I encourage that walk."

"What shall we call you?" Gretchen asked.

"Eira."

With that, Eira exited the room.

Hansel's hand found its way to Gretel's, and she was thankful for the warmth of his touch.

"The Dark Wood is filled with magic, Gretel. Magic, good or bad, can be unsettling." His voice rumbled in his chest, low and sweet—utterly familiar.

Gretchen closed her eyes and nodded. "I would like to get some air."

"How about that walk?"

The door to the greenhouse creaked when it opened, letting the warm air free from its confinement.

Gretchen breathed in the scent of stone and earth as she followed Hansel's tall frame onto a path that wound through the entirety of the structure. Butterflies fluttered through the air—dancing through the light transformed from gold to green as it filtered through the leaves. Water trickled from a nearby fountain, and Gretchen's boots scuffed on the gravel path as she made her way to observe the waters.

Sitting in the presence of Eira had been unsettling. Thinking back on the last few days made Gretchen's stomach feel as if it were filled with lead and that heavy feeling followed her into the greenhouse. Stopping short of the stone fountain, Gretchen watched the water flow from the mouth of a small child throwing crumbs from a basket in her hand. While the child's expression wasn't anything but neutral, there was something grisly about the artwork.

Gretchen shook off the feeling and tried to focus on something more uplifting. Hansel was alive, and Prince Lovis was left without a bride. The second part brought a smug satisfaction, much like making Lady Kendrick squirm at dinner.

"Do you regret your decision?" Hansel's voice came from behind her as he settled in near the fountain. She didn't turn, but she could feel the heat radiating from his body. He was standing close, but there was some emotion stirring in his words. Uncertainty?

Gretchen didn't turn to face him. "No, of course not." If there was one thing she was sure of, it was her decision to leave the palace behind. Hansel had eased her fears, but she realized she had done little to ease his. "I didn't know this existed out here." The green limbs stretched above her, overgrown and smothered behind confining glass. It felt much like the palace where she grew up. "I've spent my entire life preparing to rule a kingdom, and I had no idea witches existed in the Dark Wood." She turned, finally facing the angel in the room. His chest was still bare, wings tucked in to make room for his large form. "I suppose I wasn't really being taught to rule though. Just to be married. This entire place—you—it is all like an old fairytale from a book."

Hansel pressed his lips together before speaking. "You know most fairytales have tragic endings?"

It wasn't comforting. In fact, it reminded her of the story of Julien. Even so, Hansel hadn't died. They were together. "Do you believe *we* will have a tragic ending?" Gretchen took a step forward and looked up into his brown eyes as if she were looking for the true answer to the question. It wasn't there. "Just days ago, I was putting Lady Kendrick in her place over a ridiculous dinner roll and picturing dragging my knife across a prince's throat."

Hansel smiled; his eyebrows raised.

"Don't act so surprised," she chided. "I was so confident, and even though my future was not my own, I didn't feel what I'm feeling now."

"What are you feeling?" he questioned, running a knuckle to trace the shape of her jaw.

Gretchen didn't want to admit it. "Hansel," she began, "I'm afraid."

Hansel shifted closer until she could feel his lips just hovering before her own. Her eyes were closed as she relished in his closeness. Mere days ago, he was on death's door.

"Most people are," he whispered before placing a gentle kiss on her lips.

When she pulled back, she opened her eyes, his gaze capturing hers. "And what about angels? What about those in the kingdom above? Do they experience fear?"

Was he afraid in the same way she was, or was Hansel high above such mortal emotions?

"I was fearful when I fell from the sky." One corner of his mouth quirked up, but it quickly fell. "However, I was not nearly as fearful as I was the night

I met you. You remember. The night you were crying in your rooms. That was truly terrifying."

Gretchen huffed a laugh. "You know my mother had just passed."

His thumb glided across her jaw until his fingers twinned in her hair. "And for that, I am truly sorry." His smile had fallen, eyes flashing with something like pain.

It made her uncomfortable.

"Right," she said. "Eira. Do you trust her?"

That earned her a different expression—one dark and pensive. "Most certainly not. Witches can be dangerous—hungry." His hand left her cheek, but he remained close. "However, we have few options as it stands. We can spend a night or two here with the gold Emily added to your pack. When we feel up to it, we can leave."

That lead feeling returned to her stomach. "Where will we go?"

"Anywhere you like. We can make ourselves a home."

They walked the paths of the greenhouse, looking at the unsettling artwork. Eira must have been interested in sculpture because hidden behind much of the greenery were carvings of people—all beautiful and ominous.

Stopping at the statue by the exit, Gretchen mapped out the features of a small boy, much like the girl carved into the fountain.

"They're beautiful," she mused. "If not a bit disconcerting."

Hansel huffed a laugh, weaving his fingers through hers. "They're not nearly as beautiful as you."

When Gretchen looked up, he was staring down at her. For the briefest moment, it felt as if all would be well. She didn't fear the uncertainty of what they were doing. At that moment, surrounded by stone and earth, Gretchen felt a calm settle into her bones. It was a feeling she longed to put a name to.

It was the feeling of hope.

When Gretchen walked down the creaking wooden staircase of the bed and breakfast, she trailed one finger along the splintered railing and wondered when the future would bring them.

She had spent the night beside Hansel, encased in his embrace while his wings provided a cocoon around them, blocking the rest of the world out. Gretchen listened to his steady breathing as tears trickled down her cheeks, staining the borrowed sheets below. She hated her own sorrow.

When the scent of eggs and sausage met her at the base of the stairs, Gretchen was able to push aside the discomfort she felt at the beauty of the witch's greenhouse and finally allowed her mind to settle. Hansel was the first person she saw.

"You didn't wake me up," Gretchen said as she walked into the quaint dining room. Three places around the wooden table were set. Dried flowers rested in a vase at the center with small purple petals littering the table from where they had broken and crumbled.

"I didn't want to disturb you," Hansel said, rising to pull her hair out for her.

Gretchen sat in her chair as Hanel moved to his own, gripping her hand beneath the table. When Eira came in, her willowy form gliding through the room, she took her seat opposite them. The woman's back was stiff, a chilled expression on her face.

"Eira," Gretchen spoke softly. "Might there be a place where we could purchase some clothes? I'm unfamiliar with much of the Dark Wood. I'm not entirely sure what is out here."

Eira's cold gaze met hers, sending ice through Gretchen's veins. Hansel's expression couldn't be read, but there was tension through his shoulders.

"Do you plan to leave today?"

"That is a possibility." Gretchen offered a warm smile that didn't meet her eyes, calling on the false expression she frequently used at court.

"Of course," Eira nodded once before picking up her fork to poke at the breakfast she had prepared. "Might you join me for a walk at the pond after breakfast?" she asked. "I can then point you in the proper direction."

Hansel squeezed Gretchen's hand once under the table, revealing nothing. "We would enjoy that," he said.

Stepping out into the meadow after breakfast quenched a deep need for fresh air Gretchen hadn't realized she needed. While she was thankful for a place to stay, and the food, something was suffocating about Eira's home.

She walked hand-in-hand with Hansel to where Eira was waiting for them by the water.

"Walk with me," the woman said.

There was something quite fascinating about the owner of the bed and breakfast. While she was cold and stiff, something about her called to Gretchen, and as they walked through damp grass, the powerful pull of whatever this woman was threatening to drag them under.

Hansel's eyes were fixed at Eira's back, and something in his glazed expression made Gretchen believe he was taken by the same spell.

"You saw the greenhouse?" Eira began.

"It was beautiful," Gretchen responded.

Hansel cleared his throat. "The statues. Who is the artist?"

Eira's icy eyes peered back over her shoulder. "Ah," she said, "The statues." Golden light reflected off the pale blue water of the pond, glistening and utterly entrancing. "I made them."

"You made them?" Gretchen asked. There was a wistfulness to her tone, something that spoke of her state of mind in the woman's presence. She desperately wanted to touch the water.

"Witches are capable of beautiful works of art." Eira turned to face them, ceasing her movement around the pond. "You all plan to leave today, yes. Before you do, I encourage you to take a swim."

"In the pond?" Hansel questioned. Gretchen sensed no trepidation in his tone, and he, like herself, was staring longingly at the body of water.

Eira smiled. It was the first time Gretchen had seen this expression. Sharp and calculated, there was something off about the way the witch grinned. Even so, they could not look away from her.

"You said you were a witch?" Gretchen knew this from before. Her thoughts were bent and crooked, and she could not straighten them out.

"Yes. My statues wouldn't be quite as beautiful or unique if I weren't." She licked her lips once, a hungry expression overtaking her face. *Witches can be dangerous--hungry.* She could feel the warning bells ringing back behind whatever fog had formed in her mind, but she was helpless to react.

"How did you make them?" Hansel asked, eyes bright.

"They are dipped in the waters here." Eira gestured to the pale blue glass—still and waiting. "Take a swim, you two."

There were no thoughts in this place, nothing to stop Gretchen from shedding her clothes and boots and moving to the enticing water beyond. Hansel followed, trailing behind her.

As her toes touched the surface, a sudden panic washed over her. Something was wrong. This place was wrong.

Gretchen tried to turn, but a small hand touched her back, keeping her pinned in place. Hansel was next to her with a wild expression in his eyes. In the depths of his gaze, Gretchen saw something like realization and then regret.

Eira leaned in between them, her soft whisper sending chills down Gretchen's spine. "The fallen angel and his lover," she whispered. "What a beautiful work of art."

The last thing Gretchen remembered was being shoved beneath the surface of the water.

And then there was nothing.

Green light filtered through the glass, casting emerald over the entire greenhouse as Eira stood with her feet planted on the gravel path.

She raised a cup to her lips, drinking the sweetened jasmine tea she had brought with her during her afternoon walk around the grounds.

A small bead of sweat trailed down her back—an irritating but necessary symbol of her hard work. She wasn't fond of heavy lifting.

Before her, stood the image of a stone woman with soft curves and hope glistening through her stony gaze. Behind her, with his arms wrapped protectively around her figure, was an angel. His wings were wrapped around them—as if he were shielding the one he loved in their last moments.

"Pity," Eira whispered, a thin smile stretching across her sharp face.

She turned around, taking careful steps out of the greenhouse and toward her home, ready for her magic to guide the next unfortunate group to her doorstep.

"BEHIND HER, WITH HIS ARMS WRAPPED PROTECTIVELY AROUND HER FIGURE, WAS AN ANGEL."

About the Authors and Illustrator

NagmerrieCircus:

NagmerrieCircus is a freelance Illustrator and Character Designer based in Italy.

With a style characterized by strong contrasts and vivid colors, she seeks the fusion of folklore elements, and urban and modern scenes, creating mystical and surreal illustrations.

https://linktr.ee/nagmerriecircus

B.A. McRae:

B.A. McRae is known for her cozy yet emotionally gripping works, and also for her life-long relationship with coffee. Aside from being a busy bee surrounded by writing projects, TBR lists, and coffee ring stains, B.A. McRae adores life with her Partner, family, and close friends.

https://a.co/d/8Hv6zwV

B.V. Beuge:

B.V. Beuge is a fantasy author who was raised across the United States, but currently resides in the middle of the desert. When procrastinating at writing, she likes to drink too much coffee, lose spectacularly at video games, and whittle down her ever-growing stack of to-be-read books.

E. A. Williams

Born and raised in Houston Texas, E.A. Williams is inspired by the diverse and challenging landscape of her home state. She attended the University of North Texas where she earned her bachelor's in film. She continues to work with other artists across mediums to hone her skills.

Willow Bay:

Willow spends her time in the Sierra Mountains, hiking and eating fried fruit. Also, she enjoys skydiving, but only on very special occasions.

Monroe Wildrose (Anthologist):

Monroe spends her time juggling writing, enjoying time with her husband and two boys, and a couple of jobs to keep her busy. She loves to bake, thrift and read all things fantasy romance

https://www.amazon.com/stores/author/B09D3CCJMK

Charli M. :

Charlie is a talented and imaginative writer. When not reading or writing she can be found out with her horses or doing anything her dad thinks is cool.

J. Houser loves using snippets of dreams and a lot of 'what-ifs' to create adventures in brand new worlds and realities. She enjoys taking original fairytales, throwing them in a new setting, stripping away old, problematic themes, and breathing new life into them for our generation to enjoy.

https://www.books2read.com/TheDreamTrials

Nickole Storm:

Although Nickole is most often found behind a book like the recluse she is, she is regularly lured outside by means of coffee, and friends. Her favorite hobbies are; weightlifting, boardgames, running D&D campaigns and painting.

Emma Steinbrecher:

Emma Steinbrecher is a twenty-something mom and former third-grade teacher who loves writing stories and creating characters.

Emma writes New Adult Fantasy books with magic, romance, and spice. She also writes Romantic Comedy under the pen name Emmie J. Holland.

esteinbrauthor.wixsite.com

The Authors Acknowledgments

B.A. McRae:

I must bring our fearless and brilliant femme fairytale leader to the spotlight, Mrs. Monroe Wildrose. Monroe has become such a dear friend, and I couldn't be more grateful to collaborate on another amazing project! The way she lifts others up is inspiring, and her work is absolutely remarkable.

Willow Bay:

Thank you to my loving sister who rode my a$$ for weeks to get this done. And another thanks to her for my nephews because I love them.

J. Houser:

I sculpted this Princess and the Pea retelling, serendipitously, as I suffered from insomnia one night. My sleeplessness ended with me eating chocolate cake at 3 am & not meeting a prince, but you can't win them all.
A huge thanks to Monroe Wildrose for the push to try fairytale retellings!

Monroe Wildrose (Anthologist):

Thank you to all the beautiful authors who submit their stories to this anthology and to our readers, who keep us alive.

E.A. Williams

I wrote this story for you, because the forest is dark, and the desert is vast, but you went anyway.

Nickole Storm:

I want to say thank you to my husband for always listening to my rambles on the different ways this story could go. To my parents for always encouraging me to keep writing, and my sister Courtney and best friend Alexis for being the best beta readers ever.

Emma Steinbrecher:

I usually try to thank everyone who has ever even thought of supporting me ever, but Monroe only gave me like 50 words, so thanks to my husband for being a sugar daddy just so I can write, thank you to my bookish friends Ali and Wednesday for your wonderful—

Femme Fairytales Playlist

Femme Fairytales Poem

The Secret History – The Chamber Orchestra of London, Andrew Skeet

The Tale of Night and Day

When the Sun Loves the Moon – Reinaeiry

The Nightingale in the Temple

No Rest for the Wicked – Lykke Li

Lady Knight and the Vixen

Soul Sucker - Elise

A Witch Called Frog

Bird Song – Florence + and the Machine

Lilly's Story

Flowers in my Hair – Wes Reeve

The Dream Trials

Once Upon a Dream – Lana Del Rey

Trading Tales

Where's my Love – SYML

The Fallen Angel and His Lover

C'est La Mort – The Civil Wars

Other VIBE songs

Polonaise in G Minor – July Sunrise

Once Upon a December – Invadable Harmony

Fairground – Joby Talbot

The Flower Garden – Joe Hisaishi

www.ingramcontent.com/pod-product-compliance
Lightning Source LLC
Chambersburg PA
CBHW021623030826
48979CB00036B/1906/J

* 9 7 9 8 2 1 8 1 1 5 5 2 4 *